According to Gabriel Jackson

Peter D Birchenall

To Sue

With best wishes

Peter D Birchenall

Published in 2013 by FeedARead.com Publishing – Arts Council funded

Copyright © Peter D Birchenall

First Edition

Chapter 1

Late November 2002

Dougy MacKay had less than an hour to get him and Sara clear of their farm; otherwise, along with Sara's unborn child they would be killed, hacked down and ripped to pieces. No mercy. It had happened on neighbouring farms where entire families had disappeared. Valuable livestock had been butchered and buildings looted before being razed to the ground. Mugabe's Land Reform Policy had made Zimbabwe a dangerous place to be if you were a white farmer. Dougy had the will to resist but not the means. His priority was Sara and the baby, nothing could be more important than that.

His Land Rover had a full tank of diesel but it wouldn't be enough to get them across into South Africa. Jerry cans of extra fuel were crammed in at the side of other essential items needed to see them through the hostile environment that lay between the farm and the border. He stuffed bottles of water under the seats and anywhere else a space could be found. Sara belted herself in and Dougy floored the accelerator. Gravel spun from the wheels, pebble dashing a wicket fence as the vehicle sped away. Relying on local knowledge and luck to keep him out of the potholes scarring each side of the uneven dirt track, Dougy drove the unlit vehicle away from the farm until he felt safe enough to stop. Hidden by darkness they watched from a distance as flames engulfed their home. To them it was a sickening, gut wrenching disaster but to the whooping land grabbing thugs dancing around the edge of the conflagration it was a triumph. But now Dougy had to find a safe haven where Sara could rest, somewhere with a roof, which in their situation was a long shot indeed. He drove south towards the border; it was a border full of danger. He'd heard stories of razor wire that curled upwards to 3 metres, and about armed guards who used those caught in its murderous barbs as target practice. How much of this was true he didn't know, but it worried him just the same.

Being thrown around on heavily laden springs caused Sara to believe that she would be giving birth before her due date. It was this thought that brought home the stark truth, that like time and tide, babies wait for no one. Hers would come when it was ready, and the way things were it could easily be at the roadside. Two hours later they stopped. Their overloaded Land Rover was hitting too many deep potholes for Sara's comfort.

'For God's sake Dougy I can't take any more of this, I'm so thirsty.'

Dougy reached under his seat for a water bottle. Sara took it and drank copiously.

'I'm sorry lassie, but we have to keep going, by my reckoning we should be at the Limpopo in about 10 hours.'

Dougy knew that finding a bridge across the river would take longer but he couldn't risk Sara becoming more stressed than she already was. If he left the road to take a short cut across country they would soon be lost. He topped up the fuel tank and set off into the night.

The sun began its ascent from behind a range of hills beyond which the river separating Zimbabwe from the rest of the continent flowed. These brooding hunchbacked sentinels marked out a border along which ruthless well-armed guards patrolled. Occasionally automatic gunfire would puncture the still night air where even the slightest sound was magnified. The guards had their own way of supplementing a meagre income paid from an out of control economy where several million Zimbabwe dollars would probably buy a loaf of bread. Failure to pay the going rate for turning a blind eye was a death sentence. No one cared who lived or died because to the despot ruling the country human life was cheap.

Soon the sun would be high above them, beating down its merciless heat from a cloudless sky. Sara had slept fitfully. Yawning, she stretched her aching body as far as it would go in the cramped conditions.

'There's the border,' said Dougy, nodding towards the hills behind which the river ran.

Wiping her eyes Sara peered through the mass of dead insects on the windscreen. Distances were perceptive in this barren land. Hills that seemed near enough to touch could be miles away.

4

'How much further Dougy?'

Dougy shrugged his shoulders.

'Oh, probably 20 or 30 miles, I don't really know.'

Sara took a long swig of water and passed the bottle to Dougy.

'How much water do you reckon we have left?'

Dougy did a quick mental calculation of what they'd consumed so far and reckoned they had enough to see them across the border and half a day beyond, providing they were careful. By his reckoning the same could be said of the diesel. Driving in low gear soon eats up the fuel and he'd done plenty of that over the pockmarked road. Dougy said nothing to Sara about this, she'd only fret.

The hills sharpened in focus. Dougy knew that border guards would have seen their dust trail. The glint of sunlight reflecting from powerful binoculars confirmed his suspicion. Trained on the Land Rover they would give all the information needed about the status of its occupants. Poor black refugees would be on foot or in an ox cart. A Land Rover represented rich pickings and the guards were ready.

'*Sod this,*' thought Dougy as he swung the Land Rover off the road.

'I reckon I know another way across,' he shouted above the noise of his protesting vehicle.

'I was on a hunting trip here some years ago and there's a narrow track between the hills that takes a roundabout route to the bridge, all I have to do is find it. I don't remember it being guarded.'

Brown, sun scorched brush wood grew around the foothills and Dougy gambled that this would hide them as he searched for the way across. Nothing looked familiar; it was a last chance ploy. Sara cried out more in surprise than pain as the baby gave a sharp reminder that it was still alive and kicking. In a move that seemed out of place in such a desperate situation Sara took Dougy's hand and placed it on her abdomen. He felt not only the kick but also the power of the love he had for his wife and the baby she carried. It was a moment of tenderness, reminding him that they still had hope; it was hope that rested on a child yet to be born. He wasn't about to let them down; he'd get through no matter what.

Even with the Land Rover's air con working flat out the heat was stifling. Sara brushed strands of hair from her sweat-streaked face, pinning them beneath a hairgrip. The determined set of her jaw betrayed a toughness which would help Dougy find the bridge that would take them over the river.

'Those bastards won't beat us,' she muttered.

Dougy smiled at his wife's uncharacteristic use of bad language but he'd always admired her stubbornness, they were a team and a bloody good one at that. He cursed as the vehicle hit yet another large stone, wrenching the steering wheel from his hands. The Land Rover swerved, and then began to tilt.

'We're going over,' yelled Dougy.

The passenger side wheels spun in mid-air, searching for traction. Dougy threw himself over towards Sara as if to protect her. He didn't believe in miracles but one happened right there when the vehicle righted itself. It bounced a few yards then stalled. Breathing heavily they looked at each other and for the first time in his adult life Dougy found himself praying out loud.

'Our Father who art in Heaven...' he began.

His early Protestant upbringing had lodged The Lord's Prayer firmly in his mind, it was the only one he remembered and he recited it all the way through.

Dougy walked round the vehicle looking for signs of damage. Bodywork over a wheel arch flapped about like a crow with a broken wing but there was nothing else to concern him, well nothing he could see anyway. Sucking greedily at a roll up he sat on the rock that had threatened to end their progress. Smoking calmed him; he enjoyed the taste of strong tobacco. Idly blowing smoke into the air he let his eyes wander over the terrain. Convinced it had a familiar look he heaved himself off the rock and walked through the tinder dry brush to see if anything else struck a chord in his memory. He waved back towards Sara when she yelled at him to watch what he was doing with his cigarette. Another fire would finish them off all together.

She heard him laugh when he discovered the track, it was as he remembered, and wide enough for the Land Rover, just. Running back to the vehicle he jumped on board, started the engine then inched forward listening for the tell-tale sound of suspension damage. He thought he heard a slight knock but ignored it, the steering felt OK so he drove forward on to the track.

Bucking and rolling he moved along as fast as he could. Sara's knuckles lost their blood supply as she gripped the edge of her seat.

'Not be long,' said Dougy

He shoved the gear lever into a higher ratio. Sara said nothing; she just stared straight ahead, watching for the border fence to appear. With each pothole the suspension knock became louder, but the point of no return had long since passed. The fence loomed 200 metres ahead and beyond it the bridge. There were no guards in sight but that didn't mean they weren't there. He dropped a gear, jammed the accelerator pedal to the floor and turned the Land Rover into a guided missile. Sara's lips moved in silent prayer as the vehicle made contact with the fence. It ripped through, damaged bodywork flew past the driver's window and Dougy caught a brief reflection of himself as the wing mirror tore away from its mounting. Every movement seemed to be in slow motion. The wire wrapped itself round the Land Rover like a giant squid reluctant to release its prey.

'Come on lass, we've come this far, don't give up on me now.' As if it had heard him, the faithful vehicle dug its wheels into the soft earth and made a desperate lunge forward. Blasting through what remained of the fence it freed itself from the cloying barbs. The engine protested as Dougy pushed it to the limit, with whoops of joy and the river swirling beneath them they sped across the bridge. Two guards ran from their hut but were too late. In vain they fired after the speeding Land Rover. Already knowing his fate, a shaken guard commander called in the failure.

Small towns had sprung up along the South African side of the river and Dougy hoped there was enough fuel in the tank to find one of them. Soon it would be dark, the hills and scrubland had been replaced by hostile countryside and spending another night in the open was not a good idea. Sara needed to rest but there was no shelter. She urged Dougy onwards.

'Keep going, we'll just have to keep a watch for lights.'

Before darkness came, Dougy poured in the last remaining diesel. He knew the Land Rover was about done for so unless they found civilization soon their chances of survival would disappear. The track did not stop at the far side of the bridge, it continued into the distance. It was something to follow and Dougy took heart from this. African nights descend rapidly, the vehicle headlights pierced the blackness as Dougy struggled to stay focused on the job. Fatigue had overtaken them and Sara thought she was hallucinating when in the distance she saw lights, flickering at first but drawing closer they became brighter. Dougy coaxed more life out of the ailing vehicle, which responded with a burst of speed that surprised him. A feeling of relief seemed to come from the Land Rover's tortured engine as it propelled them towards the dark shape of buildings that Dougy guessed were at the outskirts of a border town, probably Messina. He knew about this town, it was similar to others in the area, populated by a collection of migrant workers, many trading in illegal activities such as pimping and prostitution. It served as a stopover place for truck drivers plying their trade between the border communities and for those fleeing oppression. In these border towns many who lived there had AIDS. Medical aid was available but scarce, funeral processions were a common sight.

Lights on poles leaning at odd angles shone a dim yellow fluorescent glow onto a street that once had boasted a tarmac surface. Dougy judged that it was the only way in and out of town. Neon signs advertising various types of business, some more dubious than others, flickered half-heartedly, most had letters missing, creating bizarre words, leaving punters to fill in the gaps.

One of these signs, spluttering and fizzing, hung from a rusting chain draped across the front of a dilapidated wooden structure that passed for a township hotel. What was the point in spending money on creature comforts for people who came and went? No one was asked to register; many would just disappear, some would drift into a twilight world fuelled by drugs and crime. The hotel had become a monument

8

to neglect, greed and inhumanity, marking out the godless nature of the town in which it stood.

Dougy stopped the Land Rover alongside the hotel entrance, switched off the engine and lay back in his seat. He rolled up the last of his tobacco; hot smoke hit his lungs. A sudden bout of coughing forced the smoke back into the cab. Dougy took a few more pulls then tossed the half smoked weed out of the window, watching the glowing tip as it rolled under the peeling veranda of the hotel.

'Let's go in and see if they have a room for the night.'
Sara grabbed his arm as he helped her down. She felt shaky and nearly fell as her swollen feet made contact with the uneven surface. Then, with the sort of timing that is unique to unborn babies, her waters broke. Together they struggled up the steps into the dingy hotel lobby where Dougy hit a well-worn brass bell that sat on the corner of the counter.

'Come on, anybody there, we need help.'
An unshaven, grubby looking man appeared from the gloom of an office, His English was poor.

'You have money?'
'Yes, have you a room?'
The man looked at Sara.

'Sorry, no room.'
Sara let out a yell as the contractions hit her.

'She's having a baby; for God's sake find somewhere quick.'
A door at the far side of the lobby swung open revealing a plump, hard looking woman who Dougy took to be the man's wife. Her English was better and she stated the obvious.

'Your baby is coming.'
'Get a doctor.' Dougy's voice betrayed how close he was to losing control.
The woman shrugged her shoulders.

'No doctor here.'
She beckoned; they had little choice but to follow her. In the back yard their senses were immediately assaulted by a stomach turning stench of accumulated sewage backing up from a blocked pipe

9

leaking somewhere beneath the litter strewn patch of scrubland that once passed for a patio. Sara baulked, the nightmare was getting worse.

Pointing, the woman said:

'There's a shed with some sacks, she can lay there.'

Wiping her hands on a filthy apron she went back into the hotel, slamming the door.

The moon cast a warm light across their predicament. The shed was in the same state as the rest of the place but they had nothing else. The second wave of contractions came and not long after, the third. Dougy thumbed the wheel of his cigarette lighter. Holding it at eye level he looked around the shed. A pile of potato sacks sat in one corner, an assortment of rusting garden tools lying across them. He found a tin of grease and a few empty cardboard boxes. The lighter spluttered, then went out. Sara screamed:

'It's here, the baby's here.'

The woman from the hotel reappeared; she held a few grubby towels and a storm lantern that Dougy hooked on a nail above where Sara lay. The baby's head was showing. Dougy supported his wife as she half raised herself on the rough sacks. He peeled off his shirt and placed it beneath Sara's straining body. This was her first baby; there was no telling how long it would take. Without gas and air the birth would be very painful but Dougy dismissed the possibility of complications from his mind. Sara cried out as the baby's shoulders came into view. Dougy could think of nothing else to say but 'push.'

'What do you think I'm doing?' yelled Sara.

Her labour took three hours. It was a boy just as Dougy wanted except now there was no farm to inherit. His pen knife, sterilized against the hot lamp, cut into the umbilical cord, separating the baby from its mother. The woman from the hotel took over. Wrapping the baby in a towel she placed him in one of the cardboard boxes, and then attended to Sara. Then out of the night, like a swarm of fireflies, lights appeared. The word had got around and people came to see the baby born in a shed. Some brought simple gifts; others could only marvel at what had happened that night. Dougy and Sara wept tears of joy as they looked down at their first-born. Against the ebony sky familiar constellations occupied their usual place but directly overhead an intense orange light appeared, it seemed to reach from deep within the night sky, bathing the entire town in its brightness. For a while the intensity remained, then it faded, leaving behind a gentle comforting glow.

Chapter 2

A room was found for them in the hotel. Grotty and smelly it may have been but at least it had a wash basin and they would rest on a bed rather than a pile of old sacks. The sheets hadn't seen the inside of a laundry for a while but Dougy was thankful for small mercies. Even before Sara became pregnant it was always Dougy's intention, should their firstborn be a boy, to name him after his father and so he was named Alastair James. Sara lay back against a greasy stained headboard and held the baby to her breast, and in between periods of falling asleep and waking he took his fill. A young woman from the next street gave them nappies which her own child no longer needed. Gifts brought by townspeople at the time of Alastair's birth included soft toys and discarded baby clothes. Their generosity touched Dougy's heart. In some ways it helped to ease the pain and anger of the last 24 hours, but he knew that somehow they had to get away from Messina and find a route back to Scotland.

For the next few days Sara rested at the hotel. Physically she was exhausted yet the joy of giving birth buoyed her. All babies are special but Sara knew hers was different, she couldn't explain how but she knew all the same. It may have been something to do with the orange glow still casting its radiance across Messina, fuelling rumours and speculation throughout the town, or it could be the sort of feelings experienced by most mothers when a first born arrives. Dougy had a rational explanation for the light. He'd dabbled with astronomy at university and remembered that ancient Chinese records tell of guest stars that appear without warning in places where no other stars had been before and that in time they disappear. The orange glow above Messina was probably one of these, a supernovae resulting from a devastating stellar explosion in deep space light years ago. Coincidentally the light had reached earth on the eve of his son's birth, having travelled an unimaginable distance. That's all it was, light from a dead imploded sun, nothing to get excited about. Even so, he could understand why the people of Messina were keeping a vigil on the street outside the hotel, they had their superstitions, but his baby was not the new Messiah, how could he be. The astral event of Alastair's birth had spread through the town like a bush fire.

Dougy had to get his family out this place but the Land Rover was well beaten up and the chances of acquiring another reliable vehicle were diminished because he had nothing of value left with which to trade. It was gunfire and screaming from the street that galvanized him into action. Soldiers drove their vehicles at the crowd, scattering those who were not quick enough to get out of the way. Inching aside a grubby curtain Dougy looked out. Fear gripped him as he recognised the uniforms worn by this bunch of killers; they were Zimbabwean thugs who had only one way of dealing with white settlers from the UK fleeing oppression. They shouldn't be here but the border meant nothing to them, there was no opposition, they meant business and Dougy knew his family was in mortal danger. A fat, untidy officer with an array of pips on the shoulders of his sweat stained shirt yelled out an order for the hotel to be stormed. No mercy, shoot them all.

Sick with fear the hotel owner's wife hurried to the McKay's room, she entered without knocking, and grabbing the baby from his makeshift cot, urged Dougy and Sara to follow her. The thumping of heavy boots showed there was no time to lose. They ran along a short corridor and down the back stairs into an alley where a rusting VW Golf was parked; it belonged to the hotel owner who had come to believe what others in the town were saying about baby Alastair. The woman pointed to the south.

'Head that way, we'll get rid of the soldiers and then come and find you.'

As Dougy shook her hand a feeling of dread went through him. These people would suffer, possibly forfeiting their lives to save his family. He bundled Sara and the baby into the back.

'Keep down,' he urged.

Sara clasped Alastair to her chest and sank into the footwell where there would be some protection. The fuel gauge registered half full, enough to get them a good distance from the town but not enough to avoid being stranded in open countryside. He just hoped the promise of rescue would be kept. Dougy eased the car out of the alley, keeping the revs to a minimum. He gambled that the fat officer and his soldiers were too preoccupied searching the hotel to hear him drive away, the rear view mirror confirmed there were no pursuing vehicles.

For a while longer Sara stayed crouched in the footwell, emerging only when Dougy thought it was safe. Alastair let them know he was hungry; breast feeding has its compensations in situations like this. Then Dougy's eyes were drawn once more to the mirror, a pall of dense smoke was rising from the town, the hotel owner and his wife were paying a dreadful price for helping them escape. Military that take orders from vicious dictators have one modus operandi and that is to use deadly force against anyone who opposes them. In Dougy's mind his new found friends were already being beaten or tortured in an attempt to extract information about their whereabouts. These simple people would never withstand this kind of barbarism for long; the soldiers would soon be in pursuit. The old, neglected VW was incapable of outrunning modern military vehicles, it was only a matter of time before they were captured and very likely killed. Hiding bodies in this terrain was easy and who would look at just another burnt out car more than once.

'They said someone would come and find us,' said Sara, 'we can't lose hope now.'
But Dougy felt helpless. Tyre tracks left by the car would guide their pursuers, there was nowhere to hide and he couldn't guarantee that the fuel gauge, now showing just over a quarter full, was accurate.

'OK, we'll keep going and just pray that God is on our side.'
In the distance, a dust cloud rose into the air and it was catching up.

Behind the cracked glass of the instrument panel a red flashing fuel light suggested God was preoccupied doing something else.

'Shit,' said Dougy, giving the dash board a thump. 'We're out of juice.'
Within a few minutes the car engine coughed and died. Momentum carried them forward a few metres before rolling to a stop. Without water or food all that remained was to throw themselves on the mercy

14

of people who did not know the meaning of compassion. The dust cloud was being dragged behind a vehicle much larger than a car.

'They're sending a bloody tank after us,' said Dougy.

Sara held Alastair to her breast, the futility of their position washed over her, she was quite prepared to die in defence of her son but what good would that do, they would kill him anyway.

'It's not a tank,' yelled Dougy, 'It's a truck.'

Messina was a truck stop for transport companies whose drivers came into town to rest and enjoy the bars and other distractions on offer; some were long distance trucks belonging to mining companies, the truck pursuing them was one of these. As it drew closer its horn blared and headlights flashed. It stopped alongside the stricken VW and Dougy could just about make out 'South African Mining Co' through the grime clinging to the driver's door. The window slid down revealing a black man whose bulk seemed to fill the cab.

'Want a ride?'

Not looking salvation in the mouth, Dougy helped Sara into the back of the truck before handing up Alastair. He then clambered in himself. Between them they fashioned a hurried shelter beneath a tarpaulin and hung on as the truck driver engaged first gear. He let the clutch in with a crudity that slammed the lorry's contents into the wooden tail gate. This was going to be a bumpy ride to who knows where but this driver had appeared at the right time and for that they gave thanks.

After what seemed an eternity the truck slowed to a stop. The driver was talking to someone. Dougy and Sara held their breath, hoping that Alastair wouldn't give away their hiding place. The tarpaulin was thrown back; Dougy looked up into the face of the driver who called over another man who was armed.

'You've betrayed us you bastard, how much were we worth?'

The driver smiled.

'This man will see you to safety, trust him.'

Again, options were limited. They climbed down from the truck and followed the man to a large hatch back that was parked with its engine running. They were motioned to get into the back seat. Before closing

15

the door the man reached over into the rear of the vehicle. Lifting out a basket he gave it to Sara.

'For you,' he said.

The basket held everything they needed, food, water and requirements for the baby. The townsfolk had kept their promise and to Sara's relief Alastair had a clean nappy for the first time that day.

The air conditioned hatchback was comfortable and sleep inducing. It was dark before Dougy awoke. Sara was laid across his knees with Alastair in her arms, both were asleep. Dougy leant forward to speak to the driver.

'Where are we?'

The driver remained silent but in the distance there were lights.

Chapter 3

Sara woke as Dougy's gentle hand stroked her face. He took Alastair from her; she sat up, yawned and looked to where Dougy was pointing. The lights ahead were low to the ground; this was not a town nor a village but something much different. A powerful intermittent beam reached out as if guiding them in. The driver slowed and flashed the vehicle's spot lights.

'Come on, tell us where we are,' said Dougy. But again there was no reply.

Drawing nearer they made out two rows of lights, beacons of fire stuck in the ground at set intervals gradually converging before disappearing at a vanishing point some way beyond. The vehicle stopped alongside the torches, the pungent smell of burning paraffin hung heavily in the night air. Two people ran towards the hatchback and one of them, a woman, peered inside. Reaching over, she touched Alastair lightly on the forehead.

'You're safe now,' her soft South African drawl was almost a whisper, 'stay inside and don't move from here, the soldiers are only an hour away.'

The driver left the vehicle and stood with the others. They bowed their heads as if in prayer, it was surreal yet in a strange way reassuring.

Dougy pointed towards the lights.

'It's a runway, what the hell is going on?'

Sara shrugged.

'We'll just have to trust these people, they seem OK,' she said. She changed and fed Alastair before cradling him to sleep in her arms. Then they waited.

When the distant sound of an aircraft broke the silence Dougy's natural impetuousness overcame caution and he jumped down from the vehicle. He'd had enough of this; it was time to take charge. The woman turned towards him. In the torchlight he glimpsed a young, pretty face.

'Just a little more patience and you will be safe,' she said.

17

The plane was overhead, its navigation lights clearly visible.

'Who are you, why are you doing this?' said Dougy.

'The heavenly sign, that's why; the child must live, no matter what the cost.'

The plane landed and taxied to a halt just a few metres from where they stood. It turned to face the runway, ready for take-off. The woman moved towards Sara.

'Hurry, we haven't much time.'

She held out her hands to take the baby but Sara drew Alastair close to her. Dougy stepped between them. Masterful, protective. Once airborne he knew that any control over the situation would be lost, they would have to go wherever these people took them. The woman screamed to be heard above the plane's engines.

'Come on, get on board, now, if they catch us on the ground we're dead.'

The hysterical urgency in her voice was enough to convince Sara to get on the plane.

'Help me down Dougy, we're going and that's that.'

Within a few minutes they were belted in, the twin engine Cessna reached maximum revs and gathered speed along the makeshift runway, bumping, yawing and then it was in the air. The pilot banked to the left. In the distance could be seen vehicle headlights, their pursuers had not been far behind. The young woman had been telling the truth and Sara mouthed her thanks.

In the soft glow reflecting from the instrument panel Dougy was sure he recognized the pilot. Where had he seen him before? It was when he spoke that Dougy knew who he was.

'Well my friends, we meet again.'

'The lorry driver,' said Dougy

A deep barrel-chested laugh boomed around the cockpit.

'Yes and now I expect you want to know who we are and where we are taking you.'

'It would help.'

'Well, my name is Gabriel Jackson and the people behind you are my friends. Where we come from does not matter, what matters is that you and the child are taken to a place of safety. He is precious in our sight, he is the one we have been waiting for; he is the one who will save the world.'

'Rubbish, how can you possibly say that about our son?'

'It is prophesied,' said a small quiet voice from the back of the plane.

Gabriel Jackson checked that they were still on course then continued with his explanation.

'In three hours we will land at Pretoria where you will rest and prepare yourselves for the onward journey.'

'To where?' asked Dougy.

'Home of course, to Scotland.'

Sara gripped Dougy's arm. She was sure they'd told no one about their wish to return to Scotland so how did this man know. Their lives were being decided for them by a group of religious zealots; it was as if they had been taken hostage.

'We have no money, how will we pay for the tickets.'

'It is all arranged,' said Gabriel Jackson.

'What do you mean it's all arranged,' Dougy betrayed a growing impatience.

'I mean what I say; you must leave everything to us, I will be coming with you to Scotland.'

A light touch on Sara's shoulder caused her to turn.

'He is the child's Guardian Angel, you must have faith.'

Sara's grip on Dougy's arm tightened as the Cessna flew towards a new dawn. The cabin fell silent and troubled minds gave way to sleep.

The jolt of wheels meeting a tarmac runway roused them. Gabriel Jackson brought the plane to a halt at the perimeter of a small airport. The propellers twitched to a stop and Dougy watched as an unmarked minibus approached them.

'For now you will be taken to a safe house in the city. Tomorrow we leave for the first part of our journey to Glasgow,' said Gabriel Jackson.

The house was in a grubby, run down part of the city but it contained all that was necessary for an overnight stay. Sara took first turn in the tub; the water was hot, she lay back in the steam and her mind drifted over the past few days. Had she really given birth to the saviour of the world or was it a cruel attempt at extortion? The bulge of an automatic in the pocket of their rescuer's leather flying jacket didn't seem the sort of thing guardian angels carry about but who knows, it may be how things are done these days. Neither had she expected that he would be such an accomplished cook yet the meal they ate that evening was sumptuous by anyone's standards, this isn't the way that hostages are usually treated. It was a complete change of clothes laid out across their bed that finally dispelled any lingering doubts. The garments were of good quality, in the correct size and stylish. Two brown leather cases filled with more clothes and other personal requirements stood side by side in the hallway. To each one was tied a South African Airways label with Glasgow as the destination.

'You have to look like a normal family going on vacation; it would be disastrous for you to draw attention to yourselves. I'll be sat across from you. Avoid speaking to me or showing any signs of recognition, I must keep the child in view at all times,' said Gabriel Jackson.

'OK,' said Dougy.

'We have an early start so may I suggest you get to bed, there's a cot for the child in your room.'

Sara noticed that Gabriel Jackson and his friends referred to Alastair as 'the child' never once enquiring as to his given name.

In the sultry darkness they lay together, the still air punctured by the murmur of traffic and a dog barking in the distance. As sleep came they didn't see electric torchlight casting shadows across the bedroom ceiling. Gabriel Jackson was keeping watch.

Chapter 4

It was still dark when Gabriel Jackson roused them.

'Time to go,' he said.

A powerful Mercedes saloon was at the door, engine running. The driver's features were hidden by a monk's cowl.

'The house isn't safe, they know we are here.'

Sara picked up a still sleeping Alastair and followed Dougy down the dimly lit staircase into the luxurious leather interior of the Merc. Gabriel Jackson slid into the front passenger seat and the car moved away from the kerb, gathering speed along the narrow deserted street.

'Faster,' urged Gabriel Jackson.

Tyres squealed as the driver responded with breath-taking acceleration. The car had been tuned to perfection; it was the perfect getaway vehicle able to outstrip anything on four wheels, but not on two. Like a ghost an unlit Kawasaki appeared alongside them, slugs from a Kalashnikov ripped into the car's bodywork, shattering the driver's side window. Dougy threw himself across Sara and the baby, protecting them the best way he could. Gabriel Jackson returned the fire and the Kawasaki assassins died instantly as the bike's engine shattered, cart wheeling it into a wall.

'What the devil is going on?' yelled Dougy.

'Just stay down.'

Sara began to cry; Dougy kissed her, tasting the salty tears that coursed down her face. They had escaped death this time but only by the narrowest of margins. If this man was their son's guardian angel then he'd better stay on the ball.

It was blood soaking through the folds of the driver's cowl that alerted Gabriel Jackson to an impending problem.

'How bad is it,' he whispered.

'Just a scratch, that's all.'

'It looks more than that, let me see.'

'OK but not until we reach the airport.'

The driver's blood loss was increasing.

'Stop the car,' demanded Gabriel Jackson.

The driver managed to slow the Merc to a crawl before losing consciousness. He was bleeding out from a ruptured aorta. The car smacked into the kerb and stalled. With a gentleness that belied the tough nature of his personality he lifted the now lifeless body from where it lay across the steering wheel. He got out of the car and called Dougy to help him. Together they pulled the driver's remains into the passenger seat and Gabriel Jackson took his place. At first the stalled car refused to start, Gabriel Jackson sat back and closed his eyes, lips moving in silent prayer. He tried again and this time the engine fired.

'God is gracious,' he whispered.

Within ten minutes the pulsating light of the airport control tower came into view, the car came to a halt. Briefly, Gabriel Jackson spoke to someone on his mobile phone, then he said,

'We wait here.'

Dougy knew it was useless to question anything this man said or did, so he focused all his energy on comforting his wife. Headlights came up behind the Merc; Gabriel Jackson pulled his gun from its holster, an order to 'get down' was instantly obeyed. His phone rang three times then stopped.

'It's OK,' he said.

Two people approached, each wearing overalls bearing the airport insignia. Embracing Gabriel Jackson they huddled together for a moment before one of them opened the rear door of the Merc.

'Come with me,' said a gentle female voice.

Dougy hesitated.

'It's safe,' said Gabriel Jackson, 'please go with her,'

As they left the car the woman placed two fingers on Alastair's forehead.

'Praise God,' she whispered.

The quiet electric motor of the airport passenger transport minibus ferried them to the terminal building. On the way Dougy asked about the dead driver only to be met with what had become Gabriel Jackson's stock answer,

'It is taken care of.'

Once inside they were escorted to a secure part of the building. There were no security checks; Gabriel Jackson would be taking his gun onto the plane. Alastair needed changing and feeding but Sara was not permitted to do this alone, everywhere was a potential source of danger, nothing was left to chance.

They had an hour to wait before boarding, long enough for Gabriel Jackson to clean any remnants of the driver's blood from his person. Dougy thought he'd use the time to find out what was really going on. Here they were, virtual prisoners, having been chased all over the place by armed thugs and involved in several killings all because Alastair was supposedly special. He confronted Gabriel Jackson.

'Come on, tell me, who the hell are you?'

'I suppose Hell does come into the equation.'

'What kind of an answer is that?'

'I've spent an eternity fighting evil just to be here for this moment in the history of mankind.'

'More riddles, tell me, who are you, really?'

Gabriel Jackson laughed, showing a perfect set of teeth.

'I am whoever my people say I am,'

The phrase sounded vaguely familiar to Dougy, he'd heard it before somewhere. He remembered that this man had once been described as Alastair's Guardian Angel, could this be a clue to his origins?

Sara rejoined them; she too had tried to get some sense out of the young woman who had been helpful in changing Alastair but when questioned just smiled and said,

'It's in God's hands, just wait and see.'

Time passed slowly, they waited in silence for the call to board the aircraft. Gabriel Jackson handed Dougy travel documents for him and Sara. They would change planes at Johannesburg for the flight to Heathrow, then on to Glasgow. Dougy had family living in the west of Scotland so he reckoned they would have somewhere to stay until they sorted out their affairs. Gabriel Jackson had other ideas. Once in Glasgow they would be taken to another safe house away from the city until he was sure of Alastair's safety. Nothing would divert him from his mission for he was under orders from a higher power.

The flight information indicator showed the plane was ready for boarding and a queue formed at the gate.

'Remember, act normally,' said Gabriel Jackson.

The queue shuffled forward and soon they reached the desk. Two officious men checked their documents. This seemed to take an age, passports were scrutinised, the men whispered to each other in Afrikaans then one of them beckoned Dougy towards him. Gabriel Jackson reached inside his jacket, wrapping his hand around the automatic.

'Enjoy your flight,' said the man, handing back the passports. Dougy nodded his thanks and Gabriel Jackson relaxed.

Their seats were in the tail part of the plane, near an emergency door. Dougy reckoned this was no coincidence, he'd known Gabriel Jackson for long enough now to realise this was his doing, once landed they'd be first off the plane with him directly behind them. Flight attendants went through their safety rituals, seat belt signs came on and a bilingual chief steward welcomed everyone on board. Although Dougy and Sara were aware of some extra attention by one of the cabin crew, the flight was routine. Alastair slept through most of it, waking only to be fed. Only once before had Dougy been to Johannesburg, his mind briefly returned to when he was a boy and how he'd holidayed there with his parents. Now all he would experience of this beautiful city was from the inside of an airport terminal building.

Chapter 5

The flight to Heathrow was delayed, something about a minor problem with a faulty warning light from one of the engines, nothing serious they were told but some precautionary safety checks were being carried out by airline technicians, it would take a couple of hours. It may have been genuine but Gabriel Jackson's natural instinct to believe nothing at face value made him suspicious.

An immaculately dressed young woman on the South African Airline desk remained unruffled even when confronted by a large intimidating black man who wasn't going to be fobbed off.

'Why the delay,' he asked.

'Something with an engine I think.'

'Not good enough. Get me someone who knows.'

The woman didn't argue as Gabriel Jackson had that effect on people. Her manicured voice echoed around the terminal building asking for the duty manager to come to the check in desk. Eventually a fat uniformed man ambled across from the refreshment area, his untidy beard decorated with the remnants of a sandwich. Rubbing his hands together in that ingratiating, smarmy way beloved of people who have turned patronising into an art form he spoke to Gabriel Jackson.

'How can I help sir?'

'By telling me why the London plane is delayed,'

'Minor engine problems that's all, there's nothing to get concerned about.'

'Liar. he thought'

There's something about the way people scratch their noses when lying - this man was taking the skin off his.

Gabriel Jackson looked down to where the plane was parked. Two men in a maintenance buggy were heading out across the tarmac, it all looked routine but he had to keep the child and his parents away from the plane, something was seriously wrong out there. Then an announcement confirmed his fears.

'May I have your attention; in a few minutes we will conduct an evacuation of the main terminal building. This is a routine drill. When the fire alarm sounds please make your way in an orderly fashion to the main exit. Airport coaches will take you to an assembly point.'

Gabriel Jackson had pledged to keep the child in his sight at all times yet he had to check out the plane for himself and the only way he could do this was to get on board. He had to trust someone to be his eyes and ears but there was no one. Then he remembered how attentive one of the cabin crew had been during the flight from Pretoria, she had smiled at him as if to say she knew who he was, but now she could be anywhere and he hadn't much time to find her. When she arrived to assist with the evacuation of South African Airline passengers anyone else would call it a coincidence, but not Gabriel Jackson. Ignoring all other passengers she came directly to him.

'Are you a believer?' he asked.

'The child is the chosen one,' she replied.

'Get them away from here, as far away as possible.'

He scribbled down her mobile phone number.

'I'll call you when it's safe.'

Out of earshot Dougy and Sara grew suspicious of the whispering and hand gestures that passed between Gabriel Jackson and the woman. They became even twitchier when he walked off, his pace quickening until out of sight.

The woman introduced herself.

'My name is Rachel; I will stay with you until he returns.'

'Where's he gone,' asked Dougy.

'It's all taken care of, now follow me,' she replied.

A sigh of resignation left Dougy's lips but he and Sara did as she asked.

The unsuspecting security man made no sound as he fell unconscious to the rest room floor, a half smoked cigarette rolled from his hand. Gabriel Jackson discarded an empty syringe into a waste bin then dragged the man out of sight behind a row of lockers before exchanging his jacket for the man's sweat stained uniform tunic and

26

cap. It was good enough to fool the occasional glance and in the melee of the evacuation he left by a rear door. CCTV cameras were everywhere, once in the open he'd be picked up so he gambled that in his borrowed uniform he wouldn't attract a second look. It paid off, he reached the plane unchallenged.

The buggy was parked under the 747's starboard wing, but there was no sign of the maintenance crew. He moved swiftly towards the steps leading into the rear of the plane then slipped in behind the galley door and listened as muted voices reached him from deeper within the aircraft. Along the aisle he could see two men wearing what looked like protective body armour, helmets and visors. Any conversation between them was lost in the hum of the air conditioning so he had to get nearer. He moved in the dimness of auxiliary lighting from one row of seats to the next using the seat backs as cover. In seconds he'd reached a point where urgent conversation could be overheard.

'I think it's the red wire first then black,' said one of the men.

'But you can't be sure,' said the other man.

'Ninety percent sure,' was the reply.

Gabriel Jackson knew about bombs, he'd dismantled a few in his time; ninety percent wasn't good enough.

He made his move, the click of an automatic safety catch caused the men to turn but he was on them in an instant, the muzzle of his gun only centimetres from the visor of the man who was about to cut the wire.

'Give me the cutters,' demanded Gabriel Jackson.

Without argument the man handed over a pair of wire cutters.

'Now trust me, I'm on your side so don't try anything stupid.'

The bomb was crude, unstable and large, a timer made from a digital clock showed five minutes to oblivion. Detonation would take out much of the terminal building as well as the plane.

The second officer had found the device during a last minute check before handing the plane over to the ground crew. At first it looked like a piece of innocent hand luggage left under a seat by mistake. This wasn't unusual as such things happen on long haul

27

flights, when passengers are tired they get careless. It was a faint ticking noise that had alerted him to something much more sinister. Moving the plane was out of the question, towing it to a safer place would take too long. Gabriel Jackson reached down and cut the black wire with a decisiveness that showed he knew what he was doing. The clock stopped.

He did a deal with the two men to get him off the plane and back to the terminal building. With the defunct bomb at his feet he rode in the back of the buggy until within a few metres of the building.

'Stop here.'

He jumped from the vehicle and disappeared into the shadows.

In the locker room he redressed the still unconscious security man. Propping him against a wall he positioned his cap to make it look as if the man was sleeping. Gabriel Jackson smiled at the thought of the poor fellow trying to explain this to his superiors. Retrieving his jacket he allowed himself a few seconds in front of a mirror before going off in search of Rachel and the MacKay family. Whoever had planted the bomb would not give up, assassinating the child was their avowed objective and his was to stop them, at whatever the cost.

Chapter 6

All flights from Johannesburg International were on hold. The evacuated passengers began to return but chaos was never far away as they jostled each other to get a look at the departure boards. Tempers frayed, scuffles broke out and rumours about a bomb on a plane refuelled a situation that the airport manager tried to deny. His composure evaporated, he ran for the cover of his office, locking himself in. The stories took on the characteristics of a flash flood, completely swamping the terminal building. Fear mongers spreading stories of more bombs on other planes whipped frightened, hysterical people into a frenzy. A human tidal wave swept people towards the exit doors, the cries of those who fell were ignored as common humanity gave way to panic stricken chaos. Like lemmings they swept from the building into the arms of inexplicable terror as a car bomb detonated in the unloading bay.

The violence of the blast hurled Gabriel Jackson into an advertising board that collapsed under his full weight. His head felt as if it would burst, flying glass cut his hand but he was alive and conscious. Rolling into a ball he protected himself from the panic that raged around him. Somehow he had to get out of the shattered building and call Rachel. She would not have used buses to transport the MacKay family to safety, she was wiser than that. He reckoned that her knowledge of the airport would give her the edge on safe places to hide. It was possible that she was still in the vicinity watching the horror unfolding and already grieving colleagues who may have been killed.

Within minutes two-tone horns blared through the spiralling cloud of choking dust, a well-rehearsed airport disaster response team moved into place, immediately bringing a semblance of order to the chaos. Gabriel Jackson moved among the debris, hands reached out for help, cries of terrible pain assailed his senses. Although it was in his nature he could not stop to offer comfort to the injured or hope to the dying. The bombers were still at large and the future of the world depended on him finding Rachel and the MacKays before they did. He tried to get into Rachel's mind, where would she go to be safe? He shrugged off a concerned paramedic, pointing to where he'd seen injured people; at least by doing this he could salve his conscience. Blood dripped from his hand; the paramedic tossed him a bandage before disappearing into an acrid mixture of dust and smoke.

Away from the building he dialled Rachel's number but it didn't connect. He tried again with the same result. This wasn't the plan; she was supposed to be waiting for his call. For a second he felt helpless, perhaps she was out of range or the authorities had blocked mobile phone signals to avoid another device being triggered, which would explain it. He was reassured that the child had escaped the bomb but disturbed because he didn't know where he was. Rachel would not return to the airport, it was too risky. Rachel's car was ordinary, it moved anonymously along the highway into the city suburbs, its radio playing a local station. It was when the radio station cut in with a newsflash about the bomb that Dougy leaned over and increased the volume. Details remained sketchy but casualty figures were high; there had been many deaths and serious injuries. They listened with intensity as the news unfolded. Dougy and Sara had come to trust Gabriel Jackson and the possibility of him being dead was not one they cared to dwell on.

'He'll be OK, death doesn't scare him,' said Rachel.
But to Dougy, Scotland was now an impossible dream. Even if Gabriel Jackson had survived, how would they get there? The airport would be closed and they had nowhere to go. Sensing their disquiet Rachel said,

'We'll go to my place, it's basic but comfortable, and we'll be safe there.'
She turned off the radio and drove the rest of the way in silence. Her first floor downtown pad was as she had described, no frills but homely.

Coffee and soup acted as a diversion. Cocooned in well used easy chairs, Dougy and Sara began to relax and Rachel tuned the television to a news channel. A young reporter, clearly shaken by the events at Johannesburg International, fought back tears as she described the awful events of the past hour. A camera swept around the scene focusing on the collapsed building and the frantic search for survivors. Another was broadcasting live pictures of people being interviewed.

'They're like bloody vultures, those reporters,' muttered Dougy.

Then like a startled rabbit, he sat up, coffee spilling from his mug onto the carpet.

'Look, it's him, he's trying to phone,' he shouted.

Rachel reached out to where her coat was hanging. She pulled her phone from a pocket. It showed no sign of having received a call but it was obvious from the TV pictures that he was trying to make contact.

'Come on folks, think of something,' said Rachel.

'Get in touch with the TV channel; tell them you've seen your husband on the screen and he's trying to phone you. Get them to contact him for you. They'll go for it, it'll make great television,' said Sara.

'Brilliant,' replied Rachel.

The TV channel grabbed the idea. Someone in the newsroom phoned back and Rachel guided her into where Gabriel Jackson was still tapping out numbers. A microphone was thrust in front of his face and an excited reporter pointed at the camera.

'Your wife is watching this, can you tell her you're OK.'

Gabriel Jackson knew instantly what was happening. Holding his bandaged hand up to the camera he said: -

'Hi honey, yeh apart from this I'm fine, I tried to phone but couldn't reach you. I'll try and get home the best way I can.'

'Thank you sir, your wife will be relieved that you are safe.'

The camera pulled away from Gabriel Jackson and moved to another breaking story. He had to get away and quickly. Others would have seen the broadcast and know of his whereabouts, he was separated from the child and his vulnerability would not be lost on them. The only vehicles allowed in and out of the area were emergency vehicles. If he could get to the hospital then his phone might work.

Removing the bandage from his hand he opened the wound. Blood spilled to the ground. A cursory examination by a harassed triage nurse confirmed that sutures were required. She said he may have tendon damage and bundled him into the next ambulance to leave. The hospital emergency room was overwhelmed. The army had rigged a first aid tent in the grounds; it was like a war zone. Gabriel Jackson was told he had to wait for treatment; he was in a long line of walking wounded but had no intention of staying any longer than necessary. His lacerated hand had stopped bleeding and he had a mobile signal.

Rachel's phone seemed to ring with more urgency than usual.

'Where are you,' she asked.

'At the hospital, can you get to me?'

The hospital was half an hour away and she wouldn't leave the family unprotected.

'Bring them, but be careful.' said Gabriel Jackson.

Rachel felt fear in his voice. She had to do as he asked, without his protection the child was at much greater risk. He continued,

'Access to the hospital is impossible; I'll walk a couple of blocks then call you with a street name.'

Traffic was at a crawl. The evening rush hour swelled the already congested streets and Rachel's impatient fingers drummed on the steering wheel.

'Come on,' she muttered under her breath, but it made no difference as second gear was all she could manage.   Dougy's impatience kicked in.

'Bloody hell, we'll never find him at this rate, can't you go any quicker, round backstreets or something.'

Rachel's phone vibrated in her jacket pocket, she gave it to Dougy.

'Listen carefully to where he is, and then tell me.'

Dougy put the phone to his ear.

'It's Dougy, where are you?'

Gabriel Jackson's whispered reply was relayed to Rachel.

'Victoria Street, I'm in a coffee bar next to the Astoria Hotel.'

'OK, I know it,' said Rachel.

He'd found a quiet corner yet felt that eyes of other customers were on him. His dishevelled appearance and a blood stained, dirty bandage was probably the reason why. A second cappuccino was cold by the time Rachel arrived. He got to his feet but a wave of nausea threw him back into his chair, delayed shock combined with blood loss overcame him. Others looked on or turned their backs as Rachel tried to lift him, He was barely conscious; no one moved to help her.

'Come on Gabriel, it's only a few steps to the car,' she said.

His inner strength took over as he struggled to get up. Dougy came to the café door but Rachel waved him back. Rachel bent her head towards Gabriel Jackson's face.

'The Lord's will be done,' she said.

Once more he rose from his chair, Rachel steadied him as together they reached the car. He slumped into the front passenger seat.

'You have to go back to the hospital,' said Rachel.

Gabriel Jackson shook his head.

'Too risky.'

As part of her job Rachel had had some medical training but caring for Gabriel Jackson in his condition was beyond her experience. She would take him to her apartment and let him rest, that was all she could do.

He woke at 6am; his injury had been freshly dressed even though he remembered nothing of it. Rachel let him sleep in her bed whilst she watched over Alastair and his parents who lay curled up on the sitting room carpet. She had taken Gabriel Jackson's gun knowing that if the child was attacked she could protect him. She forced a smile as he appeared, framed in the doorway.

'Thanks,' he said, looking first at her then at the sleeping child.

'The bathroom's that way,' said Rachel.

Dougy and Sara woke to the smell of fresh coffee. The microwave pinged, giving notice that several rashers of bacon had thawed enough for frying. Baked beans spluttered in a saucepan.

'I'm sorry, that's all there is but it's better than nothing,' said Rachel.

Gabriel Jackson reappeared, bits of towelling stuck to his stubble. Rachel's delicately perfumed soap only partly doing its job.

'How're you feeling?' asked Dougy

'Fine thanks.'

His pain filled eyes told a different story. This was not the confident smartly dressed man they had come to know, but to an extent his dishevelled grubby appearance mirrored their own. Apart from their travel documents that Dougy kept in his coat pocket, everything else had been lost in the blast.

Over breakfast they regrouped, grateful for having survived the horrors of the past 24 hours.

'I can't believe that those who would harm the child have not tried again, I'm sure they must know where we are.' said Gabriel.

'God will protect us,' replied Rachel.

Gabriel Jackson nodded and finished his baked beans.

Rachel made a call to her employer. A relieved telephone operator told her that Johannesburg International would remain closed for some hours until security forces completed their work, she would be contacted later in the day.

'We could be on our way this evening then,' said Sara.

'It's possible,' agreed Rachel.

The mood in the apartment lightened, Rachel's washing machine churned away, Sara attended to Alastair, and Dougy showed his skill with a steam iron. Gabriel Jackson was restless. His injury troubled him, he reflected on what the airport nurse had said about tendon damage, he wouldn't be as accurate when it came to using a gun with his left hand.

Chapter 7

The day wore on; Rachel's apartment became claustrophobic. South African Airlines hadn't called and Gabriel Jackson feared the worse. With his automatic back in its holster he paced up and down, stopping only to stare out of the window, looking, searching. Alastair had colic and a whinging baby, no matter how precious, can create tensions. TV news channels still broadcast the same pictures over and over again as if by now there were still people who weren't aware of what had happened at the airport. Expert analysis explored all angles but the reality was that the bombers had gone to ground carrying with them the knowledge that they had failed to kill their target. Conspiracy theorists phoned the TV studios with 'off the wall' views of why the bomb had been aimed at that particular terminal but none had worked out the real reason why so many innocent people had been slaughtered.

There is nothing like breaking news to inject life into a faltering story. A message crawled across the bottom of the screen announcing that a limited number of flights would recommence at 1900 hours from a different terminal. There was the usual political rhetoric about not giving in to terrorism, about standing firm. Under his breath Gabriel Jackson muttered something uncomplimentary about politicians, he had no time for them, and they'll always let you down in the end. He mused that Pontius Pilate was such a man.

'Call the airline, don't wait for them to call you,' he demanded.

Rachel made the call and was told the Heathrow flight would be the first to leave; she was expected at the terminal within an hour. In an instant Gabriel Jackson was at the window.

'It looks clear, come on let's get going.'

Rachel's bag was already in the car, the others had nothing except what they wore but there was always baby stuff on the plane. Gabriel Jackson ushered them out.

'Wait for me at the bottom of the stairs, I've a call to make, just two minutes,' he said.

When he caught up with them he asked Rachel for the ignition keys.

'I'll check the car, just a precaution.'

Staying close to the wall he edged to where Rachel's car was parked. Going down on one knee he looked beneath it, searching for anything suspicious, it seemed normal as did the inside of the vehicle. Pain shot up his arm as he turned the ignition key, specks of blood surfaced through the bandage. The engine started, he waited for a few seconds before reversing to where Rachel and the others were waiting.

'I'll drive,' he said.

Rachel eyed his damaged hand but said nothing.

Diversions on the approach to the airport took them into a heavily policed parking area. Security had been seriously tightened but the guards had photographs of S.A.A. staff so Rachel was not a problem to them. A well-built female guard led her to a staff minibus. For Dougy and Sara the interrogation was fierce and prolonged. They were separated; questions came from all directions, and their answers cross checked until the guards were satisfied. Without raising his head a self-important middle aged official stamped their documents.

'Wait in line over there,' he said.

Somehow during the interrogation Dougy had held his temper but the attitude of this official was taking him towards the edge. He took Alastair from Sara's arms knowing that if he was holding his son it would prevent him giving this imbecile the slap he so richly deserved. Dougy grunted an acknowledgment and Sara followed him to where a lengthening line of people was waiting to be taken to the boarding gate. His mind went back to the farm. He leaned towards Sara,

'Our cattle were treated better than this,' he muttered.

They looked across at where Gabriel Jackson was in animated discussion with two heavily armed guards. He was having a hard time explaining the gun and why he'd travelled in the same car as Rachel and the others. He had to use all his guile to dupe the guards into believing that he was a law enforcement officer seconded to the airline and that he lived near Rachel who sometimes gave him a ride in to the airport. His fake ID was scrutinized and handed back to him.

'Why don't we have your photograph like for other staff?'

36

Gabriel Jackson sighed; it was a sigh of contempt and his hand was hurting.

'Because you idiots, my cover must not be blown,' he said in voice low enough so as not to be heard by others.

'Why were the man, woman and child in the flight attendant's car?'

This time his answer was truthful and could be checked.

'She rescued them from the bomb and took them to her place.'

'How did you damage your hand?'

'Cut it on some broken glass, just a stupid accident.'

The questioning was relentless, as far as these guards were concerned he was a security risk and they were taking no chances. Gabriel Jackson had to take charge otherwise he'd be prevented from getting on the plane. He grabbed a pen from the guards' desk and scribbled a phone number on a scrap of paper.

'Call this number now,' he said.

'Why?'

'Do you want to keep your jobs?'

The senior of the two guards punched in the number.

It connected immediately, as if the call was expected. The unmistakable voice of the airline President gave an order.

'Yes sir, certainly sir,' said the guard, handing the phone to Gabriel Jackson.

'I spoke to you earlier; the child is in jeopardy.'

'Put the guard on.'

'He'll talk, you listen,' said Gabriel Jackson, thrusting the phone into the guard's hand.

The call lasted 20 seconds, Gabriel Jackson was waved through.

At last they were on their way, the plane climbed to its cruising altitude of 38,000 feet; it would stay above the clouds for almost 11 hours. As before, Gabriel sat opposite the MacKays; Rachel would be passing by at regular intervals going about her duties making people comfortable, serving meals, being strict about seatbelt signs. Passenger behaviour on long haul journeys is usually predictable.

Experienced cabin crew can spot problems and deal with them before they became serious, it is part of the job, and so it was with this trip. Being well fed early on in the flight settles people down, afterwards they will watch a film, listen to music or just sleep. Visits to the washroom are frequent; everyone has to go sooner or later. It is only when the engaged sign stays on for longer than is usual that cabin crew become concerned, a light tap on the door accompanied by a discreet enquiry is all that is usually necessary. They were 2 hours out of London and this time it was different. One of the toilets in the front section of business class had been occupied for too long. Rachel knocked on the door.

There was no reply. Rachel summoned assistance from her colleagues; airline regulations were specific about this. Several abortive attempts were made to communicate with whoever was in the toilet. In emergencies the door can be opened from the outside and a decision was made to do this, the person inside may need urgent medical help. The door swung open, a small slimly built black woman was staring in the mirror as if hypnotized. She hadn't noticed Rachel who reached out to touch her shoulder.

'What is the problem, can we help at all?' asked Rachel.

The woman moved her eyes to catch Rachel's reflection. What Rachel saw in those eyes caused her to shudder; there was no life in them, no recognition that someone was trying to help, just cold, dead, evil eyes staring back at her from the glass. Somehow, Rachel had to warn Gabriel Jackson, she turned to pick up the intercom phone, it was the only way but she had to do it without alarming other passengers. The woman sensed what Rachel was doing and moved with amazing speed, tearing the handset from its mounting and knocking Rachel and her colleague to the floor.

'He must die,' screamed the woman.

There was no time to question how she'd smuggled the knife onto the plane; all that mattered was the deadly threat to Alastair's life. Gabriel Jackson was puzzled that he hadn't seen Rachel for a while. She'd made a point of being in the vicinity about every twenty minutes, keeping a watch over Alastair, but her routine was broken and he wondered why.

'Cover the child,' he ordered.

Without argument Sara and Dougy did as he asked.

Gabriel Jackson moved into the aisle, blocking access to Alastair. Danger could come from any direction so he had to be ready. To discharge his firearm in the pressurized cabin would be a last resort.

Raised, frightened voices caused him to turn, facing towards the front of the aircraft. The woman was running towards him, lashing out at anyone in her way. Her knife, already blood stained, was raised ready to impale her target. It was down to one of two choices, either risk the gun or attempt to manually disarm her. The safety catch was released; he would wait until the last second before firing. His accuracy would have to be unerring; something he could no longer guarantee, one shot was all he had. Frightened passengers dived for cover as the gun shot reverberated around the cabin. The dying woman fell, still clutching the knife. Blood, frothing from her mouth, seeped into the monogrammed carpet.

'It's all over,' shouted Gabriel Jackson, holding up his badge.

Out of a shocked silence there came clapping and whooping. It didn't matter that some had crimson splatters on their clothing, they'd been delivered from a crazed killer, a terrorist had died and the man who had shot her was a hero.

Horrified, Rachel had watched as the woman made her frenzied way towards Alastair, she saw two innocent passengers fall beneath the knife because they didn't move fast enough and she'd prayed that Gabriel Jackson would protect the child. Through a secure intercom she'd alerted the captain to the danger on board. He'd locked down the flight deck and declared a Mayday situation to Heathrow control who gave him top priority to land; he wouldn't be stacking over London, straight in, no messing. The woman's body was left where it had fallen, the plane was a crime scene and everyone on board would be treated as a potential threat to UK security until cleared by MI5. Gabriel Jackson couldn't afford another delay, but he was the principal witness and despite his heroics on the plane his faked ID would place him at the head of a list of people to be investigated. Rachel would stand by him but dealing with guardian angels isn't in the MI5 handbook. International law enforcement computer records would show nothing; in hyperspace he was invisible.

Chapter 8

Emergency vehicles surrounded the taxiing plane, escorting it to a perimeter holding area. The rusting doors of an obsolete hangar cranked open to reveal a makeshift interrogation centre where identities would be checked, documents pored over and questions asked. The plane rolled to a standstill, seatbelt signs remained lit and cabin crew walked along the aisles enforcing the captain's orders for everyone to stay seated with a total authority that comes with the job. Rachel stepped over the blanket covered corpse and dropped a note into Gabriel Jackson's lap. He read it then looked across at Dougy and Sara. A slight nod and a brief smile gave out a message of reassurance, but apprehension and fear still remained. They were on home soil but it might as well be thousands of miles away for the good it was doing them.

A central door in the side of the plane swung open and men in smart dark suits and bulges under their jackets came on board, taking control in a polite yet firm way that typified the British secret service. Everyone was called sir or madam but God help anyone who made the wrong move. A bilingual agent spoke over the intercom; he left nothing to guess work. No one would leave the hangar until they had been cleared to enter the United Kingdom and he demanded full cooperation, as this would take several hours. Groans met the announcement but only as a form of protest against something that was beyond the passengers' control. Whilst he was talking, two others slid the corpse into a body bag and removed it from the aircraft. Disembarkation would be strictly controlled beginning with economy class. The first block of seat numbers that were read out included Gabriel Jackson and the MacKays.

'A coincidence or what?' muttered Dougy to his wife as they followed Gabriel Jackson down the steps. In the shadows of the hangar they saw the body being loaded into a hearse. For a second Sara felt some sorrow for the woman, there would be no flowers, no one to mourn her passing, it seemed a waste but then she shuddered at the thought of what might have happened if Gabriel Jackson hadn't killed her. A police sergeant led them into the floodlit hangar. Rows of operatives sat like automatons tapping on computers networked to a central criminal database. This was a well-practiced top secret operation designed for situations such as this. Behind the computers was a battery of machines for analysing DNA and fingerprints.

Dougy, Sara and Alastair were taken to a table where a woman was preparing to verify their collective identity and onward destination. A badge clipped to the collar of a starched uniform blouse identified her as an administration assistant working for Military Intelligence.

'Sit down please; I won't keep you a moment.'
The chairs were of the red plastic stacking sort, hard and uncomfortable.
Without looking up from the screen she held out a hand.

'Passports and tickets.'
Dougy passed them over but knew it would only be a few minutes before she'd discover their documents were forgeries and that no record existed of Alastair's birth. Gabriel Jackson had been taken away for special interrogation and Dougy had visions of deportation, without his protection, they wouldn't stand a chance of survival. The woman raised her head from the computer to answer a phone, the message caused her to stiffen, her eyes narrowed as she listened. Then, without a word of reply, she replaced the receiver and turned her attention once again to the computer. For a few seconds her fingers moved expertly over the keyboard, she stopped to read what had come up on the screen. Whatever it was, she picked up the travel documents and handed them back to Dougy. The delete button was pressed and the screen went blank.

'All seems in order; your friend will be with you shortly, you will soon be on your way.'
Dougy was taken aback, only a cursory examination of their documents had taken place, there were no questions and no body searches. He turned as Gabriel Jackson touched his shoulder.

'Come on, we're getting out of here.'

Rachel was standing at the hangar doors.

'A regular Glasgow shuttle will be leaving in half an hour, so if you hurry you'll catch it,' she said.

'You are coming with us aren't you?' asked Sara.

'No, I have other things to do, there's a police car waiting to take you. Gabriel will look after you, he has money.'
Rachel kissed Alastair lightly on the forehead and she was gone.

The police car accelerated around the perimeter road, arriving in time for them to pass through the Glasgow departure gate onto the shuttle. Apart from being allocated seats there were no other formalities, the flight should be quick and easy but uncertainty remained in Dougy's mind as to their final destination once on Scottish soil. In his mind they were homeless, penniless, and fully dependent on Gabriel Jackson for all their needs including a roof over their heads. Dougy's parents still managed a farm near the small town of Inveraray but he'd had minimal contact with them since moving to Zimbabwe. His marriage to Sara had caused some disquiet in the family. It was expected that he would marry the fine Scottish lass who'd been his childhood sweetheart. His parents had treated her as if she were their own daughter so for Dougy to marry someone else was unthinkable. He'd met Sara at the Scottish Young Farmers' September conference in Edinburgh; she had come over with a group of students from Harare University to attend the event and had danced with Dougy during the final evening's ball. She captivated him. Sara was the most beautiful woman he had ever met. Her warm brown eyes and perfect smile drew him in and one kiss was all it took to make him realise that he wanted to spend the rest of his life with her. He gave no thought as to how his parents would receive this devastating blow to the plans they had for him, it was his life and he would live it his own way. Dougy proposed there and then. Sara accepted and he followed her to Zimbabwe to be married in a small church on Christmas Day. His one regret was that his parents had not been present but perhaps now they had a grandson who bore his father's name they would accept Sara and come to terms with their dismay that Dougy had married outside his culture.

He reclined his seat, rested his eyes and allowed his mind to recall the life he and Sara had left behind, it was a life they could not return to, a combination of losing their farm and the birth of Alastair had seen to that. At the time of his son's birth Dougy had written off the 'sign in the heavens' as a coincidence but now, after all that had happened in such a short time, he was well past the point of having second thoughts. Alastair may be special, but he'd made up his mind that his son would have a childhood doing things that ordinary children do, being special was a secondary consideration. He opened his eyes and turned to Sara. She was feeding Alastair whose appetite for his mother's milk was undiminished. Dougy leant over to kiss his wife. She returned his affections with a tired smile. Alastair was taking a lot out of Sara and it showed.

The final leg of the journey was uneventful; Gabriel Jackson relaxed and enjoyed the flight, his hand was hurting less now and movement had returned to the fingers. This pleased him as he would be able to shoot straight once again. An announcement from the flight deck confirmed that they were expected to land in a few minutes and the weather was fine. Dougy felt a slight jolt as the landing gear locked into place. He looked out of the window, he could see the Glasgow sprawl and in the distance, to the west, the peaks of the Highlands. He was home but Sara would have to adjust to life in a foreign land. Dougy remembered how he felt when first moving to Zimbabwe, he would have to be patient with Sara but he knew her strength and she would soon come to terms with life in Scotland, providing they could find somewhere to live. A standard recorded message was delivered in an accent that Dougy identified as coming from the posher part of Edinburgh.

'Welcome to Glasgow, thank you for flying British Airways and we wish you a safe onward journey.'
The irony of this message dawned on Dougy. For them there was no onward journey. Although Gabriel Jackson wouldn't let them down, the most they could hope for was another safe house, probably in the Gorbals, the thought of which filled Dougy with despair. If they were to bring up Alastair in Scotland then Glasgow or any city for that

matter was not the place to do it. Dougy had spent much of his life in the fresh air by shimmering lochs; he'd bagged his first Munro at 14, he'd walked the glens and rounded up his father's sheep from barren hillsides. Alastair would thrive there and not in some crowded metropolis where drugs and alcohol ruined so many young lives, after all he was special.

Even though he'd been away from his homeland for quite some time, as soon as he put a foot on Scottish soil it was as if he had never been away at all. Sara held Alastair close to her as together they walked through the arrivals gate. Gabriel Jackson was not far away, alert and instinctively ready to deal with any threat that may arise. Death could come from any direction yet nothing happened, perhaps those who would harm Alastair were waiting elsewhere ready to strike when the time was right, or they had given up.

Taxis ferried some passengers away, others went to people holding name boards and some just kissed those who'd met them. Soon there was no one left, apart from Gabriel Jackson and the MacKays.

'What now?' Dougy asked but he already knew what the answer would be. *Everything was taken care of so there was no need to worry*, but they'd been shot at, nearly blown up, had come within inches of being annihilated by a crazed woman with a knife so Dougy had good reason to be just a little concerned.

'Just sit there and wait,' said Gabriel Jackson pointing to a bench.

'What for, Christmas,' replied Dougy.
The sarcasm was lost on Gabriel Jackson who by now was talking on his phone. As always with this man the conversation was one way. He motioned Dougy and Sara to follow him to the taxi rank. The thin pasty-faced driver of an old, red Mondeo at the head of the queue reluctantly put down his copy of the Sun, stretched himself and started the engine, he didn't move from his seat. Gabriel rapped impatiently on the driver's window, it slid to half open.

'Where to mate?' asked the driver in a broad Glaswegian accent.

'Oban ferry terminal.'

There was menace in Gabriel Jackson's voice and his 'full on' posture brought about a swift attitude change. 'Sir' replaced 'mate' and the driver became nauseatingly helpful to the point of opening the doors and giving Sara a blanket to cover her knees. Gabriel Jackson settled into a front seat, it sagged under his bulk. The driver felt a compulsion to turn his head towards him, and was transfixed like a rabbit caught in the glare of a car's headlights. He would remember nothing of the journey.

Chapter 9

Taxi drivers the world over like to talk, and this one was no different. Gabriel Jackson ignored him. His mind, closed to diversions, was preoccupied with the task that lay ahead. It wasn't going to be easy convincing Dougy and Sara that the only way to keep the child from harm would be for them to stay at a place dedicated to the spiritual life with an added bonus of being surrounded by a natural moat. He'd wait until they were on Mull before telling them.

Once through Crainlarich the scenery began to change. Sara stared in wonderment at the rugged misty topped mountains that went on forever into the distance and at waterfalls cascading into fast flowing rivers that were almost within touching distance. Back in Zimbabwe Dougy would constantly speak of his beloved Highlands and now she could see why. This countryside was truly magnificent, but deep within her was sadness at having to leave a homeland that in its own way was just as beautiful. Two and a half hours is long enough cooped in a beat up old taxi smelling of pine from a deodorizer that dangled from the driver's mirror. Sara felt some relief as Dougy exclaimed:

'Connel Bridge, we're nearly there.'
Memories once again flooded back. This was the place of childhood holidays, of ice cream, fish and chips, jumping off rocks into the sea and racing his father up to the top of McCaig's Tower. He wondered if the shop that sold homemade Scottish tablet had survived the years, his mouth watered at the thought.

There was no tip for the driver, just the exact fare. He made a 'U' turn on the narrow quay before joining the traffic heading out of town. By the time he'd gone a dozen miles his memory of the journey was fading; soon all he would remember was the way back to Glasgow. There was already a queue forming at the ticket desk for the afternoon sailing to Mull. The ferry would be busy with commuters and school children whose return trip was their equivalent to the school bus. Keeping the MacKays close to him Gabriel Jackson paid for the tickets. So as not to spook Dougy or Sara he bought returns, they would know soon enough of his plans for Alastair.

Once on board they followed him to the main lounge. Seats were scarce but they found two together and Gabriel Jackson stood with his back against a bulkhead. He could see everyone from there; nothing would escape him. A long blast on the horn signalled the ferry's departure. It moved slowly from its berth and turned into the deep water channel that took it across the bay into the open sea. All seemed normal, people read their newspapers, drank coffee and giggly schoolgirls talked of boyfriends, yet Gabriel Jackson was uneasy, it was that sixth sense again. He cursed himself when Dougy signalled that he and Sara needed sustenance. Why hadn't he bought water and sandwiches before getting on the ferry, how stupid of him, but he couldn't allow either of them out of his sight. He'd noticed a coffee machine in the stairwell and judged that if he used that, Dougy, Sara and the child would still be visible but a lot of people would be between him and them. If anyone was watching and waiting for an opportunity then to go to the coffee machine would be foolhardy. Gabriel Jackson shook his head, he was staying right there, no point in taking risks especially on a sea crossing as short as this. He would buy something once they'd docked on Mull, but Dougy had other ideas. His wife was hungry, she needed to keep up her strength to feed and care for Alastair. Scottish rebelliousness replaced common sense; he approached Gabriel Jackson, his hand held out for money. For a moment the view was blocked, long enough for a small wiry African man to make a move towards Sara. Gabriel Jackson's arm sent Dougy sprawling into a group of passengers scattering them like ninepins. He was on to the man, pinning him to the floor, the muzzle of his gun firmly embedded directly above the assailant's carotid artery.

'One move, that's all, one move,' threatened Gabriel Jackson.
People were yelling and falling as they scattered for cover, blocking the doorway in their panic. Girlish giggles had turned to screams, a frightened steward picked up a wall phone to call the bridge and the

ferry skipper signalled 'all stop' to the engine room, the 'Lord of the Isles' would not be docking on time this afternoon.

Dougy had found his way back to Sara who sat shivering with fear; she was holding Alastair, rocking him to and fro, a natural protective movement inborn in mothers since time began. The passenger lounge cleared but panic spread throughout the boat. This was a terrorist attack, something that happened in other parts of the world but not here, not on the Oban to Mull ferry.

'I'm so sorry,' whispered Dougy to his wife, 'that was a stupid thing to do.'
Sara managed a weak smile, he'd done it for her and she understood. Gabriel Jackson was not so forgiving, his pent up fury ploughed into Dougy like machine gun bullets. Never before had he been spoken to in such a manner, his entire self-respect was stripped away leaving him contrite, almost begging for forgiveness. At least he wouldn't be making that mistake again.

Gabriel Jackson dragged the man to his feet. He pushed him onto one of the red plastic benches lining the lounge, warning him again that any move towards the child would be his last this side of eternity. The man's eyes were glazed, He'd seen a similar look in the eyes of the woman on the plane; she was a suicidal killer just like this man and Gabriel Jackson prepared himself to defend the child. As the man lunged towards Alastair the same cry came from his distorted features,

'He must die.'
It took three bullets to stop him; blood sprayed across the seats, he staggered backwards through a narrow opening leading to the observation deck. He was already dead as momentum took him over the rails, and like a broken puppet his body tumbled into the cold waters of the Firth of Lorne. It was the last of Gabriel Jackson's ammunition; his gun caused no more than a ripple as it followed its final victim into the water.

Where there had been violence and bloodshed there was now stillness. The immediate danger had passed but the sound of a police helicopter overhead and the bow wave of a fast approaching coastguard launch meant Gabriel Jackson would have to be at his most persuasive to talk his way out of this one.

'Tell the truth, you were protecting Alastair' said Sara.

'That's right, we're all in it together,' agreed Dougy.

A humourless smile flitted across Gabriel Jackson's lips, they were so near to their destination, it was the only place on earth where Alastair would be under heavenly protection and he was driven to complete his divine task. Of course there was always God who could be called upon for help but as in the past when such a call had been placed, the response was never clear-cut or immediately helpful, it was just a matter of faith. Gabriel Jackson moved to a corner of the lounge. As he prayed, armed police from the special operations branch had already abseiled from the helicopter and were lining up on the deck.

Dougy heard a whispered 'amen' then Gabriel Jackson walked through the lounge entrance into the stair well.

'Where are you going, you're not leaving us here?' shouted Dougy.

'To get us a coffee, it might be the last we'll get for a while.'

They sat together, drinking from polystyrene cups, waiting for the authorities to burst through into the passenger lounge. Minutes passed, Sara changed Alastair, and their coffees were finished yet still no sign of the police.

The ferry skipper stayed at his post on the bridge. At his side was a senior Argyll and Bute police officer directing operations through a secure frequency. Iain Sherrie was young for a Chief Inspector but his ability was not in doubt. Experience had taught him not to rush things. He didn't want needless deaths, too much paperwork. The skipper was on another secure line to his bosses who demanded to be kept completely informed about developments. They could keep it from the media for so long but within the next ten minutes the ferry would fail to dock so it was only a matter of time before local news editors starting asking questions.

A green light flashed on the control panel, the skipper picked up the phone.

'No sir, nothing yet,' he said.

He listened as a barrage of instructions came at him. His brow furled and he sat down.

'Well, you're the boss, but I'm in control of the boat so I'll call the shots.' The skipper's voice had a definite edge; he didn't take kindly to being dictated to by someone from behind a desk in Glasgow.

'What's that all about?' asked the Chief Inspector.

'The bloody fool wants me to keep a lid on things and take the ferry into Mull where someone from the office will be waiting to take over, he says can you tell your people to stand down.'

'Nobody leaves the boat until I say so, not even you' said the Chief Inspector.

An order was given and the engines started. Gabriel Jackson raised his eyes,

'Thank you,' he whispered

God works in mysterious ways and he was sure that once the ferry had docked, safe passage would be granted, someone in authority would see to that.

Under the expert hand of its skipper the ferry slid effortlessly into a mooring position and ropes thrown down to be secured around capstans by men who gave the job more urgency than they would normally. The bow doors remained closed and exits to the gangway locked. Mobile phone messages giving distorted accounts of what had gone on ensured that news of the incident had spread; rubber neckers mixed with anxious relatives lined the quayside, standing silently, waiting for the drama to unfold. Such things rarely happened on Mull so it was something not to be missed. They would hardly notice the small helicopter as it buzzed over their heads; neither would they pay any attention to the old bus with a crash gear box that carried visitors to nearby Duart Castle grinding to a halt in a reserved parking place, anyway why would they bother with what was a common occurrence. Today though, the more observant amongst the crowd would notice it had a different driver. A woman had replaced the general handyman who normally drove the old charabanc to and from its owner's ancient pile. She kept the engine running, hands resting lightly on the steering wheel as a soberly dressed man wearing a clerical collar got off and walked through the crowd to where passengers exited the ferry. He encountered no resistance from police officers guarding the gangway. Having reached the locked door he stood, head bowed and motionless, as if waiting for a body to be carried from the boat.

The skipper answered his phone, listened and replaced the receiver. His orders were unequivocal; failure to carry them out to the letter would have dire consequences for him. He turned to the chief inspector,

'The black man and his friends must not be prevented from leaving the boat, OK.'

'What the hell is going on here, I said before, nobody leaves without my say so and that stands,' said the policeman.
The phone rang again.

'It's for you,' said the skipper.
The Chief Inspector grabbed the receiver.

'Yes, who is it?' he shouted.

'Oh right sir, sorry sir,' he spluttered.
Yet again, the conversation was one way, his authority had been countermanded. The Chief Constable had taken control. Gabriel Jackson and the MacKays were immediately escorted from the ferry and handed over to the priest. The crowd parted to let them through and as they climbed into the bus a familiar face turned to greet them.

'Hello again, still attracting trouble I see,' said Rachel.
Sara felt relief at seeing the woman with whom she had developed an earlier friendship, but this was a different Rachel. Gone the efficient flight attendant and in her place was a softer more gracious, sensuous woman. Long auburn hair cascading over her shoulders and the natural beauty radiating from her suggested a halo would not be out of place. Her voice no longer had that edge of authority but was soothing, almost hypnotic. The look that passed between her and Gabriel Jackson was deeper than one of recognition; it was a look of love but

not of the physical kind. They shared a common spiritual bond that went through them to Alastair; he was the object of their affection.

Rachel guided the old bone shaker away from the quay side and headed along the coast towards Duart Castle. Dougy had been there before; he remembered it as a cold place offering few creature comforts. He recalled being shown the dungeons and regaled with stories of torture; he remembered standing in driving rain looking over the parapet at the grey sea. It was a part of Scottish history, no more than that, not a place where a child could be nurtured. Through the rear view mirror Rachel caught the frown on Dougy's face; she guessed what he was thinking.

'It's OK, you'll see,' she said.

Sat on the back seat Gabriel Jackson appeared relaxed, more like a tourist than a man on a mission. Idly he thumbed through a few of the information leaflets scattered on the seats more for something to do than anything else. The bus trundled on for about a mile then Rachel steered it onto a private single track road leading to the castle. Gabriel Jackson walked to the front of the bus and gave instructions to Rachel.

'Get as close as you can to the helicopter,' he said.

Already the rotor blades were turning as Rachel drew alongside, she yanked the handbrake over its ratchets and opened the doors. Then, for a brief moment, the former efficient self-assured flight attendant took over.

'As quick as you can, follow me.'

The firmness in her voice brought about an immediate reaction. Battling against the powerful downdraught they ran to the helicopter, Rachel was there ahead of them, helping, directing, and ensuring that Sara and Alastair were belted in. Dougy squeezed in at the side of his wife and Gabriel Jackson joined the pilot in the cockpit.

The journey time was short, so short in fact that it was only minutes before their destination came into view. They hovered over Iona, a small, sparsely populated island where a restored Abbey stands partly on the same spot as the original built in 563 by St Columba. Over the centuries the Abbey has been sacked by Vikings, pulled down and rebuilt by various religious factions and had its ownership disputed by the MacLean clan of Duart and the Campbells in the shape of the dukes of Argyll, who acquired it by force in the late 18th century. It now rests under the guardianship of Historic Scotland.

Early versions of St Columba show him to be single minded, ruthless and wholly committed to seeing through what God had directed him to do, he didn't worry about the occasional sacrifice here and there, a bit like Gabriel Jackson. What he began on Iona still continues. The pilgrimages, the religious retreats, the never ending influx of tourists that once exposed to the influence of this place usually leave having been permanently changed, some returning year after year. It is a place of burials where kings and political leaders lie side by side with ordinary folk. It is a place of folklore, ghostly apparitions that appear out of the sea mist catching people unawares. But now powerful political and ecclesiastical voices had colluded to close down Iona to tourism, isolating it from the outside world, giving Gabriel Jackson total authority to use the Abbey and its surrounds in whatever way he saw fit to ensure the survival of the child. He planned to live on the island, guiding, directing and making all the decisions. But first, the helicopter had to be landed safely.

The pilot, his features concealed behind a full face visor, brought the aircraft in over the stretch of sea separating Mull from Iona and with consummate skill, hovering above a patch of grass close to the Abbey, he brought it down with the precision of an eagle delivering food to its young in a nest balanced on a ledge hundreds of feet above a shear drop, it was effortless. This pilot really knew his business, but then he was one of a selected few, Alastair's whereabouts would remain a secret with him. Standing in the shadows of a side entrance a brace of nuns and a young priest waited for the rotors to stop before moving forward to offer their welcome. This holy trio would ensure that Gabriel Jackson's wishes would be honoured to the letter; compromise was out of the question. They greeted him with reverence usually reserved for visiting dignitaries, bowing and kissing his hand. Then, virtually ignoring Dougy and Sara they turned their attention to Alastair who, having slept for the entire journey, was beginning to wake. They knelt before him, eyes facing the ground, muttering a prayer. Then one of the nuns stood and held out her hands as if to take Alastair from his mother. Dougy stepped between them; his son would not be leaving their protection, not now or ever if he had his way. This nun's actions sent a message to Dougy; he would have to be on his guard against any attempt to take Alastair away, facing up to Gabriel Jackson was not something he looked forward to but Alastair was his son and as far as he was concerned carried human genes and not those of a heavenly deity to be worshipped by these people. He knew this island and the only realistic way of escape was by sea. An intermittent ferry service existed but locals generally used their own boats to move between Iona, Mull and neighbouring islands so possibilities existed, he would have to bide his time, there was no other way of wrenching Alastair away from Gabriel Jackson's increasingly tight grasp. By now the others had risen from their knees.

'Please follow us, we will take you to your rooms,' said the priest in a distinctive Irish accent.

One of the nuns took Sara by the arm as if to lead her. Dougy smiled as Sara resisted.

'Good girl,' he whispered.

'Where are you taking us, where are these rooms,' asked Dougy.

Whatever the priest said in reply was drowned out as the helicopter took off. The loud swish of the rotor blades grew in intensity, throwing up dead grass and dust. It turned and within seconds was just a speck as it headed out over the sea.

When it had gone, Dougy repeated the question but Gabriel Jackson stifled any attempt the priest may have made to answer it.

'You'll be very comfortable and well cared for, now follow the priest.'

It was Gabriel Jackson at his most dictatorial. Dougy and Sara, who was holding Alastair close to her chest, followed the priest, flanked by the two nuns, through the main door into the gloom of the place where they would stay for weeks, months or years.

Well-trodden stone steps led up to two rooms that had been set aside in a part of the Abbey usually reserved for pilgrims. Despite comfortable beds, soft furnishings and a sea view, Dougy felt imprisoned. The stone walls told their own story, these rooms had once been cells where monks, isolated from the world, had spent much of their time in penitence, rising at some ungodly hour to pray then after a sparse breakfast and more praying would engage in some kind of backbreaking menial work before being called back to prayer once again. It was a daily cycle of devotion that went back to the days of the Abbey's founders and Dougy shuddered at the thought of having to defend his son should Gabriel Jackson have a similar life plan mapped out for Alastair. This place wasn't home; it was nothing less than incarceration. They would soon discover that contact with anyone other than Gabriel Jackson and his followers had been cut off, any attempt to reach out beyond the rocky shores of this isolated place would be impossible. The Abbey was now out of bounds to tourists and the only people remaining on Iona would be those who lived there and they had already been warned that loose talk carried severe penalties. Supplies would be ferried to the island by helicopter and the Abbey would revert to its roots. The media had been told that a new order of monks was to be trained there and the sea ferry would be called into service only if an emergency arose.

It was the sound of the ferry's horn that drew Dougy to the window. This would be its final docking before being taken out of service. Evening mist rose from the water as the gangway crashed down onto the concrete and a small group of people walked away from the ferry and up the gentle slope of the jetty. Heading past the ruined nunnery they came into view of the Abbey. Huddled together as if seeking protection from a non-existent cold wind they shuffled, in step, along the dirt road, their vestments merging to give an impression of a large black stain moving ever closer to the Abbey. Each had a cord tied loosely around the waist from which hung a large silver crucifix. Their shuffling gait caused the crucifixes to swing in unison, catching the evening sunlight. As far as Dougy was concerned those crucifixes could have been keys. The sound of a Taizé chant came from within their midst, repetitive and hypnotic.

'The jailors have arrived,' he said.

Sara moved to the window.

'It's just a bunch of monks, perhaps they live here,' she replied. Dougy grunted and turned away from the window. They had fled one dictator, now here they were in the hands of another, the difference being that this one did not wish to kill their son but Gabriel Jackson would take his life anyway.

'Give me the boy until the age of seven, I will give you the man,' Dougy muttered.

'What's that,' asked Sara.

'It's an old Jesuit saying. Once a boy has been under their total influence for seven years they will have him for life, so I reckon we are here for that length of time. This bunch believes they have the reincarnated Jesus Christ and see it as their duty to prepare him to fulfil religious prophecy.'

Sara drew Alastair to her and she began to cry, silently at first then as the stresses of the past few weeks caught up with her she broke down into uncontrollable screams of frustration, anger and fear. It was a fear not for herself or Dougy but for Alastair who she had become convinced would be taken from her to be treated like some force-fed caged animal being fattened for the slaughter. Holding Alastair ever tighter to her body she stormed around the room until falling exhausted into Dougy's arms where he held her until the paroxysms calmed. He struggled to keep his own feelings under control. Age had matured him but a Scottish temperament lurked beneath the surface and given the right mixture of circumstances it would emerge and take over. Sara's heartbreak was enough to set things in motion, they had to flee from here, remaining was not an option.

Chapter 10

The monks reached the Abbey precincts, their chanting becoming more audible. Gabriel Jackson strode out from the main entrance, greeting them as one would long lost brothers. He wore the habit of a Benedictine Abbott, marking himself out as the man in charge.

'Welcome, welcome all of you, come let us dine together,' he boomed.

Joining in with the chant he swept them into the building. They followed him to the refectory where thirteen places had been arranged six to a side and one at the head of the table, each place had a bowl, a spoon and a heavy pot mug. For centuries countless monks and pilgrims had eaten in this place but in recent years it had taken on the characteristics and feel of a coffee shop, serving tourists and others who came to the island. It had become a place to rest weary legs and engage in light-hearted banter over a meal and a drink. Now it more resembled the refectory used by Columba and his monks, austere, lit only by candles. All decoration had been stripped away; a heavy scrubbed pine table and crudely fashioned stools replaced the veneered tables and elegant dining chairs.

Gabriel Jackson motioned for the monks to sit; he clicked his fingers in the direction of a small kitchen next to the dining area. The two nuns appeared carrying jugs of soup and home-made bread, warm from the oven; the young priest followed holding a pitcher of red wine. When all had been served Gabriel Jackson stood, he extended his arms as if drawing the monks into himself.

'Let us bow our heads in prayer,' he said.

With arms still outstretched and the palms of his hands facing upwards he prayed.

'Lord, our Father we are a brotherhood in your service, give us strength and direction as we begin the task you have set before us. Vanquish those who seek to thwart your Holy will and make this a place where prophecy is fulfilled. Amen.'

The 'amen' was collectively repeated and they ate in silence. When the meal was over they rose at Gabriel Jackson's command and fell in behind him as he left the refectory. The monks had been allocated quarters on either side of the rooms occupied by Dougy and Sara. It was a stifling, suffocating arrangement, no chances were being taken. Gabriel Jackson had thought of everything.

As night fell, the distant gentle sound of waves running up the tiny beach calmed Dougy's troubled mind. Sara, still fully dressed and holding Alastair in her arms had curled up on the bed, both were asleep. From the window Dougy looked across at the dark shape of Mull, it was only a short distance away and to reach its shoreline undetected would give them a real chance of escape. Islanders' boats were tied up alongside the jetty and Dougy considered that to take one would offer a way of getting his family to safety, but it was too simple, Gabriel Jackson had planned his strategy to perfection and the boats would probably be disabled or alarmed to alert their owners of any attempt to take them. But he had to find out.

Making a sortie under the cover of darkness appealed to him. The moon was bright enough to offer some light and he could dodge in and out of the shadows to escape detection. Some lights in the building had not been replaced by candles; a fire exit light at the end of the corridor glowed softly, it would see him safely to the steps. The door creaked as he eased it open. Ordinarily the noise would go unnoticed but with so many ears tuned to detecting the slightest sound, he immediately found himself explaining to an inquisitive monk why he'd left his room, particularly at night.

'I need some fresh air.'

The monk nodded then offered to go with him, to keep him company. Dougy agreed. They walked in silence to the Abbey door. The monk reached up and from a hook concealed behind the door frame produced a key. The door swung open. Dougy stood for ten minutes on the grass bank, inhaling the clean air thinking that even if he'd made it past the monk unchallenged, the locked door would have barred any further progress. But knowing where the key was kept gave him the edge; perhaps Gabriel Jackson wasn't so clever after all. Back in his room Dougy settled into an easy chair and catnapped.

It was the sound of footsteps outside in the corridor that startled him. They gradually disappeared as the monks made their way to the chapel. The luminous dial of a bedside clock said 5.00am. Dougy guessed that this was time for a regular act of worship, he gambled on a free run to the main door. Placing a hand lightly over Sara's mouth, Dougy woke her.

'Come on, we're getting out of here.'

'How, what time is it?'

'Trust me,' was all that Dougy would say.

He opened the creaky apartment door but this time he wasn't challenged; the corridor leading to the steps was quiet and deserted. For a moment Dougy listened, satisfying himself that the way was clear. This was Gabriel Jackson's second mistake and he meant to exploit it to the full.

'C'mon lass.' Dougy beckoned Sara to follow him.

Sara pulled a shawl around the still sleeping Alastair, hoping that he would not wake, at least until they were clear of the building. The fastidious monk had replaced the key on its hook, which Dougy gratefully exploited. A cooling breeze came from the sea carrying with it the smell of decaying seaweed that littered the shoreline in large quantities. To Dougy it was the smell of freedom, with luck he would find a boat that would take them across to Mull and from there the chance of escape. Staying close to the walls of the ruined convent they made their way to the jetty. The early morning light picked out the shapes of a number of small boats bobbing on a slight swell and Dougy could hardly contain his excitement when he noticed that one of them was tied loosely to a mooring post and the owner hadn't removed the outboard motor.

'Wait there a second,' he said to Sara.

Dougy removed his shoes and socks, rolled his trousers above the knees and waded to the boat. He almost laughed out loud when he saw an ignition key protruding from the dashboard. He took hold of the mooring rope and dragged the boat to shore. Dougy held Alastair whilst Sara climbed into the boat then clambered in himself. Because the noise of an outboard motor firing up would carry to the Abbey he cast off and allowed the boat to drift on the tide until some way from shore. He turned the key, nothing happened. He tried again with the same result. Just as he was to try for a third time a beam of light lit up the boat. Dougy shaded his eyes against the blinding light.

'Going somewhere?' shouted a familiar, mocking voice.

'Shit,' muttered Dougy.

He slumped back in the driving seat, guessing that the battery had been removed. Sara rocked gently, almost in unison with the marooned boat, she was crying again.

'Wait there, I'll come and get you.'

Gabriel Jackson took a bunch of keys from his pocket, a motor started and within minutes he drew alongside. The stricken craft was towed unceremoniously back to its mooring place. Once on shore Gabriel Jackson put his arms around both of them.

'I'm sorry you feel the need to run away but the safety of you and the child rests within the Abbey, oh and by the way,' he said, turning his large smiling face towards Dougy, 'I'd put my shoes on if I were you, it's a sharp walk back.'

'How did you know we had left the Abbey?' asked Sara.

'I just knew, call it intuition,' replied Gabriel Jackson.

'You bastard, you set us up,' said Dougy, choking with anger.

'Well, think what you like, but I can tell you it won't happen again.' Gabriel Jackson's voice had moved from bonhomie to threatening. His determination to keep Alastair from leaving Iona was reinforced when he locked the Abbey's main door behind them. He pocketed the key, grinning as he did so.

'From now on you won't go outside unless I give permission, and then you will be supervised. Your meals will be brought to you, and one of the nuns will be on hand at all times to help look after the child. Please comply and you will stay safe and we will remain friends.'

With that he turned and walked away. By now the monks had returned from their devotions and were at breakfast. Despite their monastic life they ate surprisingly well. The appetising smell of fried bacon had reached the McKay living quarters, fuelling Dougy's appetite.

'I could eat some of what they're having,' he said.

In return he received the sort of look that suggested now was not the time to be thinking about his stomach.

'Well, we have to keep our strength up don't we, you never know when the next opportunity will come,' he said.

But the island had been locked down, no further opportunities would arise and Sara knew it.

'Tea,' she said.

'Aye, OK,' replied Dougy in a voice edged with Scottish impatience.

Sara put Alastair in his cot and switched on the kettle.

They sat in silence, gaining comfort from wrapping their hands around the hot mugs; the tea was sipped as an afterthought. A gentle female Irish voice disturbed their daydreaming.

'Good morning, breakfast anyone?'

A nun stood at the half open door holding a tray of food.

'I've been given the task of feeding you, I'm afraid the choice is limited.' she said.

'It didn't smell limited about half an hour ago,' said Dougy.

'Special rations are given to those who do the heavy work and everyone else has to make do with what is left,' replied the nun.

Sara responded angrily.

'So that's his game is it, we are being punished.'

The nun refused to be drawn and handed the tray to Dougy. It contained two bowls of cereal and a jug of milk. Then with a slight bow she left the room, the square heels of her shiny black shoes click clacking along the corridor as she went about her other duties. She would return at midday with more meagre rations and then again in the evening.

The swish of rotor blades drew Dougy to the window. The supplies helicopter was setting down on the grassy area that by now had become a makeshift heliport.

'More grub for the monks I suppose,' he grumbled.

It was then that he saw a passenger jump to the ground. Even from a distance he recognised Rachel and his mood lifted.

'Rachel's here,' he said.

Sara interrupted Alastair's evening feed and came to the window. Several monks approached the helicopter and helped Rachel and the pilot to unload a dozen or so of wooden crates that were carried to the abbey. It was obvious from the way they were lifted that each crate weighed more than one monk could carry alone. Dougy quipped that it was probably heavy food for those who did heavy work but he realised that these crates contained something other than cabbages or potatoes.

As Gabriel Jackson greeted her, Rachel led him to where they could not be overheard. Her urgency was justified, whilst on Mull she had received reliable information that an attempt on the child's life was imminent.

'Have you any more information?' asked Gabriel Jackson.

'None, except that it will happen very soon.'

'Arm everyone,' he said.

Each crate was smashed open and Heckler and Koch MP5's handed out.

Dougy watched in disbelief as the monks checked and loaded their weapons. These men were highly trained. *'What the hell is going on?'* he thought.

Gabriel Jackson had to know more about the planned attack so he questioned Rachel with an intensity that scared her.

'Let's go over it again, who told you about the attack, where did the information come from?'

'I was staying at the castle and one of the cleaners fetched me to the phone.'

'And…'

'A disguised voice told me that the boy would soon be dead and so would all those who protected him.'

'Think Rachel, think, did the voice give any clues as to its origin?'

Rachel closed her eyes and went over the message in her mind. She'd heard many different languages in her life but this voice was so well camouflaged it was almost impossible to tell, yet there could have been a faint hint of a familiar dialect. Deep concentration was etched on her face.

'I can't be sure but it could have been South African, certainly male, but there is one thing I remember, the voice said they will come for the boy at night.'

'OK, we don't know when but they'll be fanatics just like the others, we don't know how many there'll be but we have to be ready for them, we have to stand between them and the child. There's two ways they will come at us, either over the water or from the air and we have to be ready for both, first blood is vital.'

'We have to get the child and his parents to a safer place, any ideas?' asked Rachel.

Gabriel Jackson took Rachel by the arm and almost dragged her into the Abbey.

'I will show you.'

He took her to the refectory.

'Wait here, I won't be long.'

He returned carrying what Rachel took to be a scroll. He unrolled the fragile parchment across the dining table.

'What is it?' asked Rachel.

'It's an early plan of the Abbey graveyard going back hundreds of years. I noticed a stone in the wall of my bedroom that looked as if it didn't belong, so I loosened the mortar and removed it. The graveyard scroll and other things were in a cavity roughly chopped into the wall.'

'What other things?' asked Rachel.

'No time for that now, but look at this.'

Gabriel Jackson positioned a finger above the image of a large cross then moved it slowly to the right.

'What does that look like?' he said.

Rachel could hardly believe what he was showing her.

'Is it a tunnel?'

'Yes, a ley tunnel that begins in St Oran's Chapel and leads to a chamber below the ruined convent.'

'You went down into it,' said Rachel.

'Not on my own, I took one of the brothers with me in case there was more digging to do, but there wasn't, the tunnel is lined with stone and the chamber is large enough to take four adults, but what the map doesn't show are the steps leading from the chamber up to the convent, the perfect hiding place and escape route, so I'm putting you in charge of getting the child to safety if and when we are attacked.'

Rachel smiled at the thought of what really went on in the secret chamber but insisted on seeing the tunnel for herself. If the attack was to come in the dark she needed to have knowledge of its layout. At the tunnel entrance Gabriel Jackson dragged aside a large flat stone, then stooping, they made their way to the chamber. Rachel held a powerful torch that lit the way and once inside the chamber she was amazed at being able to stand upright. Whether it was a place built for survival or secret liaison a small number of people could remain out of sight here for days rather than hours. Fixed to the walls were the remnants of corroded metal brackets that once held flaming torches. Ingrained smoke stains showed the chamber had been used frequently. Back in the chapel, Rachel cleared her lungs and asked Gabriel Jackson not to replace the stone over the entrance; if it became necessary to use the tunnel then speed would be critical, also they would need a supply of breathable air.

Gabriel Jackson returned to the Abbey and summoned the heavily armed monks to meet him in the refectory. He addressed them in a sombre tone.

'The enemy is coming. Are you prepared to fight and if necessary die in defence of the child?'
Automatic weapons were raised in the air and together the monks pledged their lives to the cause.

'I would have expected nothing less, your names will live forever, now we must mobilise the others,' said Gabriel Jackson.

Organised in shifts, the islanders were part of a permanent lookout, posted at every point from where an attack could be mounted. Men sitting in boats out at sea, women standing on high ground watching the sky and monks surrounding the Abbey, formed the first and last line of defence. The lookouts had flares with orders to launch them at the first sign of trouble. Gabriel Jackson told them not to hesitate even if it turned out to be a false alarm.

Darkness had settled and the lookouts were in place. Rachel felt mixed emotions of fear and excitement as she readied herself to protect the child; the tunnel would be a last resort. Propping her chair against the wall next to the MacKay's quarters she waited; it could be tonight, tomorrow or next week, but she was ready when called upon to do her duty. In the quiet of the night she prayed for strength.

Chapter 11

No one took a second look at Banga and Rudo Chiku strap hanging on their way to Glasgow University Campus. They each carried identical blue and black rucksacks that looked to the casual commuter to be full of books and other paraphernalia that students haul around with them. Students of all nationalities are a familiar sight in this part of the city; mixing with other commuters during the morning rush hour. The subway train slowed as it approached the University stop, the brothers moved to the door. Most carriages will empty here, students spilling onto the platform, clogging the escalators as they bustle their way towards busy exits. Subway staff cast cursory glances as tickets and passes are flashed under their noses; they are pleased to see the back of students, until the evening when they return for their homeward trek, often to cold, sparsely furnished accommodation in less attractive parts of the city. Banga and Rudo Chiku had ridden the subway each weekday for the past six months, they'd attended lectures, took notes, chatted up girls, acting normal, yet somehow had managed to stay inconspicuous, which is what sleeping killers are meant to do.

Today they didn't go to their lectures; instead they hung around outside the station, Banga Chiku looked at his watch.

'They'll be here in five minutes,' he said.

Rudo Chiku began to show signs of agitation; his brother reached out, touching his arm.

'Calm down, we'll soon be on our way, remember we are doing this for the glory of our leader, he is relying on us, the boy must die.'

Rudo Chiku smiled; it was a humourless rueful smile, knowing this could be a one-way trip his gut churned. A red Vauxhall Zafira hatchback carrying two other young men drew up at the kerbside. All four had trained together at a location deep inside Zimbabwe before being 'parachuted' into the UK as students. The driver lowered his window.

'Put your bags in the back and get in,' he ordered.

67

Rudo Chiku lifted the hatchback and carefully placed their rucksacks against two others that lay on a blanket. Another blanket was thrown over them, a deadly arsenal of micro Uzis, Glock semi-automatic pistols and stun grenades were completely hidden. The Chiku brothers climbed into the car and fastened their seat belts. Everything had to appear normal; four young men going about their business, nothing suspicious to attract attention. Tap, tap, tap. The driver lowered his window. A traffic warden was already writing the ticket.

'You're in a no waiting zone, didn't you read the notice.'
Stay calm, don't attract attention.

'Sorry, I didn't see the sign.'

'You can appeal sir, I would advise that you read the instructions on the back of the ticket,' said the Traffic Warden.
Smile, be respectful.

The car pulled away, they had gone about a mile when Banga Chiku leaned over, touching the front seat passenger on the shoulder.

'Pass that ticket over here,' he said.

'He was no traffic warden, this is our final instruction, that's why he told you to read it,' he said.

'Read it to us then,' said the driver.

The instruction, written in Afrikaans gave the postcode of where Alastair was being kept, the strength of resistance they would encounter, and the location of a high powered boat, fuelled and ready for use. They were instructed to make their assault that night because fog over Mull was forecast. Clipped to the ticket was a map of Iona. An arrow pointed out Martyrs Bay, where in the year 806, Viking invaders reputedly slaughtered 68 monks. The carnage on this infamous day may have given the sand a permanent thirst for blood, so this ancient killing ground was an ideal place to mount their lethal quest, the omens would be good. They were no longer a sleeping unit, what they had been trained to do was now a reality. The boy had to die along with anyone who stood in their way.

'Long live our glorious leader,' yelled the driver, raising a clenched fist as they sped westwards to meet their destiny.

A blue flashing light in the rear view mirror and the penetrative wail of a police siren brought an expletive from the driver.

'Shit, now what?' he growled.

'Just stop, plead ignorance, we're tourists unused to British speed limits; remember we have a ferry to catch' said Banga Chiku.

The car was brought to a stop, its nearside wheels running along the steep grassy verge that lined this part of the road. They sat in nervous silence, waiting. A tall, robust female officer emerged from a police 4x4, chromium plated sergeant's shoulder stripes reflecting the blue light that flashed across the top of the vehicle. For the second time that day the driver lowered his window at the insistence of a uniformed official.

'Is this your car sir?' inquired the sergeant in a pronounced regional accent.

This opening gambit usually precedes more in depth discussion, especially if there was some doubt as to the true ownership of a vehicle.

'Yes,' replied the driver.

'OK sir, can I see your documents; you know, licence, insurance and MOT certificate.'

'They're at home.'

Another officer had left the police vehicle and was circling like a hungry buzzard. He looked at the tyres, checked the tax disc and inspected the body work whist his colleague continued the conversation with the driver.

'Where's home?' asked the officer.

'Glasgow, we've rented an apartment there.'

'Can I have a look in the back please sir?'

Rudo Chiku felt fear, they were about to be discovered, the mission would be in danger of failure.

'Why, there's only our rucksacks in there, we are going to hike around Mull,' said the driver.

'Aye, well, that being the case sir you won't object to me taking a look then will you.'

The second officer returned to his vehicle and made a call.

'PC McDougal to base, we've stopped a car just outside Taynuilt. It contains four IC 3 youths who say they're on a hiking holiday. Sergeant Grant is talking to them now. Can you do a vehicle check please? Over.'

The registration number was quickly relayed to police HQ and within seconds the officer knew the car was stolen. It had been taken from outside a university lecturer's house earlier that day.

'Can you send backup, I've a feeling we might need it, over'

'Sorry, we're stretched to the limit, there's no one to send so can you deal with it, over?'

'I'll expect we'll have to, out.' The radio receiver clattered into its cradle and PC McDougal walked to where he'd last seen his sergeant at the rear of the Vauxhall. What he didn't expect was a silenced semi-automatic pistol pointed at his chest. Stab vests wouldn't stop a slug at this range so he did as he was instructed, falling to his knees then forward to lay prone on the ground alongside his dead sergeant. Seconds later he took a bullet to the head. By the time their bodies were found in the back of the police 4x4, half submerged in Loch Etive, the assassins were already well down the single track road to Iona.

Chapter 12

There was still some light in the day when the gang arrived at the small ferry terminal of Fionnphort. Ditching their car behind several large bushes, they made their way down to the beach in search of their boat. The small rocky beach was deserted apart from a woman exercising her dogs. One, a young Springer Spaniel, paid excited attention to the rucksacks that had been dropped on the sand, but was called away and ran towards the far end of the beach where it found an abandoned Vauxhall to sniff around.

Their boat was secured to a buoy a few metres from the beach, a rigid inflatable with a potent 250 horse power Yamaha outboard engine capable of up to 30 knots. A powerful hand held spotlight lay in the foot well.

'We can't go yet, not until darkness falls,' said Banga Chiku.

'The police know we're on Mull because we were stupid enough to tell them, that copper would have radioed it in before you shot him,' said Rudo Chiku to his brother.

'Mull's a big place,' said the driver.

'They're not stupid, it's only a matter of time before they find the bodies, we need to do what we are here for, and fast,' said Banga Chiku.

They settled down behind some large rocks and even in their hyped up state were impressed by the quiet beauty of the place. Across the water they could make out the Abbey's outline, the focus of their operation, they would burn it to the ground if necessary.

Evening shadows lengthened across the sand and daylight soon faded into dusk. Mist hung around over the water but it was not as dense as had been forecast. A pale moon began its slow climb over Staffa.

'C'mon, let's get ready, as soon as it's dark we go, we can take them by surprise.' said Banga Chiku.

The boat was dragged to the beach and quickly converted into an assault craft. Then it was refloated. The four assassins, now masked, sat facing forward, adrenalin pumping through their bodies. Almost inaudibly they chanted in unison. *'The boy must die, the boy must die.'* On the island, lookouts were in place. From the moment Rachel had brought the news of an impending attack, each night was treated as the time when assassins would invade. Martyr's Bay was the likeliest place for an attack so well armed monks patrolled there, working in shifts.

Darkness fell and the sound of an outboard motor bursting into life alerted a lookout in his fishing boat. Normally, this would not be out of the ordinary, Mull is an island and motor boats are common place, but he recalled his instructions not to take any chances and immediately sent a flare into the misty sky. It arched, leaving a stark red message that the attack could be coming. By the time the flare had fallen back towards the sea; the assassins were halfway across the bay. The lookout responded with a second flare. It was an action that made him the first sacrifice of the night. Gunfire raked the small fishing craft. It exploded and a ball of orange flame threw the assassins' unlit boat into stark relief as it carried four young killers towards their rendezvous with fate.

'Get them into the tunnel,' yelled Gabriel Jackson.
Rachel hurried the MacKays from their room and down through the main Abbey door from where they ran the short distance to St Oran's Chapel. Horror crossed Dougy's face as he saw the remnants of the burning boat. The realisation that someone had died out there protecting his son made him want to join the fight. He was a clansman, not used to skulking away in some smelly hole in the ground, but Rachel had other ideas.

'We are to stay together, the child may need your protection before this night is over,' she said, giving him a hand gun.
Once in the tunnel Rachel took full control.

'Walk quickly until you reach a small atrium.'
Torch light created grotesque shadows on the tunnel walls as they moved forward. Sara held Alastair close, she was petrified; being buried alive was not her idea of how she wanted to end her days. Rachel sensed Sara's fear.

'You will be OK, trust Gabriel, he knows what he is doing,' she whispered.

'I bloody well hope so,' snorted Dougy, whose opinion of Gabriel Jackson had plummeted since the earlier episode on the beach. The atrium came into view and they settled down to wait. Rachel switched off the torch to preserve its batteries. Apart from the luminous face of Dougy's watch, total blackness and stale air enveloped them.

The powerful outboards had put the assassins within one hundred metres of Martyr's Bay, their spotlight picked out hooded figures on the landing jetty.

Banga Chiku hurled himself over the side. He swam under water until his body's demand for oxygen exceeded his resolve to stay invisible. Surfacing he witnessed a brief burst of semi-automatic gunfire from the boat, hopeless, pathetic. Bullets raked the sides of the rigid inflatable. In panic the others had thrown themselves into the well of the boat but there was no protection; the motor drove them forward into a merciless hail of bullets that ripped the craft to shreds. Death came instantly. As it sank, Banga Chiku briefly mourned his brother then turned and swam powerfully towards the shore. A pistol and sheath knife tucked in his belt would be all he needed.

Satisfied they had destroyed the threat to Alastair, the monks retreated to the Abbey. Gabriel Jackson was waiting at the door. Grim faced, he'd watched as the lookout's boat had been destroyed and had heard the automatic gunfire coming from Martyrs' Bay. He did not share the monks' confidence; it had all been too easy.

The tide was in as Banga Chiku dragged his exhausted body over a rocky outcrop leading towards a grassy shoreline where, undercover of a line of cottages, he made his way towards the Abbey. There was enough moonlight to help him and he was soon in sight of his target. Low voices alerted him to drop below a perimeter wall. Cautiously he raised his head in time to see Gabriel Jackson's silhouette moving towards the tunnel entrance. He climbed down, leaving the tunnel uncovered, unprotected. Banga Chiku waited momentarily as the monks went inside the Abbey, leaving him a clear run across to St Oran's chapel. In seconds he was in the tunnel.

Gabriel Jackson's torch lit up the atrium, alerting Dougy to face the light, gun cocked, ready to fire.

'Don't shoot, it's me.' His whispered voice was recognised and Dougy lowered his weapon.

'The boy is safe, the assassins are dead.'

'Not all of us,' screamed Banga Chiku. He pointed his gun at Alastair and fired.

The speed at which Dougy moved was electrifying. He threw himself between his family and the assassin. The bullet missed Alastair but grazed Sara's arm. In an instant Dougy fired back, his shot, slightly off target, smashed into Banga Chiku's leg, rupturing his femoral artery. The assassin, red frothy blood spurting from his wound, fell to the floor of the chamber, screaming and writhing in agony.

'Get them back to the Abbey,' shouted Gabriel Jackson.

Rachel obeyed and stepping round the wounded man led the family along the tunnel. Gabriel Jackson allowed enough time for them to clear the chapel entrance, screwed a silencer to his pistol and with a single shot to the head dispatched the assassin to eternity. He dragged Banga Chiku's lifeless body through the tunnel opening. The corpse could not be left on consecrated ground so it was dumped against the perimeter wall. He'd sort it out later.

In the grey light of dawn, Banga Chiku's remains, weighted down with rocks, were taken out to sea and dropped over the side of a fishing boat. A more formal ceremony would be held for the boatman who had died. Alastair's life had again been spared, but the closeness they had come to disaster convinced Gabriel Jackson that drastic steps must be taken to ensure total security of the Abbey.

Chapter 13

Next morning Chief Inspector Iain Sherrie hung his coat behind the office door and dropped into a well-worn leather chair, facing a desk full of work. The down side of taking leave was always a full in-tray, but he'd been owed the time and his boss insisted he took it. His phone rang.

'No peace for the wicked,' he muttered, picking up the receiver.

Iain Sherrie's jaw twitched as the Divisional Commander unfolded the happenings of the previous day. In a voice choking with emotion he began by describing where and how the two officers had met their deaths. He told Iain Sherrie of how the vehicle that had been stopped earlier by the murdered officers was later found abandoned near the Fionnphort ferry terminal. A woman walking her dog had reported it. In disbelief he listened how terrified local residents had overwhelmed the 999 service with reports of automatic gunfire across the bay, emergency flares in the sky, the destruction of a fishing boat; he described what eyewitnesses said were high powered assault rifles being fired at a speedboat in the area of Martyr's Bay and then made what to Iain Sherrie was an even more incredible statement. Even as officers raced to the scene, high ranking politicians had intervened, creating a blackout of all media coverage and putting MI5 in charge. The Home Secretary had ordered that security in this part of Scotland be raised to level one terror alert with Mull and its neighbouring islands being placed under continuing satellite and ground surveillance. This was by far the most serious incident ever to have happened in the Argyle and Bute police district and they could do nothing but sit it out whilst faceless spooks from London took control over their own backyard.

'We're to leave it alone, it's out of our hands.' said the Divisional Commander.

'Like that killing on the ferry, what the hell is going on round here,' replied a disbelieving Iain Sherrie.

'Higher powers have decreed it, that's all I can say, leave it Iain, for now anyway.'

His boss rang off and Iain Sherrie slumped against the wall of his office, drained and angry. He was sure the big black guy he'd met on the ferry was somehow implicated in this and sooner or later he'd prove it, if he ever got the chance. In the meantime there would be two funerals to attend.

As dawn broke over Iona the monks assembled in the Abbey chapel to give thanks to God for their deliverance from the evil that had threatened to rain so much destruction upon them. A fully robed Gabriel Jackson stood in front of the altar, arms outstretched, his eyes focussed on an ancient gargoyle's face grimacing down from high on a pillar at the crossing of the chapel. It was the face of a tortured soul that Gabriel Jackson likened to the face of a desolate Christ as he hung from the cross, abandoned and left to die in agony.

The monks knelt in silence. Gabriel Jackson prayed.

'*Father in Heaven, This night you did not abandon us but delivered us from evil. We give thanks that you are always here to protect and guide. Lord we give our word that the promised one will be guarded even though some of your faithful ones may die. Instil in me great Master, the wisdom to make the right decisions and not to allow distraction from doing what is right. Amen.*'

The monks rose, leaving in single file to return to their rooms, all but for two. One moved to a corner of the chapel and climbed a flight of stone steps leading to a Monks' Watch Tower that gave a clear view along the road leading to the Abbey from the direction of the Street of the Dead. From now on, this small cold primitively furnished room would be manned round the clock and a direct radio link maintained with Gabriel Jackson. The other monk made his way to the MacKays' living accommodation.

Rachel stayed with the MacKays in their room; she was a good counsellor, which under the circumstances, she needed to be. Sara held Alastair tightly to her body, so tightly that Rachel was concerned that he would suffocate. She reached towards Sara who pulled away sharply, her eyes full of anger and fear. Dougy's feelings were fully exposed; he paced the room cursing Gabriel Jackson and everything that had brought his family to this forsaken hole in the middle of nowhere. At one point his voice rose to almost a scream.

'That swine Jackson could've killed us, he led that man into the tunnel, he should have been more careful. Why the hell can't we be left alone, Alastair is special to us that's all, for Christ's sake let us be.'

Rachel tried to calm him but he would not listen, he was beyond reason and it was only when Sara begged him to stop that he sagged into a chair and stared out of the window, tears welling in his eyes. Then, after a few minutes he got to his feet, walked over to where Sara and Alastair sat and held them to him, his entire body shaking with emotion.

The monk tapped on the door, he was armed and was to stand guard; from now on a sentry would always be present. The monk bowed slightly as Rachel left the room. She went directly to the Abbott's House. There would be no sleep until she was satisfied that Gabriel Jackson had everything under control, but Rachel was not prepared for the shock of finding out what he really had in mind. Sitting in the quiet of a small study she listened as Gabriel Jackson told her that on the first anniversary of Alastair's birth, the child would be baptised and removed from his parents' control. The following day his education into the faith would begin. At that point he said, quietly and deliberately, that Dougy and Sara would become expendable.

'What do you propose to do with them?' asked Rachel.

'As yet I do not know but the Lord will show the way.'

Rachel felt a strong conflict fuelled by a mixture of guilt and loyalty. As a woman she felt compassion, particularly for Sara, but she was a servant of the Lord and his word, delivered through Gabriel Jackson, was paramount. However, she had enough experience of the way this man served the Lord to know that he was ruthless and dedicated. He was a man who would kill without flinching to bring about God's kingdom on earth. She despised yet admired him but could not stand by while he plotted the elimination of two people she had come to respect. Rachel thanked him for telling her of his plans and then returned to her own quarters. She prayed and then, fully clothed, fell into a light troubled sleep. She awoke with a start, her sleep lasting just two hours. Somehow she had to warn Dougy, but how could she do this without undermining Gabriel Jackson? Rachel slipped from her bed and walked the short distance to the MacKay quarters. The guard stood to one side as she knocked on the door. Dougy let Rachel in then latched the door behind her, sliding the bolts silently into place.

'What is it now, we are trying to rest,' whispered Dougy, glancing towards his sleeping wife and son. The conversation continued in a hushed tone.

'I'm sorry, but there is something I must discuss with you,' replied Rachel.

'Has Gabriel Jackson sent you?'

'No, but you must listen. Your lives may still be in danger. I believe there will be another attempt to kill you but this time it will come from a direction that you least expect, the enemy may already be on the island, already amongst us.'

'Now you are scaring me, what more do you know?' asked Dougy.

Rachel could not answer truthfully without betraying Gabriel Jackson's plans for Alastair; the monk on guard duty will already have alerted his master as to Rachel's whereabouts and he will surely ask for an explanation of her visit. She will not lie to him; he can read her face as if it were an open book. All Rachel can hope for is that by alerting Dougy in this way he and Sara will maintain a vigil and by some miracle are able to avoid becoming another grim statistic.

'I must go now, you still have the gun I gave you, keep it to hand and please be careful' she said.

In her room she stood at an open window. The view was tranquil with only the sound of gulls and the gentle whoosh of waves running up the sand, breaking an otherwise total silence. Yet tension crackled around the Abbey like a log fire on a cold winter evening, it could be felt everywhere. Such was the aftermath of the attack and Gabriel Jackson's increasingly powerful grip on the lives of all who came within his influence that this ancient place of worship would once again become a closed institution with only the supplies helicopter making its secret, well-guarded flight to the mainland and back.

Chapter 14

Dougy glanced at his sleeping wife and son. Sara had heard nothing of the conversation between him and Rachel; he must get them away from the island, but how? Gabriel Jackson had locked the place down, escape was impossible yet if what Rachel had said was true then he must find a way. His mind turned again to his parents and to Inveraray where they lived. If he could somehow let them know that their son, his wife and grandson were being kept against their will on Iona then something might happen. The MacKays were a bloody minded lot with a history of rebelliousness, if anyone could raise awareness about their plight it was his father. But he was now elderly, his powers may have waned, yet Dougy could think of no one else who could help. He had left Scotland some years ago and time had eroded whatever relationship he once had with his friends, only family could help him now. His thoughts turned to Rachel; he recalled their conversation, she really cared about them, maybe enough to put her own relationship with Gabriel Jackson on the line and get a message out to his father. It was fanciful but what other choices did he have?

Sara stirred and opened her eyes. She yawned, stretching her arms.

'What time is it?' she asked.

'Oh, it's the middle of the afternoon; do you want anything to eat?' replied Dougy.

'OK, as long as you make it, and don't forget your son,' she said pointing to Alastair who was stirring beneath his comfort blanket on the couch.

Dougy noticed a smile flicker across Sara's lips. He felt relief that his wife could still smile even after what they had been through. Later, when they had eaten, he would tell her of his conversation with Rachel.

Sara listened without interruption. It was hard for her to believe that anyone on the island would want to harm them. Earlier, many people had risked their lives to protect them, a man had been killed, so what did Rachel mean when she had said that 'this time it will come from a direction that you least expect?' Dougy had his theories, it had to be Gabriel Jackson, he wanted Alastair to himself and he was single minded enough to achieve this through any means possible. Under these circumstances it is easy to develop paranoia, looking under the bed, jumping at every sound and seeing everyone as a potential enemy. Such things can eat into the mind, creating delusions that no one can be trusted, not even those close to you. He began to harbour thoughts of making a last ditch attempt to escape by boat and living rough in the mountains and glens just as his forefathers did, anything but staying on Iona to face possible death at the hands of a madman. Then rational thought calmed him. It was a stupid idea, they wouldn't last long, and Gabriel Jackson would have them hunted down like animals. They were trapped, and persuading Rachel to get a message to his father became the only thing that made any sort of sense. He resolved to work on Rachel's sense of justice, hoping that her close ties with Gabriel Jackson could be loosened enough for her to see his point of view. All he required was a few minutes with a mobile phone; he carried his father's number in his head. This tiny spark of hope was all he had.

Jackson had been annoyed that Rachel had visited Dougy and Sara without asking him first. He summoned her and she felt like a naughty child being scolded by a head teacher as he made it clear that any future visits could only be made if they were checked out with him beforehand and the reasons made clear. He stopped short at describing any form of punishment that would befall her if she disobeyed his instructions but she felt intimidated enough not to risk angering him again.

Dougy became increasingly depressed that he couldn't get near to Rachel. Whenever he and Sara took their daily walk around the Abbey grounds an armed monk followed them. He was stood at their door when they went to bed and was there, standing exactly in the same spot when they awoke in the morning. Days became weeks and still no contact. Rachel kept her distance until one morning she arrived unannounced to speak to them about what Gabriel Jackson had described as 'a matter of great importance.'

Sara recalled what Rachel had said to Dougy about an attempt on their lives coming from a direction they would least expect. Could this be it, was Rachel really a Judas in disguise? The monk positioned himself in the open doorway. His automatic firearm, visible and menacing, was lowered, pointing at Sara. She bent and lifted Alastair from the floor where he was playing and turned away, shielding him from harm. Sara moved towards Dougy and stood by him, she trembled in anticipation that something dreadful was about to happen.

'The child is nearing the first anniversary of his birth and he is to be baptised,' said Rachel.

Sara drew Alastair closer.

'Baptised, what the hell are you talking about, baptised as what?' said Dougy, his anger beginning to rise.

Rachel did not answer directly, instead she said,

'The first baptism was by John in the River Jordon, this time it will be by Gabriel, the child will be baptised in the sea. Now follow me.'

'Where to?' said Dougy.

'Just do as I ask.'

'No.'

The monk stepped forward, the muzzle of his gun inches from Dougy's chest.

'OK, but tell that goon to lower his gun,' said Dougy.

Rachel nodded to the monk who turned and began a slow walk along the corridor.

'Follow him,' demanded Rachel.

Dougy took his son from Sara and they fell in behind the monk, Rachel brought up the rear a few steps behind. It was to Dougy as if they were being marched to their execution, never to be heard of again. Many people had disappeared in Zimbabwe, their bodies burned. He was sure it was their turn now. How stupid they had been to put any sort of trust in Gabriel Jackson, he was no better than the people who had burned their farm. Dougy bent and kissed Alastair lightly on his face.

'Don't worry wee man we won't let anyone hurt you,' he said. The monk led them towards the Abbott's house where Gabriel Jackson was waiting at the door.

'Please come in,' he said. The tone of his voice was gentle and in a strange way, reassuring, but it cut no ice with Dougy.

The monk moved to one side and stood by the door, his firearm still threatening. Dougy followed Gabriel Jackson through the gloom of a hallway into the living area. It was a small, sparsely furnished room, a single bar electric fire glowed in a hearth where once there had been an open fire. Gabriel Jackson motioned towards two easy chairs.

'Please sit.'

A nun brought tea and scones from the kitchen, placing the tray on a small coffee table at the side of Gabriel Jackson's chair.

'Have some refreshment, the scones are freshly made.'

'No thanks, we've eaten,' replied Dougy.

'Very well, but I hope you don't mind if I do.'

Gabriel Jackson cut a scone in half then spread a thick layer of butter on each piece. They watched as he ate, washing each mouthful down with a gulp of tea. It seemed an age before he spoke again. The tone of his voice was cold and deliberate.

'I'm going to baptise the child into God's church. He will be named Joshua which means 'God is Salvation' and directly afterwards he will be taken into our care.'

'His name is Alastair James, after his grandfather, it is a good name and you will not change it and you will not have him,' yelled Sara.

Gabriel Jackson smiled.

'Tomorrow the child is one year old and he will be baptised at dawn, a record of which will become part of a new gospel.'

'No, no,' screamed Sara.

Lunging forward she snatched Alastair from Dougy's grasp and ran to the door; Rachel stood in her way but was knocked aside by Sara's momentum. In blind panic she reached the door but got no further. A muscular arm held her; she struggled but was held firm in the monk's grip. Dougy moved towards the monk, fist clenched.

'Let her go,' he yelled.

Gabriel Jackson raised a hand and Sara was released. Still holding Alastair she staggered backwards into Dougy's arms. They crashed against a wall; Dougy's head struck the corner of a picture. As the heavy wooden frame fell towards the stone floor, Gabriel Jackson made a desperate lunge to catch it, but failed. The glass shattered, tearing at the fragile oil painting that lay beneath, and the lifeless, vacant eyes of the crucified Christ stared upwards. Gabriel Jackson fell to his knees, weeping and praying.

Dougy helped Sara to her feet and when he was satisfied that she and Alastair were unharmed he took them from the house. He felt nothing but fear and deep apprehension at the consequences for his only son once the baptism had taken place. The tenacious monk followed, this nocturnal sentinel watched as Dougy and Sara reached the Abbey. He let them in and then stood to one side, allowing access to their accommodation. As the door closed he took up his position, cradling the Heckler and Koch across his body. Alastair would be baptised in the morning, it was inevitable, and nothing on earth could prevent it.

It was Rachel knocking on the door that woke them. Darkness was still over Iona but she had come to prepare the way for Alastair's baptism. Draped across her arms was a white handmade cotton robe. Rachel said it had been sewn by the nuns then blessed and prayed over by Gabriel Jackson. He insisted that Rachel dress the child and bring him to baptism herself.

'He is my son, I will bring him,' insisted Sara.

'No, once in this robe the child becomes holy, you cannot touch him after that,' replied Rachel.

'Superstitious claptrap, who the hell do you people think you are,' demanded Dougy.

'It is not who we are but who the child is,' replied Rachel.

She woke the sleeping boy who immediately reached for Sara but Rachel picked him up. Alastair protested, calling for his mother but the firmness of Rachel's hold prevented the struggling child from breaking free. The monk's looming presence ensured compliance as Rachel removed Alastair's pyjamas, replacing them with the baptism robe.

'He will be washed in the Holy waters of the sea,' she said.

Dougy shrugged and turned away, this time he controlled his emotions, the baptism meant nothing to him, he was inwardly reassured that a quick dip in the sea could not harm his son but it was the thought of losing him to these determined crazy people that ate into him. They would take away his son's proud Scottish name, replacing it with their own. Alastair's ancestry would mean nothing; he was to be changed through a spurious ritual into something else, a spiritual transplant or systematic brainwashing depending on whose point of view determined the boy's future. Deep in his gut Dougy accepted that the dominant point of view was Gabriel Jackson's but only because his controlling influence was backed with a significant array of firepower and an army of monks who would kill at his command.

It was this army of monks that arrived to escort them. Damp rooftops reflected early dawn as they moved in step from the Abbey door, stopping for a moment to bow before the cross of St John, then processing along the pathway leading to the ruined nunnery and onward to the sea. Behind the monks followed Rachel carrying Alastair. Behind her, hand in hand, walked Dougy and Sara, with two nuns bringing up the rear. The monks sang a special anthem of praise written for the occasion by Gabriel Jackson. The anthem, chanted in Latin, drifted in the stillness of the cool morning air to where Gabriel Jackson was waiting, already immersed to his waist in the clear cold waters of Martyrs' bay.

'Bring the child to me,' he boomed.

Rachel waded out to him and he took Alastair from her. She noticed how gently he held the child, this was a different Gabriel Jackson, he was to baptise the one they had waited so long for; this was a special day, it was the pinnacle of Gabriel Jackson's long life in which he had faithfully carried out the will of God.

Dougy and Sara watched horrified as he held their son high above the waves, then they heard Alastair laugh, he thought it was a game. In the distance thunder rumbled around the hills of Mull and then, as if preordained, fork lightening unleashed its frightening power directly above them; it seemed to come from nowhere. As one, the monks raised their hands towards the grey, rain filled sky and chanted 'God is gracious,' over and over again. Gabriel Jackson responded to the chant, shouting triumphantly,

'God is certainly gracious. In His name I baptise this child whom He has given to us and who henceforth will be called Joshua.'
Gabriel lowered Alastair into the sea, fully immersing him. By the third immersion Alastair no longer thought it was a game and screamed for his mother. Sara ran through the waves towards her son but Rachel had already taken him, wrapping him in a blanket she passed him to one of the monks who, along with the others, turned and walked towards the Abbey singing joyously.

'The transition is complete, Joshua is no longer yours,' she said.
Gabriel Jackson waded to where Sara stood, shivering. He put an arm around her and led her to the shore.

'Please believe me, he is safe, whilst here he will be nurtured and only when we are sure he is ready will he go out into the world.'
Sara was too cold and shocked to respond, it was only later that the full impact of what Gabriel Jackson had said would hit her.

From their room, Dougy and Sara could hear the celebrations taking place in the refectory. Rachel came upstairs, inviting them to join in; at least they would get the chance to see their son again. This was too much for Sara who launched herself at Rachel, targeting her eyes. Dougy managed to catch his wife's dress as she went past him, holding her long enough to allow Rachel an escape route.

'That would solve nothing, we must give ourselves time to think,' he said.
Sara was near to the edge; somehow Dougy had to find a way of helping her but she needed to hold her son again and that was now impossible.

'He is still our little Alastair, nothing will ever change that, and we'll get him back you wait and see,' he said.

But Sara shook her head violently,

'I know I'll never see him again, never, never, never.'

Her voice was so full of anguish that Dougy felt completely helpless. He tried to comfort his wife but she pushed him away and threw herself across the bed, burying her face in the pillows as if trying to block out the reality of it all.

Losing Alastair this way was, to Sara and Dougy, as if he had died. The feelings of grief were the same; they had been plunged into a bottomless pit of despair. Numbness, sleeplessness, anger, gut wrenching pain and bouts of weeping that would take them by surprise filled their days; time had no meaning without Alastair. They railed at Gabriel Jackson, Rachel and the monks; they even turned on each other, anything to ease the burden of loss. Rachel was sent to spend time with them, to absorb their grief and to reassure them that their son was in safe keeping. She even suggested that in time they will come to accept that Joshua, as she now calls him, is the chosen one and they, along with the whole world, will kneel at his feet in supplication.

Chapter 15

Iain Sherrie, up to now, had reluctantly obeyed the order to leave things to MI5. Armed with their top of the range computers and other technical stuff a couple of officers had taken over his office. A senior officer had moved into a large meeting room on the next floor. To his disgust, Iain Sherrie had been decanted to the equivalent of a broom cupboard further along the corridor and his only contact with MI5 officers was in the kitchen at brewing up time. They seemed friendly enough but didn't say much to him apart from passing the time of day and the occasional comment about the weather. He was amazed at how much tea they consumed. His personal stock soon disappeared and he was reduced to keeping a supply of his precious Yorkshire tea bags hidden away in an old brief case. He kept busy with investigating general reports of local crime. His clear up rate was impressive; he led a good team who in turn respected him.

He was a policeman who had come up the hard way. He'd never wanted to be anything else. As a cadet he'd been attached to various departments, picking up knowledge and learning his way around the place. He developed a feel for the job that impressed his mentors and at nineteen completed basic training at the Scottish Police College at Tulliallan Castle. Three years later he joined the Criminal Investigation Department of the Argyll and Bute Police; he was a natural detective, inquisitive and thorough. The rare attribute of a 'copper's nose' led to many successful prosecutions and promotion was inevitable. By the time he reached the position of Detective Chief Inspector he was a fully grounded investigator, nothing fazed him, he'd seen it all, until now that is. The happenings on and around Iona were beyond his experience and, being unable to investigate the shooting of his two colleagues, stuck in his craw. He had nothing to offer apart from condolence but swore that one day he would get to the bottom of it and bring closure to two grieving families. Iain Sherrie was not a man to tolerate loose ends.

There is a saying that alcohol loosens the tongue and he discovered that tea had a similar effect on two rather bored MI5 officers. His timing was perfect; he waited until they had run out of tea bags and then magnanimously offered to give them some of his. His ruse was to get into their office and put his copper's nose to work. It was a cache of rich Scottish shortbread that finally got him through the door. Ingratiation was something he despised in others but there was a time and place even for this reprehensible aspect of human behaviour. The men in crumpled dark suits saw him as being a good chap and within a couple of days Iain Sherrie was drinking tea, dunking shortbread and sharing jokes with them. He encouraged their southern prejudice of him as just a country copper stuck in the Highlands investigating nothing more serious than sheep rustling - he was no threat to their security.

He listened to office chatter, read computer screens, absorbed snippets from phone conversations but there was nothing that gave any real clues as to what was going on. He gained an impression that apart from maintaining surveillance there was little more for MI5 to do, so why had he and his colleagues not been trusted with the job in the first place? Frustration eventually took over and the veneer of a bumbling flatfoot was stripped away. It was his pointed questions that alerted the MI5 officers to his true intent and at nine o' clock the following morning Iain Sherrie found himself on the carpet, facing an angry Divisional Commander.

'What the hell do you think you were doing Iain, didn't I tell you to leave it,' he said, his face reddening with anger.

'You were at the funerals, didn't you feel anything,' asked Iain Sherrie.

His comment was caustic and accusatory.

'Of course I bloody well did, but I know how to follow orders; I should throw the soddin' book at you.'

Iain Sherrie took a deep breath and waited for the inevitable, he'd seen what suspension could do to people. It saps professional confidence; the whispers, the innuendos, the fear that things will turn out badly ultimately leading to the sack. He was the wrong age to be thrown onto the scrap heap. He stood rigidly to attention, waiting for the axe to fall on his career. The Divisional Commander's voice was formal, his tone stern.

'Chief Inspector Sherrie, late last night I received a call from the Chief Constable. '

Iain Sherrie felt the blood drain from his face, this was serious.

'Yes sir.'

'We spoke at length about your conduct and why an officer with an impeccable record such as yours should see fit to act against the specific orders of a senior officer, knowingly putting his career in jeopardy. However, he shares our disquiet about the involvement of MI5 and the way we were blocked out, but his orders come from the Home Secretary who obviously has a much broader view of things.'

'Where's all this going sir?'

'Just listen. He's arranging a temporary transfer. From immediate effect you are promoted to the rank of Detective Superintendent and will join forces with MI5. They need someone on the ground with local knowledge. The Home Office rates the possibility of another terror incident as high and because you know this area like the back of your hand the Chief Constable reckons you are the best person for the job, so the way has been cleared for your secondment, but first you'll need to go on a firearms refresher course, after which you will be thoroughly briefed.'

The Divisional Commander shook his hand but all Iain Sherrie felt was the vulnerability of being backed into a corner, there was no alternative, no time for him to consider the promotion; it was as if he'd been hung out to dry.

'Thank you sir, I look forward to the challenge,' was all he could say.

***

It was quiet on Iona; two weeks had passed since the renaming and taking of Alastair from his parents. Christmas was almost upon them and had things been different Dougy and Sara would be on their farm celebrating the birth of Christ and enjoying Alastair playing with his new toys. Yet on Iona the celebration had been about a different boy,

90

newly baptised and being held up as the Promised One. Although Dougy and Sara had more freedom they had only once glimpsed Alastair as the nuns walked and played with him on the grass at the front of the Abbey. Sara called out but one of the nuns covered the boy's ears with her hands and hurried him away. It all added to the heartbreak of losing Alastair but at least she had seen him and Sara clung tenaciously to the hope of one day getting him back. Dougy had promised that he would do everything he could and she trusted him, but Gabriel Jackson was strong, he had powerful allies. The movement that supported him was global and rich yet his enemies had sworn to eradicate everything he stood for; they had good intelligence and should a chink appear in his protective armour, they would exploit it.

Although Gabriel Jackson felt relatively secure, surrounded as he was by a natural moat and protected by well-armed monks, he was not complacent. A further attack may succeed and his Machiavellian mind told him that the surest way to offset such an event was to wrong foot his enemies. Sometimes simple strategies are the best and he felt that his prayers had been answered when Rachel brought unexpected news.

'Sara is pregnant,' she announced.

Gabriel Jackson did not reply immediately, his face remained impassive as if allowing the news to sink in. Then he spoke.

'This second child will not be holy, only the first born carries heavenly inheritance. The woman was a vessel, nothing more. The child she now carries is of human inheritance but I'll say this, the second born may well be instrumental in saving Joshua's life.'

'What do you mean, is this some kind of prophecy,' asked Rachel.

Gabriel Jackson didn't answer, his imagination was already at work and Rachel feared for the safety of Sara's unborn child. Sacrifice was at the heart of Gabriel Jackson's beliefs and as before, Rachel found herself torn between loyalty to him and her feelings for two people who were now at the mercy of whatever this man chose to do with them. Whatever it was, she was sure the best interests of the MacKay family would not be his first consideration. As it happened, she would not have to wait long before finding out what he proposed to do.

Dougy answered a heavy, determined knock on his door to see Gabriel Jackson standing there. The big man was smiling, almost benevolently. Dougy slammed the door shut.

'It's Jackson, what the hell does he want,' said Dougy, turning to Sara who half rose from her chair.

'Well, you'd better ask him,' she said.

Dougy opened the door a few inches, he half expected Gabriel Jackson to shoulder his way in but he stood back allowing Dougy some space.

'What do you want?'

'I would like to speak to you both.'

'What about?'

'Rachel has told me of your good news; I just want to congratulate you.'

'We don't need your congratulations,' said Dougy, his hackles rising.

'Let him in,' said Sara.

Gabriel Jackson's frame filled the door as he moved inside. He stood facing the window, looking out.

'Rachel is experienced in the matter of childbirth but is concerned that you will not receive adequate medical attention here on the island should things not go to plan, so I have decided to grant you safe transport, to go anywhere you see fit,' he said.

'We won't leave without Alastair,' said Sara, her voice carried a firm determination.

'He is Joshua and he stays here,' said an equally determined Gabriel Jackson, still gazing out of the window.

'Then we will stay,' said Dougy.

'I have offered you the chance to go, I won't offer it again, and Rachel will call by for your decision within the hour.'

He backed out of the room, closed the door and walked away.

'What's he playing at? It's not that long ago he stopped us from leaving and all this stuff about your welfare is rubbish, he doesn't give a damn about us now that he has Alastair,' said Dougy.

Sara said nothing; she just stared into space, her mind in turmoil.

'Well lass, what do you think, we've only got an hour,' urged Dougy.

Her eventual reply surprised him.

'I think we should go, staying here would only drive us mad, at least we would be free of that man.'

'OK, that's what we'll do,' said Dougy.

On the hour Rachel came to their room.

'What have you decided?' she asked.

'We're going, but first I want to make a call to my father?' said Dougy.

Rachel handed him her mobile phone.

'Just one call, that's all,' she said.

Dougy punched in the number. He hadn't spoken to his father for a while, not since leaving Zimbabwe, he was anxious and it showed. Dougy waited for the number to connect, praying that it wasn't engaged. It rang several times before his father answered.

'Hello Dad, it's me,' said Dougy.

His father became emotional and called out to Dougy's mother.

'Mary love, it's Dougy.'

'Dad, please listen, we're in Scotland, on Iona. It's a long story but can we come to you for a few days?'

The questions came back in a torrent.

'Iona, what are doing there, how long have you been in Scotland, is Sara OK, are you well?'

'Yes dad, but can we come and stay please?'

'Of course my boy, of course you can, when will you arrive?'

'Tomorrow, but I don't know what time.'

'Your mother is here, please speak to her, you can tell her the news yourself.'

Dougy spoke to his mother; she was overcome with emotion at the prospect of seeing him again after all this time. Alastair wasn't mentioned, that would come later.

Handing back the phone Dougy asked Rachel what help she could offer. He figured that Gabriel Jackson had put them in this position, so he should at least provide transport for them, all the way to Inveraray.

Rachel went to the window and pointed to where the supplies helicopter was landing.

'There's your way out, you leave at dawn.'

Dougy was puzzled, even though the flight would be a short one and the thought of seeing his parents again pleased him, it had happened far too quickly. Why the sudden change of heart to let them leave, why had the helicopter been put at their disposal, what was Gabriel Jackson up to?

Chapter 16

The night dragged. Dougy could understand Gabriel Jackson's reasoning for wanting them off the island. Once they'd gone his hold over Alastair would be complete but Dougy had no intention of letting it rest, he had given Sara his word and he meant to keep it. He prowled around like a caged animal, muttering. His mind racing ahead to the dawn when they would fly from Iona, away from their son whose malleable young mind was already being warped by the religious zealots who had kidnapped him.

'Yes, that is what they've done, kidnapped him and for that they will pay.' His mutterings had become more audible, disturbing Sara.

'Come to bed Dougy, you are doing no good wandering around like that.'

Dougy did as Sara asked, she snuggled into him and he held her close. Sleep was impossible and by the time Rachel had arrived to escort them to the helicopter, they were dressed and ready to leave. Rachel gave Dougy a leather wallet containing enough money to see them through the first few days then they would be on their own. She was like a mother hen clucking round her chicks, checking that they had packed all their belongings and each had warm clothing for the journey.

'Gabriel wants to say goodbye, he's waiting by the helicopter,' said Rachel.

'I bet he does,' responded Dougy.

'I don't care what he wants, I want to see Alastair, to say goodbye to him and to tell him we love him and that we will see him again soon,' said Sara who was on the edge of tears.

'Come with me,' said Rachel.

They walked across to the helicopter, an armed monk following at a distance. Gabriel Jackson stood with the pilot, they were in deep conversation but broke off as Dougy and Sara approached. Whatever they'd been saying was for their ears only. Gabriel Jackson's trademark smile appeared as he made to shake Dougy's hand but this empty, meaningless gesture was refused. As he bent to give Sara a hug a hard slap left no doubt as to the contempt she felt for him. Gabriel Jackson flinched, his face stinging.

'You'll see, both of you, it is for the best,' he said.

Then from the direction of the Abbey a nun appeared. She was carrying something wrapped in a blanket. Whatever it was, she carried the object as one would carry a small child. Sara's hopes rose but were soon dashed as the package was placed on a rear seat and secured with a belt. Once inside the helicopter the pilot checked they were comfortable and then started the engine. The blades swished, increasing in speed and then they were airborne, heading over to Mull away from Iona, then on towards Inveraray.

A few minutes into the flight Dougy began to recall some of the things that Rachel had said about the enemy already being on Iona. His thoughts strayed to the package on the back seat and the truth hit him.

'Jackson wants someone to think that Alastair is on board,' he yelled over the din of the engine.

The pilot handed him and Sara a headset each, indicating where to plug them in.

'What was that?' asked the pilot.

Dougy decided to trust the pilot and explained his fears.

'He knows the island is being monitored and is using us as a decoy.'

So that's what all the whispering had been about. The pilot explained that Gabriel Jackson had told him to fly through Glen Coe as it was the most direct route. Glen Coe was a perfect place to bring down a helicopter. The mountains in that region are hostile, having already claimed many lives and as no flight plan had been recorded it would be very difficult to identify any remains. Dougy was convinced that Gabriel Jackson had used his contacts to leak details of the flight to the enemy who, believing that Alastair was being taken to another place, would intercept the helicopter as it flew along Glen Coe, and a ground to air missile would do the rest. They, along with the pilot, were being sacrificed; only the mind of a ruthless sociopath could have dreamed this up and Dougy had no doubt that Gabriel Jackson fell into this category. He'd win no matter what happened. If the helicopter was destroyed with all on board then information would immediately reach the assassins' political masters that the mission had been accomplished and any further attacks on the Abbey would be pointless. Should the helicopter escape being blown out of the sky then murderous action would be directed at Dougy and Sara, which could well implicate Dougy's parents.

Certain that his helicopter was being tracked the pilot decided to take evasive action. His experience of battlefield flying came into its own as he flew so low that the helicopter almost merged with its own shadow cast by the morning sun. The countryside flashed beneath them at an alarming rate. In military speak the aircraft stayed under the radar, invisible to detection. This was a flight of survival; the pilot had to get his passengers to safety before finding a way of disappearing. Ten minutes of fast flying got them to within a mile of Inveraray. Dougy recognised the terrain, his father's farm was just over the next hill, they were almost home.

The helicopter circled over the farm buildings before touching down in a field adjacent to the barn. By the time it had landed, Dougy's father was halfway across the yard, heading towards where his son and daughter in law were climbing down from the helicopter. As he got nearer, the downdraft almost took him off his feet but he steadied himself enough to grab Dougy in a bear hug, his emotion clearly showing.

'Let's get to the house dad, we'll be able to talk there,' said Dougy.

The pilot off loaded the bags and gave Dougy a thumbs up before climbing back into his seat. The helicopter lifted from the grass, turned and headed in the direction of Inveraray Castle, the ancestral home of the Duke of Argyll, the sound of its engine gradually dying away, leaving behind complete silence.

'The pilot's a good man,' said Sara.

'Aye, a good man indeed,' said Dougy.

They reached the farm house to find his mother waiting on the step. Dougy was surprised at how much she'd aged, but her voice was still as strong as ever and with arms extended, she said,

'Give your mother a kiss then wee Dougy,'

Dougy laughed, it was a while since anyone had called him 'wee Dougy' but after all she was his mother and no matter how tall and strong a son becomes, to his mother he will always be a small boy. Dougy cupped his mother's face in his hands and kissed her forehead. It was a lingering, gentle kiss that said he was pleased to see her, and his mother's tears showed the same in return. She then turned to Sara whom she barely remembered except from letters and photographs.

'Hello Sara, my goodness it's grand to see you, come in you must be ready for a cup of tea, we've lots to talk about.' she said.

It was a traditional 1920's farm house with a spacious kitchen that was almost as Dougy remembered it. The Aga stove, the scrubbed table surrounded by six high backed dining chairs, and an antique Welsh Dresser had become permanent features. The only nod towards modernisation was a set of fitted plain wooden wall mounted cupboards with glass fronted doors behind which Dougy's mother displayed a willow pattern tea set and other prized crockery.

A pair of substantial rocking chairs flanked the stove. The kitchen had a warm, homely feel that drew Sara in. She remembered the hostility of her first and only meeting with Dougy's parents, but today she felt at ease, particularly when Dougy's mother said,

'You can call me Mary and Ally won't mind if you use his first name will you dear.'

'Aye, that's fine,' he said.

'I thought his name was Alastair,' said Sara.

Mary laughed but not in a mocking way.

'Ally is a shortened version, he prefers it.'

Within minutes, food was on the table.

'Let's have lunch first then we'll catch up on things,' said Ally.

Mary and Ally had known of Sara's first pregnancy but had no idea of the outcome. In shocked, almost unbelievable silence they listened as Dougy and Sara told of the attack on their farm, how they had to run

98

for their lives and the details of Alastair's birth, the bright light that appeared overhead and the attempts made by uniformed Zimbabwean thugs to kill them. Ally felt a lump grow in his throat as he was told that his grandson bore his name. Emotions changed as the story of Gabriel Jackson and Rachel unfolded. Dougy told of the further attempts on their lives and how someone still wanted to kill Alastair. He explained how Gabriel Jackson saw Alastair as the Messiah sent from God and that it was his mission to bring biblical prophecy to fulfilment and that he would sacrifice anyone who got in his way. Earlier bonhomie was replaced by anger as the events leading to Alastair's 'rebirth' and naming were revealed, causing Ally to go almost apoplectic and he appeared to point the finger of blame at his son.

'You shouldn't have left him Dougy; he's only one year old. You could have done something.'

Patiently, Dougy explained to his distraught father that he and Sara had tried everything possible to rescue Alastair from Gabriel Jackson's grasp but had failed. It was then that Mary moved closer to Sara and took her hand; the bond between them would strengthen, particularly as a new grandchild was on the way.

Afternoon gave way to early evening and they moved from the kitchen to the comfort of a sitting room furnished with a three seater high backed couch and an easy chair. Dougy noticed the plaid throws draped across the furniture, they were woven in the MacKay tartan as were the curtains. His father was a proud Clansman who despite his age gave off an aura of strength and dependability. The scuffed wooden floor was original; at one time it had been sanded and polished but not recently. The floor and an open fire place gave the room character and charm. In the corner, next to a potted plant, was an old colour television and almost as if to give himself a respite from the family traumas, Ally switched it on to watch the early local news.

'I like to keep up with things,' he said, lowering himself into the easy chair.

Mary, Dougy and Sara watched from the couch as BBC Scotland began its broadcast.

'Good picture dad,' said Dougy.

'Aye,' muttered Ally in a voice that suggested to Dougy that he should keep quiet whilst the news was on.

The bulletin began with some breaking news. Against the backdrop of blue flashing lights a reporter was broadcasting from the scene of a serious incident.

'Just after two o 'clock this afternoon an aircraft was reported to have come down in the Glen Coe mountain range. A villager walking his dog said he heard what sounded like a helicopter flying directly above him then there was an explosion; he looked up and saw what he described as a huge ball of flame falling from the sky. Mountain rescue teams are currently searching for wreckage but a spokesperson said it will be a long drawn out job before anything is known, particularly as bad weather is forecast for the area within the next two hours. Now back to the studio.'

Dougy and Sara looked at each other, they were both of the same mind.

'Whatever possessed him to fly back that way,' said Dougy

'He was a brave man. He saved our lives but finished up getting himself killed,' replied Sara.

'We don't know it is him yet,' said Dougy.

The next news item shocked them even more.

'We have heard today that Iona will soon open again to visitors. The island and its historic Abbey have been off limits to the general public for some time now. This, we were told, was to allow for a new order of monks to be trained and that continued tourism would have been disruptive. We believe the monks are now leaving the island but their destination has not been disclosed.'

A few minutes of old footage showed the ferry making its way to Iona and tourists walking around the Abbey grounds looking at gravestones and other things of interest, then the bulletin ended.

'They will take Alastair with them to God knows where,' said Dougy.

Sara went deathly pale, the shock of losing her son to Gabriel Jackson had been bad enough, but now the thought of never knowing where he was drove her near to hysteria. Dougy held her until eventually she stopped shaking.

'I promised I would get him back, and that is what I'll do.'

'You can count me in son,' said Ally.

'Thanks dad, but we'll have to work fast.'

Mary made another pot of tea, the first of many as they talked into the night.

Chapter 17

Upon hearing of the helicopter's destruction Rachel wept bitterly. In her heart she had been close to Sara, she identified with her and felt her pain. Believing they were dead, she prayed for their eternal souls vowing to take on the child's welfare and love him as if he was her own. She told herself that soon he will forget his earthly parents and come to see her and Gabriel Jackson as his true guardians. She'd ensure that he will know the joys of being a child, of fishing in rock pools, creating make belief with toys. He will learn to read and enjoy books. Sharing the Abbot's house with her and Gabriel Jackson his would be a simple life with simple pleasures unspoiled by growing up too soon.

That evening Gabriel Jackson and Rachel walked along St Columba's Bay at the southernmost tip of Iona enjoying its peace and tranquillity. It is rumoured that St Columba's curragh or boat is buried here. Walking among the many small stone cairns that are a feature of this beautiful bay they talked of the future and of Joshua but more immediately about the coming days when tourists returned; there'd be journalists, reporters and camera crews creeping around trying to uncover headline making stories. After all, one of the most visited places in Scotland had been off limits for a considerable time with just barely credible reasons given and questions were inevitable. They'd meet a wall of silence, of people shaking their heads when asked about happenings on the island. Gabriel Jackson's presence was enough to dissuade even the most talkative of islanders from giving away information. He'd warned of inducements being offered, of ready cash being available that must be resisted if Joshua was to remain undetected. He'd cautioned them that another armed assault could overrun the island and no one was stupid enough to risk that. He'd reassured them of an eventual return to normality whilst knowing this to be impossible. Despite what the news report had said the monks were staying on Iona, they'd been billeted with islanders, hidden from view, remaining fully armed. The priest remained embedded in the

Abbey from where he could keep a watching brief on comings and goings.

Gabriel Jackson stooped to pick up two stones, one to keep as a symbol of the grace and spiritual significance of Iona, the other he cast into the sea. Legend was that as the stone sank it took to the depths all that was negative and unwanted; to him it represented fresh beginnings because here at the edge of the sea near to the place where St Columba came ashore in 563 AD he'd build the new church with its foundation stone hewed from local marble. Turning, he faced Rachel.

'Do you recall that when I found the map showing the Ley tunnel down which you hid from the assassins, I mentioned there were other things there with it?'

'Yes.

'Rolled up at the side of the map was another scroll. It was a crude but recognisable drawing of a heap of stones. In itself this would mean very little but above the stones a bright celestial body is shining.' Rachel's silence invited Gabriel to say more. He began to rant.

'It is a message from God. Remember the light that appeared above where Joshua was born, well this is the same light, it leads here, this is where God wants His new church to be built.'

He fell to his knees. Rachel let him go on about how it was the fulfilment of his long awaited destiny, how he had been chosen as God's representative to prepare the way for Joshua's ministry, a ministry set to destroy all evil and restore righteousness to the world. Remaining oblivious to the tide as it crept up behind them he began to speak in tongues; he used a language that was undecipherable, even to Rachel. She stood with him as the sea began to lap at her feet, she tugged at his coat collar but Gabriel Jackson was in another place. Within minutes the water had covered his legs and Rachel felt the first signs of panic. She couldn't let him drown but had no intention of waiting around until they were cut off from the path that led down to the bay. She had a duty to Joshua and this became her prime motive for leaving Gabriel Jackson to his fate. Rachel paddled to safety, and watched as grey salty water lapped at his chin. It was probably a wave breaking over his head that shook him back to reality. He stood, then pushing against the water that threatened to engulf him he stumbled, trying to swim but his waterlogged coat dragged him down. Regaining his feet he shouted to Rachel for help. For the first time in their relationship she was seeing this strong, opinionated man out of his depth. This was different from when Joshua was baptised, he was in control then, the water was shallower, but not now. The sea was in charge, it threatened to do what assassins had failed to do. Rachel went into the water, reaching out to him. Behind her, a small patch of sand still waiting to be covered became their only refuge, she had to guide him to it or they'd both perish. Their fingers touched and grabbing his hand she pulled Gabriel Jackson towards her. It was enough to get him to safety. They scrambled a few yards along the path then sat for a minute, shivering, regaining their breath. Rachel expected some sort of thanks.

'God saved me, I was in no danger.'

'It didn't look that way to me.'

'You were His instrument; He saved me through you, it was a test of our faith.'

Together they made their bedraggled way back to the Abbey. It was a long walk, about an hour, and darkness was falling. By the time they arrived a nun had prepared Joshua for bed. He was fractious and unsettled. Rachel hushed the child then kissed him lightly on the forehead; she whispered a prayer thanking God for Joshua and tucked him into bed. Forty miles away his mother also prayed, but her prayer was not one of thanks but one screaming out for the deliverance of her son from the evil that had taken him.

Rachel began to sing. The lullaby was hypnotic and Joshua's eyes closed, but then, is if fighting sleep, they opened again. He turned away from Rachel, hugging a Teddy that Sara had left for him; he cried out again for his mother. Reaching towards the distressed child, Rachel stroked his head. Her act of compassion caused him to retreat even further, seeking security in the soft toy that had become a powerful link between him and his mother. Unaware that Gabriel Jackson was listening from the doorway, Rachel continued singing. Crying was soon replaced by the regular breathing of a sleeping child.

Rachel leant over and kissed him, gently pulling a blanket across his shoulders.

'You certainly have a way with him,' whispered Gabriel Jackson.

'A child needs a mother and I'm the nearest he has got to one now.'

As well as sorrow Gabriel Jackson detected hostility in her voice. Grabbing her arm he led Rachel from the room, his grip tightened.

'Put aside any sentiment you may have, by all means be a surrogate but do not let it cloud your judgement, Joshua is here for one purpose and one purpose only and so are we, never forget that.'

A shudder went through Rachel's body; Gabriel Jackson smiled knowing that his message had been received. It was a message that said 'betray me and suffer the consequences.'

'You're hurting me,' she said.

His grip was vicelike.

'Just so you don't forget,' he said, then let her go.

Rachel ran to her room, she was scared. Gabriel Jackson had made a pastime of killing anyone who opposed him. His reason for each killing was always the same. These were evil people and the child sent from God must be protected. Rachel still believed him but he had tapped into her vulnerability. What if he interpreted her maternal feelings for Joshua as an act of disloyalty or even betrayal? She'd be at his mercy and if past experience was anything to go by there'd be very little mercy on offer.

She lay awake, listening as one or other of the nuns regularly walked by her door, keeping watch on Joshua, their own safety depending on no harm coming to the boy. Rachel had always admired their dedication but she knew they were driven by fear. Redness where Gabriel Jackson had gripped her was forming into a blue and purple reminder of their earlier encounter and in the darkness her fear turned to anger. She raged inwardly, yet outwardly she must stay calm and dutiful. In the morning Rachel took the Glock from a drawer in her bedside table, she checked it was loaded and slipped it into her bag. 'No more bruises.' she said to herself, 'no more bruises.'

Chapter 18

The farmhouse had plenty of unused living space and a spare double bedroom was brought back into service. Over time it had become a junk room, all houses have at least one and it gave Ally and Mary an opportunity to sort out stuff they'd long forgotten. There were old toys, board games and photograph albums. Dougy's old cot was stashed away behind cardboard boxes crammed with everything from clothes to books. Mary was a hoarder, throwing anything away was a sin; there was nothing that wouldn't 'come in handy' one day. She occasionally wondered why Ally hadn't made a bonfire of it all long ago but what she didn't know was that he'd seen her sat among the boxes with the photo albums open across her knees. He'd seen her crying as she looked at pictures of Dougy cradled in her arms, he watched from a distance as Mary worked her way through her son's childhood, his schooldays and smiled as he listened to her talking to the fine young man looking up from the photographs. The bedroom had become a place to relive the past, to become maudlin and to wish for the impossible, but now her son was back home, the circumstances were not as she would have wished but he was here and not thousands of miles away. Photographs are a link with the past; they conjure memories from deep recesses of the mind where, like junk in a spare bedroom, they had lain dormant for decades.

Even with Dougy and Sara helping, it took a full day to restore the bedroom, everything was sifted, nothing could be discarded until Mary had given it her full consideration and even then she had numerous changes of mind. Eventually, what remained had a purpose. The photograph albums, some toys, the cot, a number of Mary's dresses survived, as did Dougy's Christening robe, which was carefully folded and given to Sara.

'When we get Alastair back we'll do the job properly and he can wear this,' said Mary.

'Thank you, we can use it for both of them,' replied Sara, patting her tummy.

Furnishing the room meant a trip into Inveraray.

'You'd both better stay here, it wouldn't be good for you to be seen in public for a while, we'll sort out a bed and some drawers, anyway I can get a good discount,' said Ally.

'He hasn't changed, always the tight fisted one,' muttered Mary.

Dougy smiled, but he agreed with his father, the longer they remained incognito the longer Gabriel Jackson would believe they had died in the helicopter crash. He had eyes everywhere; if their cover was blown any chance of rescuing Alastair would go with it.

'I still believe Alastair is on Iona, there's no way that Jackson or his cronies will leave, the Abbey is a sacred place to him. He firmly believes that Alastair is the saviour of the world and he didn't go to all that trouble to get him to Iona only to leave at the first opportunity,' said Dougy.

Sara grasped at the straw.

'Then let's go and get our son, we could mingle with the tourists, somehow disguise ourselves, you could grow a beard, I could dye my hair. Gabriel Jackson's never met your father, come on let's try.'

Dougy urged caution.

'No, must bide our time.'

'Why?'

'Jackson would know immediately we boarded the ferry, before we do anything we have to be sure that Alastair is on the island and I have no idea how we can do that, we may have to wait a few months, perhaps Jackson's guard will drop long enough for us to grab Alastair but then there's the problem of getting him clear.'

Sara sank to her knees; suddenly a tiny piece of hope had existed but only for a moment, then it melted away.

The next day, true to his word, Ally shook hands on a deal with the owner of the only furniture shop in Inveraray. A king size double bed complete with matching furniture bought for a knock down price represented a new start for Dougy and Sara. Apart from the money given to them by Gabriel Jackson they had nothing. Everything they had worked for in Zimbabwe had gone; they now relied entirely on the generosity of Dougy's parents, who didn't disappoint them, but Dougy was not one for taking charity.

'I'll pay you back dad, I promise.'

'I know you will, but in the meantime let's concentrate on things that really matter, you can earn your keep by putting the farm on its feet, it's gone downhill and needs a younger man to sort it out, at the same time we can all concentrate on finding out where Alastair is and work on getting him back, how does that sound?'

'OK dad, you've got a deal.'

The farm wasn't in such bad shape; Ally had maintained the machinery and Mary looked after the stock. Anyone locally visiting the farm wouldn't immediately recognise Dougy as he'd been away for so long and had taken his wife's advice to grow a beard. Sara's pregnancy wouldn't present much of a problem either. Mary called in to see her doctor and explained things to him. It was a risk but she'd been on his list for many years and he could be trusted with patient confidentiality.

For three months Dougy toiled on the farm, Sara stayed well but no tangible progress was made towards rescuing Alastair. Ally remained glued to his television watching for the tiniest snippet of information that would give him a clue to his grandson's whereabouts but was disappointed. Iona had returned to normal and rarely featured on local news channels.

Living together in the farmhouse worked well but Sara wanted to make a proper place for her new baby. She didn't want to bother Dougy with her thoughts but as time drew near to the birth she became more unsettled at the thought of a newborn disrupting the lives of two elderly people who had been so good to them. Anyway, she wanted a place to call home where she and Dougy could rebuild their lives.

Historically, the farm had employed labourers who'd lived with their families in tied accommodation. Those were the days when local farms thrived, providing a good living and jobs for men who were prepared to work all hours in all weathers, but now neglected cottages were all that remained as a marker of better days. Sara had walked across the field to where the derelict cottage stood. Her mind moved beyond the roofless pile of debris that confronted her, instead she visualised an idyllic cottage with a garden and washing pegged to a line, drying in the warm summer breeze. She pictured Alastair playing on a swing and the new baby tucked up in a buggy, warm and contented. Dougy had once renovated a farmhouse in Zimbabwe, so putting this cottage back together should be well within his capabilities.

She put her idea to him and he didn't reject it, he'd been carrying similar thoughts about the old cottage and surprised her even further by discussing it with Ally and Mary who agreed without argument, suggesting they begin work immediately, before winter came.

'We'll have to get permission first, which could take ages,' said Dougy.

'Nae worry about that,' replied Ally, 'I've already got it.'
Dougy looked puzzled.

'How?' he queried.

'A couple of years ago your mother and I thought about cashing in on the tourist trade so we decided to rebuild the cottage and let it out.'

'So, what happened?'
Ally shrugged his shoulders.

'Well you know how it is, the best laid schemes o' mice an' men gang aft a-gley.' he replied, quoting Rabbie Burns.

'Aye, but it means we can get on with it,' said Dougy.
Ally's local contacts meant that materials were obtained quickly and cheaply, he even convinced a friend to lend him a cement mixer and a JCB. Tiles and wood for the joists had to be purchased but existing bricks could be reused. Dougy and Ally cleared the site and within a month the first course of bricks was laid. Four weeks later the roof was on and a St Andrew's flag flew proudly from the chimney. Rebuilding the cottage had kept their minds on Alastair, what a wonderful place for him to live; he could thrive here away from Gabriel Jackson and his big ideas of religious domination. Autumn was giving way to

winter as the final lick of paint was applied. A week after they'd moved in Sara went into labour. This time, although there was no bright celestial body to announce the birth of a boy who they called Farai, meaning 'happiness', a different light was about to shine into their lives. The light of hope was on its way.

December 2004

Low grey clouds masked the hill tops, sharp winds and sleety rain gave the landscape a barren look. It was the sort of weather to stay inside, feet halfway up the chimney, reading or snoozing, but farmers were not permitted such a luxury. There was always a job to do, cows to feed, sheep to check on, vermin to keep down. It was the latter that brought a local police officer to the farm to carry out an annual inspection of Ally's shotgun licence. Ally watched from a window as a police 4x4 carrying two men stopped on the driveway leading to the farm house. As both men walked the short distance to his front door, the uniformed Sergeant Angus Burns was immediately recognisable but the other man, in plain clothes, bothered Ally. Whether it was the way he stood, his strong features or just his general demeanour, there was something vaguely familiar about him.

Ally didn't wait for a knock before opening the door.

'Hello Angus is it that time of year already,' he said, offering his hand in greeting.

'Aye, time flies as they say,'

'You've got company I see,' remarked Ally, nodding towards the other man.

'Aye, this is Detective Superintendent Iain Sherrie, he decided he wanted some fresh air and it doesn't get much fresher than out here,' laughed Sergeant Burns.

'Good God,' said Ally, a broad smile spread across his face. This time the hand shake was much firmer, it was the sort of hand shake between people who hadn't seen each other for a long time. Sergeant Burns looked bemused, there was more to this than a day away from the office, this meeting had the clandestine stamp of a hidden agenda, he guessed that inspecting Ally's firearms licence was not the only business they would engage in today.

'So how long have you known each other?' he asked.

'Iain's dad and I went to the same school, hung around with the same group of friends for a while. Then I married Mary, and Jackie Sherrie married a lassie from Glasgow and went to work there and we lost touch for a while, but a year or two later after Iain was born they came back to Inveraray, by which time Mary and I had produced wee Dougy. We worked on the same farm for a while, our son's played together then I decided to buy my own place and things were never the same after that and our friendship cooled,' said Ally.

'So how is Dougy?' asked Iain.

'He's fine and you seem to have done well for yourself, it's good to see you but what really brings you here,' he asked.

'I'm conducting enquiries in this part of the region so Sergeant Burns has been given the job of ferrying me around, can we go inside please.'

Over a dram the formality of checking the shotgun licence was soon completed.

'Is Mary not about?' asked Sergeant Burns.

'She's out on the farm,' lied Ally, for he knew she was over visiting Dougy and Sara but he wasn't about to say so.

'Before we go can I ask you something,' said Iain Sherrie.

'Aye, of course you can,' replied Ally.

'A while back a helicopter crashed into the mountains over at Glencoe, you may have seen it on the news. At first it was thought to have been a tragic accident but that was wrong, it was shot down.'

'What's this got to do with us?' asked Ally.

'Probably nothing, but at the time a walker recalled seeing a helicopter flying low around here as if the pilot was looking for somewhere to land, did you see anything?'

'Can't say I did,' said Ally.

He'd already lied once and his obvious unease was not lost on Iain Sherrie who persisted with his gentle probing.

'Are you sure, please think about it, it's really important that we get to the bottom of this incident.'

'You said it was shot down, any idea who did it?' asked Ally.

111

There was no point prevaricating any longer, Iain Sherrie made the decision to tell Ally the whole story. Old loyalties stay strong in the Highlands, he had knowledge that would cause great concern to Ally but had to be shared otherwise the older man would never know what had happened to his grandson. This way there was a possibility that one day he may yet see Alastair but the strategy carried a high risk, not least for Iain Sherrie. Not wanting to compromise his colleague he asked Sergeant Burns to leave them for a while, then the two men sat across from each other and Iain Sherrie began to speak. He told of the murder of his colleagues and how the attack on Iona had been kept out of the press, of how a cordon of secrecy had been thrown around Iona and the surrounding area. Ally listened as the son of his old friend confided about his involvement with MI5 and how this had given him access to top secret computer files containing information that was only available to operatives with high level security clearance. Iain Sherrie was one such person and the policeman in him respected the need for secrecy, yet he had to investigate the shooting down of the helicopter, knowing that those who did it had a direct connection to the murderous bunch responsible for the killing of his colleagues. He then told of the worldwide coup being planned by a powerful group of politicians and church leaders to eliminate the Zimbabwean dictator whose administration was central to the evil being unleashed on the Christian church.

To MI5 this had all the hallmarks of a crusade, the spectre of millions of Christians rising up against the infidels had to be eliminated otherwise the entire planet would be engulfed in the flames of a nuclear holocaust. This was the maelstrom into which Iain Sherrie had been plunged and in some way had to play his part in stemming the inevitable tsunami of terror that would sweep everything before it. Intelligence reports had already identified that Alastair was probably still alive, and that only one body, or what was left of it, had been recovered from the burned out helicopter. There were spies everywhere and this knowledge would already be in the hands of terror command centres. Alastair's whereabouts remained unknown but the location of the MacKay farm and its connection to the boy caused great concern to the security forces. Known terror groups were under intense scrutiny but it only takes one to slip through the net and an attack on the farm was not out of the question.

Upon hearing this, Ally decided that now was the time to place his trust in the integrity of the intense policeman who sat before him. His grandson must be saved from this madness; he was an innocent child with no idea of the catastrophe unravelling in his name.

An hour later Iain Sherrie had the whole story and using a secure satellite communication system relayed it to his MI5 bosses who ordered him and Sergeant Burns to stay with the family until round the clock police protection could be organised. Two assault rifles and boxes of ammunition were transferred from the 4X4 into the farmhouse and Ally took his shotgun from its case, he was a crack shot and vermin stood no chance where he was concerned, even if the next time he used it the rats would be scurrying around on two legs. He watched as the police 4X4 was hidden inside the barn.

'No need to advertise our presence,' said Iain Sherrie.

'God knows what Mary will make of this,' muttered Ally, slipping two cartridges into the breach of his shotgun; the barrels locked into place with a satisfying well-oiled click.

Iain Sherrie reconnoitred the house, making a note of its weak spots. It was an old house with a stone walled cellar used for storing meat before refrigerators became commonplace. The white painted house had open fields on all sides making it vulnerable to attack so the cellar may come in handy. Iain Sherrie offered Ally the option of relocating the family to a safer place where they could be properly guarded. This offended Ally, it suggested to him that he was incapable of defending his family; after all he was the head of the house and as such it was his responsibility to decide what was best for the family. It was then that Mary returned and Ally knew it would be her calling the shots. As seems to befit Scottish women she had a strong mind and over the years he'd come to respect her resilience, particularly when facing up to adversity. He'd noticed that since Dougy had returned, Mary had rediscovered a vigour that he thought had gone forever.

Greetings were exchanged and Ally put his wife in the picture. For a moment she seemed lost in thought, as if processing the information. Then she spoke.

'We must talk to Dougy, let him make the decision.'

Iain Sherrie nodded in agreement.

'We'll both go over, it's a wee walk so let's take the tractor,' said Ally.

At full throttle the well-used Massey Ferguson had a fair turn of speed. Mary hung on for grim death as the old machine bucked and rocked across the rutted fields, shuddering to a halt outside the cottage. Ally alerted his son to the danger facing him and his family but without hesitation he made the decision to stay. Dougy's inherited stubborn streak showed through, after all it was only speculation that an attack would come, this was their home and they would defend it, Zimbabwean thugs had wrecked his life once before, he'd die first before allowing it to happen again.

'I want to see Iain Sherrie. If Alastair is still on Iona then he can help us get him back, he'll have the fire power.' Dougy's voice was firm and resolute.

Meeting each other for the first time since childhood provoked some emotion but there was no time for lengthy reminiscence, this wasn't a schoolyard game with pretend guns and flamboyant dying, this was for real. Both men had agendas that somehow had to become compatible; Alastair's rescue depended on it. Dougy's powerful gut reaction that his son was still on the island convinced Iain Sherrie to at least listen whilst possible weaknesses in Gabriel Jackson's human defences were outlined. He remembered the carnage following a full on attack by that group of young assassins whose deaths were violent and ruthless.

'We have the element of surprise, he probably thinks me and Sara are dead, so you and I could latch on to a group of tourists and hide until dark.

Iain Sherrie remained unresponsive so Dougy prompted him.

'C'mon Iain, what do you say, that's what friends are for.'

Dougy's attempt at emotional blackmail wasn't lost on the experienced police officer. He stayed cool, weighing up the chances of

114

such an operation succeeding. He shook his head, the plan was fanciful, it might work in the movies, but in real life, no chance.

'Answer one question, where do you propose we hide once we are on the island?'

Dougy described the ley tunnel he'd once hidden in.

'That tunnel is the last place Jackson will think of looking. It's perfect.'

'Let's be rational about this, was Alastair abducted, kidnapped or did you leave him with Jackson voluntarily?' asked Iain Sherrie.

Dougy's reply was forthright.

'Even though we knew where he was, Alastair was abducted; he was taken from us at gunpoint. We feared for our lives so we had no option but to leave. Even when we'd left Iona he tried to have us killed but thanks to a brave helicopter pilot he failed.'

'OK, technically on the evidence we could arrest Gabriel Jackson and his cronies on suspicion of abducting Alastair, but it's not that easy'.

'Why the hell not, are you saying this man has special immunity? Who is he anyway, he just appeared in our lives and took over, now he's taken Alastair as his own, surely to God the law can do something about it.'

'It's complicated,' was all the policeman would say.

Dougy felt a sense of helplessness, his son would change and any lingering memories he may have of him and Sara will be wiped away, his mind altered forever. The sooner they retrieve him the better. Then grim determination gripped him.

'Well, if you won't support me I'll just have to go it alone. Dad will stand by me but he'd be better off staying here to help guard mum.'

In an instant, Iain Sherrie made a decision. As soon as back up arrived he'd leave Sergeant Burns in charge then take the 4X4 and drive Dougy to Oban town centre from where the ferry terminal is a five minute walk.

'I'll go over with the 4X4. Once you are off the ferry, turn left and walk along the quayside to the police station, I'll meet you there,' he said.

'What then?'

'I've a pal in the Mull police, someone I trained with, he has a boat moored at Fionnphort. He knows the Sound of Iona like the back of his hand. He'll take us across to the far side of the island. From there we can tack our way to the Abbey, staying unseen all the way. When we are ashore I'll ask him to wait. If we're lucky we might not need your tunnel.'

For the first time since leaving Iona Dougy felt a real sense of hope. His body tingled with excitement.

The old tractor was again pressed into service, taking Dougy to the cottage. The plan was explained to the others and straight away Ally said he was going with them, but there were strong arguments for him to stay behind. Reluctantly he agreed. Sara had seen Gabriel Jackson in action and if the plan failed… she replaced the thought of not seeing her husband again with the image of Alastair in her arms. It was an image worth holding on to.

An hour later 'back up' arrived in the form of two police officers wrapped in warm hiking clothes. Stooping under the weight of bulging haversacks they'd walked from the main road, giving the impression of hikers looking for somewhere to rest. Instead of the usual paraphernalia carried by serious walkers their haversacks held an arsenal of weaponry. Iain Sherrie quizzed them as to the possibility of an attack. Intelligence reports said there was no sign of any terrorist activity in the area. That was good enough for him and the police 4X4 was at the cottage door in minutes.

'C'mon Dougy, If we go now we'll make the afternoon ferry,' he shouted.

Before leaving, Iain told Sergeant Burns to keep everyone at cottage. It would be easier to defend than a large house.

Chapter 19

Flurries of snow whipped up by a cold wind kept the windscreen wipers busy as they drove across to Oban. As planned, Dougy was dropped off in the town centre, leaving about 20 minutes to reach the ferry terminal and buy a one way ticket to Mull. He waited in line as vehicles were driven on to the ferry; then it was his turn. The lengthy queue wound its way along a roped off walkway leading to a covered gangway. A crewman gave Dougy a long hard look, as if he recognised him, and then let him through. Dougy knew from the way this man had stared at him that he'd probably been on duty the day that Gabriel Jackson had killed the assassin on this same ferry, he may even have witnessed the body falling into the sea. Whatever had caused him to take a second look was disturbing and Dougy merged with other passengers in the cafeteria trying to avoid this man's inquisitiveness. He adopted the same tactic when leaving the ferry by engaging himself in conversation with another passenger, turning his head away whenever he spotted the man. He walked along the quayside and within minutes had reached the police station adjacent to a small railway station that in summer plied its trade along a 2 kilometre small gauge track to and from Torosay Castle. Iain had passed Dougy on the road and was already in urgent discussion with a uniformed officer when he arrived.

'Dougy, this is Inspector Mike Fletcher, the man I told you about,' said Iain Sherrie.

Dougy received a curt nod of greeting from a tall, broad shouldered officer who looked as if he'd spent most of his life in the open air. Mike Fletcher was still smarting about being kept out of things when the shooting had started on Iona but when he'd learned of Alastair's abduction he was willing enough to offer what assistance he could. It was only when he discovered that should Alastair still be on Iona, he would be guarded by an army of monks equipped with assault rifles, that he questioned the wisdom of a rescue attempt. He asked Dougy to step outside whilst he talked it through with Iain.

'What about the islanders and people staying at the Abbey, we can't afford them being caught up in any cross fire, Jesus Iain, we're risking too much here, how did you manage to get yourself involved in this mess?'

Iain went into more detail about his connection with Dougy's family and how he wanted to help.

'That's OK, but I can't afford to lose my job, in fact we could both finish up on criminal charges if things go wrong.'

Outside in the cold, Dougy heard the buzz of conversation inside the police station and worried that things were not going well. Ten minutes later he was invited back in. Iain Sherry was apologetic.

'Sorry about kicking you out like that but Mike says he will take us across to Iona in the morning. We'll stay over tonight in the hotel across the road.'

'That's OK, but how do we get onto and off the island. If Alastair is there and we grab him, what then? Gabriel Jackson is a cold blooded killer; I don't rate our chances if he catches us, we'll need a quick getaway.' Dougy replied.

Mike Fletcher was uncompromising.

'I'll drop you off at St Columba's Bay and then make my way to Martyr's Bay and wait for you there, but I can't stay all day you understand,'

That was the deal and Dougy had to agree to it.

By 6.30 the next morning they'd had breakfast, paid the bill and were waiting outside the police station for Mike. Daylight was making a struggle to assert itself and the threat of snow was in the air. Pushing his hands deeper into the pockets of his all-weather hiking coat he was harbouring doubts that Mike would turn up.

'Don't fret man, he'll be here,' said Iain.

A Land Rover towing a trailer upon which was mounted a small dark blue fishing boat with an outboard engine, turned in from the main road, swung round and stopped. The name 'Tantrum' etched in gold paint on the side of the boat filled Dougy with apprehension. Was this just a favourite name or was it indicative of unpredictability. Mike motioned them to get in and before the passenger side door had slammed shut he was accelerating along the narrow road towards Fionnphort.

'How fast can that boat of yours go?' asked Dougy, not wishing to sound too alarmed, for he knew that Gabriel Jackson had access to boats capable of high speeds.

'The old girl will surprise you,' replied Mike.
Dougy remained unconvinced, but beggars can't be choosers, as the old saying goes. He remained quiet for the remainder of the journey.

By the time they arrived at Fionnphort the early mist had developed into a thick fog. Visibility across the Sound of Iona was down to a few metres but Mike didn't seem perturbed, he was used to this sort of weather. He was excited at the prospect of going out in conditions that would deter others. Fog creates a silence that brings an eerie atmosphere to being on the water. Senses become finely tuned, picking up sounds that in fine weather may not be so perceptible. The fog would protect them from detection but Dougy still harboured doubts.

'How will we see our way across?' he asked.
Mike's reply was brusque, bordering on irritability.

'Because I know what I'm doing, you'll just have to trust me.'
Trust was all Dougy had, he had to trust that Mike was a competent sailor and that Iain would stand by him if things turned nasty. He had to trust that Alastair was still on the island and, should he be rescued, that Mike could outwit Gabriel Jackson when it came to seamanship. A tap on the shoulder jolted him back to reality.

'C'mon, let's get this boat into the water.'
Unhooking the trailer they guided the fishing boat along hard white sand to the water's edge. With hardly a sound it slid into the tiny waves lapping at their feet. The trailer was made ready for a quick getaway on their return, every second would count.
Mike stowed a can of fuel under his seat then pulled the starter cord. The Yamaha outboard motor was surprisingly quiet but in the fog the sound would carry a good distance.

'OK, all aboard, Iain with me in the wheel house and you at the stern. Keep your eyes and ears open, we can't risk a collision,' ordered Mike.

Dougy didn't argue, he was quite happy just to be on his way.

'I'll tack our way across, that way we'll draw less attention to ourselves,' said Mike.

To Dougy it was uncanny how this man navigated so accurately in such poor visibility but an hour later they were standing on the rocky beach of St Columba's Bay. Iain took charge.

'Synchronise watches,' he said.

'I can wait three hours, no more, then I'll be off.' said Mike.

The boat disappeared into the fog, marooning them, at least for a while. Iain patted the outside of his coat pocket.

'Just thought I'd bring along a wee bit of insurance,' he said, producing a standard police issue handgun.

'Bloody hell, Iain,' exclaimed Dougy.

'No worries man, it's for, well you know, just in case.'

In a way, Dougy felt some relief that his friend had the weapon but was appalled that he may have to use it. He wouldn't give a damn if Gabriel Jackson took a hit but when shooting starts, bullets don't always find their intended target. Once again he feared for his son's safety.

'Well, what's the plan of action,' asked Iain.

It was not so much a plan but a trust in luck and good fortune that would guide the outcome of their search for Alastair. Fleetingly, Dougy recalled the times when Gabriel Jackson had bleated on about God being gracious, well perhaps just for once this graciousness might apply to him.

The path was well trodden and easy to follow. A breeze sprang up, lifting the fog slightly, just enough to see a group of walkers heading towards them. Instinctively, Iain reached into his pocket; the gun was readied for firing.

'Hello there, not good weather for being up here,' said one of the walkers. His accent was distinctly English, a bit too posh for Dougy's liking.

'Aye,' grunted Dougy.

The man insisted on chatting further. He disclosed that he and his friends were on retreat at the Abbey and visiting St Columba's Bay was an essential part of their pilgrimage. This could be the luck that Dougy had wished for. He dropped his unfriendly, dour façade and began probing about the Abbey, pretending that he had little knowledge of what went on there. Pilgrims the world over love to evangelise and it wasn't long before Dougy had infiltrated the group and his inquisitiveness paid off. With great difficulty he suppressed his anger when they spoke of the man, woman and child living at the Abbott's house, saying what a nice family they were and how the little boy was a credit to them. It took all his willpower not to tell them that the child they spoke of was his. Feeling Iain's grip on his arm he took a deep breath, they had to get going and time was against them. Bidding the group farewell they hurried along the path. This chance encounter had filled Dougy with renewed vigour, he felt Alastair within his grasp and as long as the element of surprise remained with them anything was possible.

Eventually the Abbey, shrouded in mist, came into view and they slowed to a gentle walk.

'Here, have a look through these,' said Iain, handing Dougy a pair of small, powerful binoculars.

Dougy scanned the Abbey precincts, picking out a few people milling around the grounds. Through the binoculars there were no recognisable faces but then he tensed with excitement, he felt adrenalin build up as he focussed on a woman and a child leaving the Abbey by the front door. Alastair had grown and the woman was definitely Rachel. A looming figure emerged behind them, although partly in shadow he was instantly recognisable. This was the man they would have to outwit if Alastair was to be liberated.

'C'mon, this is our chance to grab him.' Dougy was really pumped up; his emotions had taken over but Iain knew that an impulsive action now could ruin everything.

'Stay down and wait,' he said.

'What the hell for man, that's Alastair, we'll not get a better chance.'

'We'll take it a step at a time; just don't do anything stupid.'
Gabriel Jackson watched as Rachel and Alastair made their way along to the main gate then returned to the Abbey. Inside, he checked on the monk posted in the observation room.

Reaching the road Dougy and Iain ambled towards the ruined nunnery, keeping Alastair and Rachel in sight. With coat collars pulled up to disguise their faces they tagged onto a group of people heading in the same direction, their camouflage was almost perfect but not perfect enough to prevent Alastair who, turning towards the footsteps coming up behind him, recognised his father. With a yell he yanked his hand from the startled Rachel and ran towards Dougy.

'Come back Joshua,' shouted Rachel.'
Dougy picked up his son and began running to where Mike would be waiting. Rachel looked with disbelief at the man she thought had perished in the helicopter crash. As he barged past her Dougy was certain he heard her whisper 'good luck.' In the Abbey, Gabriel Jackson had been alerted to what was happening out there on the road. Bellowing with rage he set off along the Street of the Dead, determined to reach Dougy before he could escape. He screamed at Rachel to give chase but she feigned injury and lay on the ground, being attended to by concerned walkers. Iain caught up with Dougy who had begun to flag under the weight of carrying his son and together they ran towards Martyr's Bay. Taking a shorter route through gardens belonging to a group of cottages, Gabriel Jackson soon had them in range.

'Stop or I'll shoot,' he yelled.

'Keep going, I'll hold him off,' shouted Iain.
Summoning his last ounce of strength, Dougy hurtled towards the bay and the relative safety of Mike's boat. Iain dropped behind a large rock and trained his Glock on the rampaging Gabriel Jackson. His police firearms training had taught him to fire only if his own life or the lives of others were in danger. Making an instant decision he squeezed off a round that passed through the fleshy part of Gabriel Jackson's right

thigh, bringing him down like a wounded bull, but only temporarily. The bullet missed the femoral artery yet the wound bled freely. Ignoring the bleeding he struggled to his feet, firing back. Iain felt the closeness of a bullet that zipped past his head but had put enough distance between him and his pursuer to reach the boat. Dougy and his son were huddled together on the wheelhouse floor. Leaping into the boat he dropped below the stern and loosed off a volley that had the wounded Gabriel diving for cover. Mike rammed the throttle wide open, taking them into the mist and out of range. In pain and terrible anger Gabriel Jackson screamed that he would hunt them down to the ends of the earth if necessary, but his words were lost to the wind.

For a small fishing craft Tantrum had a fair turn of speed and soon they were well out into the Sound. Dougy felt safe enough to stand up. Keeping Alastair close he looked out at the swirling mist that kept visibility down to a couple of hundred yards. He turned to look astern, fearful that Gabriel Jackson had set off after them. Almost by instinct Mike could tell if other boats were about so he reduced speed, cutting down the noise from Tantrum's motor. For a few moments he listened.

'I can't hear anything but I'm taking no chances,' he said, before pushing the throttle to its maximum setting.
Dougy had developed a respect for Mike, this was a resolute man who kept his word and if anyone could get them to safety it was him.

Chapter 20

Partially stemming the bleeding from his injured leg, Gabriel Jackson limped towards the Abbey where Rachel took the full force of his rage. He yelled abuse at her, blamed her for not holding on to the boy, he raised a blood stained hand as if to lash out but then, pushing her to one side, he stumbled through the main door before falling to the stone floor where he lay, unable to move. Iain Sherrie's bullet had left entry and exit wounds that would heal themselves, given time, but time was a commodity in short supply; he had to retrieve Joshua so he told Rachel she must stitch the wounds. Horrified, she backed away; this was something outside her experience. Gabriel Jackson's mood changed, he pleaded with her to carry out the procedure. What would she use? Any equipment available to her was rudimentary, she had a sewing box in her room but that was all. Gabriel Jackson's pleas became even more insistent and she eventually agreed. On her way to collect the sewing box she encountered one of the monks, at least there was someone to hold Gabriel Jackson down. Taking a candle from its holder she sterilised the needle and set about the task. Gabriel Jackson's disciplined mind took over and he barely flinched as the needle entered his wounded flesh. The monk held him, more in compassion than anything else until the final stitch went in. Together, Rachel and the monk supported the wounded man as he struggled to his feet and helped him to his room. Pale and in pain he lay on his bed to recover.

The taking of the boy known as Joshua had reverberated around the island and that same night the monks were summoned to meet Gabriel Jackson in the chapel. Despite his ordeal he stood before them. They were ordered to make ready for a mission that must not fail, his discovery that Dougy was still alive had shaken him. His security arrangements had been found wanting and finding this out the hard way fuelled his anger to the point where he was on the verge of losing control. Rachel stood outside the chapel listening to the ranting from within. The monks cowed before their leader as he threatened each one with the ultimate price of failure. Rachel moved to the shadows as they filed out, heads hidden beneath their cowls. Gabriel Jackson showed little sign of his injury as he force marched them towards where the islanders' boats were moored. Three of the more robust craft were commandeered and they set off in pursuit. Rachel listened until the roar of powerful outboards had faded, then she made a call on her mobile. The call was to a number that had been dormant in the phone's memory since the time Dougy had called his father before leaving the island.

With no thought for the safety of others the holy army smashed through the mist in its reckless attempt to retrieve a desperate situation. Gabriel Jackson stood at the prow of the lead boat like some ancient Viking chief spurring on his warriors to even greater efforts. If he caught up with Dougy whilst still at sea then recovering the boy would be that much easier. The firepower he commanded would be over whelming; Dougy and his helpers would have no choice but to surrender Joshua to him. He would then finish the job that the assassins who shot down the helicopter had failed to do.

This was his second miscalculation of the day. Mike's superior seamanship had seen them across to the other side where he hurriedly concealed 'Tantrum' beneath tarpaulins taken from the Land Rover. Local knowledge of the bends and twists in the road kept them on track as they made the journey to Craignure police station in record time. During winter months mainland ferry crossings are less frequent than at the height of the holiday season and a wait of several hours confronted them.

'Iain, follow me in your vehicle, we'll go to my place, you should be OK there and the wee lad can have something to eat. Dougy can call his wife if he likes,' said Mike.
If it were possible, the emotion generated from that call would have melted the phone lines as Dougy told his wife that Alastair was safe. Sara said that a distraught Rachel had called, telling them what had happened, pleading with them to get the boy to safety and that she would pray for him. Dougy recalled what Rachel had said as he ran

past her. She had wished him luck and it was only now that he knew she meant it.

'Put Alastair on, I just want to tell him I love him,' said Sara. Dougy held the receiver to Alastair's ear and he watched his son's reaction

at hearing his mother's voice again. Alastair didn't say anything but his tears told their own story. They'd got him away from Gabriel Jackson's clutches in time, permanent inroads had not been established into Alastair's mind and the more he listened to his mother's voice the clearer this became.

Gabriel Jackson worked out from tyre tracks on the beach that he'd been out manoeuvred and his quarry had escaped. His men were ordered to return to the Abbey and he would go on alone but not before a local man, confronted by a persuasive monk, was given no option but to hand over the keys to his Mercedes, and then in a bizarre fashion received a bow and thanked for his help. In less than an hour a determined, highly dangerous Gabriel Jackson was at the ferry terminal with one thing in mind and that wasn't to wish Dougy and his allies a safe crossing.

Annie Fletcher, a generously proportioned woman, sorted out some food and comforted Alastair whose needs were not lost on someone with three bairns of her own. She knew from her husband what Alastair had gone through and the dangers that still faced him and it was she that suggested they stay for a few days to throw Gabriel Jackson off scent. Dougy was tempted by the offer but couldn't risk placing Mike and his family in mortal danger, apart from which, Sara would be on tenterhooks, desperate to hold her son again.

'It'll soon be time to go,' said Mike.

One thing was certain, Gabriel Jackson would be on the quayside watching and waiting for any sign of Dougy and Alastair. He would scrutinise every face and every vehicle boarding the ferry. He watched as a police 4X4 rattled its way along the loading ramp, the uniformed driver concentrating on parking close to a builder's wagon in front. A large touring coach bearing the markings of a highland holiday company parked up behind, shielding the 4X4 from view. Iain Sherrie removed the tunic he'd borrowed from Mike, stuffing it under the passenger seat. He locked the vehicle's doors manually to avoid setting the alarm and joined other drivers as they made their way up to the passenger lounges. Staying with vehicles was prohibited but patrolling deck hands wouldn't see Dougy and Alastair huddled together beneath a swathe of blankets in the back of the police 4X4. A liberal dose of Phenergan administered by Annie Fletcher now had Alastair sleeping soundly in his father's arms.

In desperation, Gabriel Jackson drove the Merc up the ramp and boarded the ferry. He would keep searching, looking everywhere; he wasn't the sort to give up, especially with so much at stake. From a distance, Iain watched as the large black man hunted for Dougy and Alastair. He followed him around the boat and down towards the vehicle deck, tripping over an unconscious deck hand who unwisely had stood in the way. He watched as Gabriel Jackson went from vehicle to vehicle, peering in them, trying doors, going on one knee to look beneath them, grimacing with pain from the gunshot wound still oozing blood. Iain's sweaty hand closed around the butt of his semi-automatic pistol as the police vehicle came under scrutiny, yet for some reason Gabriel Jackson didn't dwell on it, continuing on down the line, disappearing out of sight. Iain had to take the chance that Dougy would have the sense to stay beneath the blankets as any attempt to warn him would be too risky. Using the touring coach as cover he waited and watched.

The throb of the ferry's powerful diesels lessened as it approached the shelter of Oban Bay where it would dock, offload its passengers then make ready for the return trip later in the day. Iain had become nervous about Gabriel Jackson still being down there, but drivers had begun reuniting with their vehicles, engines fired up and the stern doors swung open to let them off. Iain slipped from behind the coach; walking slowly he moved to the police 4X4 and let himself in.

'OK Dougy, it's time to go, but stay under the blanket, Jackson's on the prowl,' he said.

Dougy muttered a response, the journey had been a nightmare but somehow ignoring the cold and his cramped up muscles he'd remained hidden and silent. He'd held his sleeping son close during the crossing, keeping him secure but the Phenergan had worn off and Alastair was stirring and beginning to whimper. Wearing the borrowed police sergeant's tunic Iain drove behind the touring coach down the ramp and onto the roadway, acknowledging a brief wave from a crewman with a bandaged head. The sooner they were out of town and heading back to the farm the better. Gabriel Jackson had only one thing on his mind; he'd know exactly where they were heading, which put the fear of God into Dougy. Iain Sherrie lit up the blues and twos and driving at speeds well in excess of the limits he cleared the town. Once in the country he stopped briefly for Dougy and Alastair to regain some comfort then pushed on to the farm. On the approach everything seemed quiet, yet Iain's instinct told him something was wrong, he wouldn't have expected to see any movement especially as Sergeant Burns and the others were at the cottage but things just didn't add up.

'I don't like the feel of this. The glasses are in the glove compartment, let's have a look at the house,' said Iain Sherrie.

Dougy swept the binoculars across the farmhouse and surrounding area, nothing. He focused on the house for a few minutes; the curtains were open, he scanned the windows for movement, again nothing, except several lights were burning.

'I'm sure we didn't leave any lights on, let me phone the cottage,' said Dougy.

Iain passed him his mobile. No signal.

'Shit, they could be in trouble,' muttered Dougy.

'Let's not jump to conclusions; signals are always 'iffy round here. I'm taking us in so get in the back and stay down.'

Iain slipped the 4X4 into drive and moved to within 15 metres of the house and stopped.

'There's a bullet proof vest in the back, pass it over will you,' he said.

Dougy fumbled around before finding the black bulky vest lodged beneath a first aid box. It didn't feel heavy enough to stop a bullet but these vests are standard issue and thoroughly tested under all manner of conditions.

'I'm going to have a look, you and Alastair stay out of sight,' said Iain.

There was no cover between the 4X4 and the house, it was a sort of no man's land and Iain was going over the top. It was a brave yet foolhardy thing to do. If he was shot then Dougy and Alastair would be at the mercy of whoever was in the house, the prospect didn't appeal and he was scared.

Iain slid out of the driver's door and immediately dropped low, gun in hand. From this position he hailed the house.

'Armed police, come out with your hands up.'

He waited then repeated the order, this time louder and with greater urgency. His command was greeted with silence. Then with natural agility he broke cover and ran in a zigzag pattern across open ground, dropping below a window. He crept towards the front door and reaching up, pulled on the handle. The locked door resisted his attempt to open it. Staying low he went round the back but everywhere was locked, just as they'd left it. He returned to the vehicle.

'Let's go to the cottage,' said Dougy

Even though it was a marked police vehicle approaching them, Sergeant Burns and his colleagues took no chances, just as they had taken no chances of leaving the farmhouse looking unoccupied. It was Ally who had switched on the lights. Muzzles of high velocity rifles trained on the 4X4 until the identities of its occupants could be verified. Iain Sherry ran into the cottage.

'Dougy's outside, he's got Alastair.'

Officers were pushed aside as Sara rushed between them out into the yard where Dougy stood holding Alastair. She wrapped herself around them, holding them, hugging them as if she would never let go. Dougy touched her face, feeling the tears. They embraced then walked towards Ally and Mary and under a grey, snow filled Highland sky, the family were together, united for the first time.

'Let's get inside; Jackson can't be that far behind,' urged Iain Sherrie.

Snow began to fall as the stolen Merc pulled up at the kerbside on Inveraray High Street. The car and its occupant attracted scant attention, someone stopping off for a meal at the Crown, that's all it was.

Chapter 21

The landlord and regulars of the Crown Hotel had never encountered anyone quite like Gabriel Jackson; his bulk framed the low doorway to the bar from where he demanded directions to the MacKay farm.

'Who wants to know?'

Gabriel Jackson faced the questioner, a young muscular man who was sat at a corner table with two older men.

'I am Gabriel Jackson, a messenger of the Lord, answer my question.'

A sniggering retort came from one of the older men.

'Och aye and I'm Robert the Bruce.'

Laughter rippled around the room and others joined in, rebuking Gabriel Jackson in a way that could only have one outcome. He moved liked lightening, the man found his head forced down, face squashed into the sticky veneer of the table at which he sat. A gun pressed to his temple dissuaded the others from getting involved.

'Now will someone answer my question or do I have to kill this man,' said Gabriel Jackson, his voice low and controlled.

No answer, so Gabriel grabbed the petrified man, pulling him to his feet.

'I won't ask again.'

'OK, OK,' yelled the landlord, 'let him go, I'll tell you.'

Gabriel Jackson hurled the man backwards, smashing him against the wall.

'Right my friend, write down the directions.'

The landlord hastily drew a map on the back of a bar meal menu. Gabriel Jackson studied the scrawl, it made little sense. He pointed his gun at the landlord.

'Come, you will take me.'

A stuttered refusal cut no ice with Gabriel Jackson and a hapless landlord soon found himself behind the wheel of the Merc. Snow was falling and the landlord argued the futility of driving across farmland in this sort of weather.

'Get me as near as you can, I'll walk the rest of the way.'

If he needed any further proof that he was in the clutches of a maniac this was it. Being caught in the open in these conditions without the right equipment was suicidal, but why should he care, all he wanted was to be free of this man so he stopped about a mile from the farm.

'That's it, I'm going no further, you need to be over there,' he said, pointing across snow swept fields.

Gabriel Jackson left the car, pulled his coat tightly round his girth and set off. Blocking out the cold he walked until the farm buildings loomed into view. Lights burned behind closed curtains giving an impression that the house was occupied but any action would wait until morning. The barn became his refuge for the night. He burrowed into an ample stock of winter hay; eventually he felt life return to his frozen extremities and went to sleep. Any pain from his wound was nullified by the cold.

At daybreak the landscape was one of deep drifts and impassable roads. Gabriel Jackson put his shoulder to the barn door but snow had heaped up against it. Time and again he ran at the door until a gap appeared wide enough for him to see through. He was faced with an impossible task of reaching the farmhouse; the snow was piled too high. He foraged around the barn looking for something - anything to dig with. An array of tools hung from rusty hooks screwed to the barn wall but they were not substantial enough. In a corner he came across a well-stocked tool chest, a bag of assorted nails lay at its side. Further investigation yielded an assortment of wood that he began to fashion into a makeshift snow plough but he knew that even to clear a path of only a few metres would take time and most of his strength. Desperation left him with only one thing to do; he fell to his knees and prayed.

Iain Sherrie made an encrypted mobile phone call, checking in with his MI5 boss. He was economical with the detail; he'd fill her in later with all that had happened. His main priority was keeping Dougy and the family safe. MI5 had some knowledge of Gabriel Jackson's whereabouts; they had information about the stolen car and his visit to the Crown Hotel. Upon his return the landlord told a local reporter about his experiences at the hands of Gabriel Jackson. The reporter, sensing the story of a lifetime immediately alerted BBC Scotland and within minutes the drama was broadcast across the entire region. The fact that the gunman was still at large made the story more compelling and before long this quiet little town would become the centre of media speculation. A description given by the landlord of the man who had held him and his customers at gunpoint was soon turned into a photofit image and sent around the television channels. There was a hunger for this story, the media were still smarting over the news blackout that had hit them over the earlier Ionian incident and they weren't letting this story get away from them. Regardless of the weather, OB units were already manned and on the way to Inveraray.

Within a few minutes of the broadcast, antiterrorist officers working undercover had reported a sleeper group becoming active and then disappearing off the radar. Iain Sherrie was immediately informed and he let it be known to everyone that they were in mortal danger. There was enough firepower in the cottage to mount a vigorous defence against a head on assault, but Gabriel Jackson was different and he was close, very close. Reliance on prayer had renewed his strength and in the face of persistent and heavy snow he'd dug his way across to the house. The door gave way beneath his bulk and finding no one inside, he shook the snow off his clothes and searched the kitchen for food. Half a dozen eggs eaten raw soon had strength returning to his aching muscles, then drawing the back of a hand across his sticky mouth he turned his attention to working out where his quarry might be. His eyes settled on several photographs pinned to a kitchen notice board. They showed Dougy posing next to the farm cottage in its various stages of reconstruction. A local phone number was scribbled across the bottom of one of them. The hills in the background gave Jackson the direction to take. He smiled, 'Not long now,' he said to himself as he settled in Ally's chair, switching on the television, waiting for the snow to stop.

In the best traditions of the Argyll and Bute police Iain Sherrie put the safety of Dougy and his family before his own and that of his officers. He had to get them out of what may become a death trap. His pleas for a helicopter rescue mission had been denied, it was much too dangerous to risk a crew in this weather. He was ordered to stay put and defend his position until such times as help could be mobilised. Dougy recalled his South African history, to him it had already begun to feel a bit like the Siege of Mafeking but he hoped it wouldn't take as long for relief to arrive. However it is always the unexpected that turn things on their head, things like answering the telephone and being spoken to by someone you least expect to hear from. Reception had improved and the voice was unmistakable.

'Hello Dougy how are you and the family enjoying the snow?' Under normal circumstances the greeting would be cordial but in a voice that held such menace it was far from that. Dougy stayed silent, it wasn't deliberate he just didn't know what to say. His mind raced as he tried to compose himself.

Sara moved across to Dougy.

'Who is it?' she asked

'Well, aren't you going to tell her?'

'You're not getting Alastair back you bastard, I'll see you in hell first,' blurted Dougy. Sara gripped his arm.

Dougy's response was met by loud mocking laughter that could be heard around the room. Iain motioned to Dougy to hand him the phone.

'Give it to me, I'll talk to him.'

He spoke in a formal and uncompromising way.

'Jackson, this is Superintendent Iain Sherrie of the Argyle and Bute Police, I am armed and so are other officers here with me so I warn you to stay where you are. Any attempt to reach us will be met with force.'

'Yes I'm sure it will, so I wish to propose a compromise.'

'What kind of a compromise?'

'You are caught in the middle, me on one side and a gang of assassins on the other. They know where you are and will not give up. In my care Joshua will achieve a Heaven sent destiny that is linked with mine. A new church is already being raised in his name; mortals such as you oppose the will of God at their peril.

'Bullshit,' said Iain Sherrie.

Jackson ignored the invective.

'The compromise I propose is that Joshua is returned to me with a caveat that his parents and grandparents can see him at any time that is convenient.'

'Oh yes, convenient to you I suppose?'

'Yes of course, I am his spiritual guardian; the Lord has placed that great onus on me.'

In disgust Iain Sherrie handed the phone to Dougy.

'The crazy idiot is ranting again; he wants to do a deal. If I have my way he'll be locked up for a very long time.'

'Tell the Superintendent he's in no position to make idle threats, now listen to me; I have never disclosed to you the positions of people who are backing me. They are powerful, controlling everything in what you know as the free world. They are convinced that Joshua is the chosen one who is sent to destroy the evils of corruption, terrorism, poverty and create a new order within which his faithful ones can live without fear of annihilation,' said Gabriel Jackson.

At this Dougy lost his cool:-

'You really are a bloody nut case,' he yelled.

As if he hadn't heard this, Gabriel Jackson ploughed on with his monologue.

'Ask your policeman friend if he has ever heard of the Bilderberg Group, then get back to me, you know the number.'

The call was terminated.

'Does the Bilderberg Group mean anything to you Iain?' asked Dougy.

'Yes.'

'Well what is it?'

'You won't like this but if this group is backing Jackson then we are in trouble.'

Iain Sherrie seemed reluctant to share any more than this but Dougy had to know, it was his son's future that was at stake.'

'OK, I'll tell you what I know but there is so much in the way of conspiracy surrounding this group that the real truth behind its existence remains unknown, but if it is putting money and power behind Jackson then perhaps the reality of why it was formed is becoming apparent.'

For a moment he was silent as if collecting his thoughts, and then in carefully measured words he continued.

'This is a group of leading politicians, media chiefs, powerful industrialists and other people of immense global influence that meet on a yearly basis in secret. It is thought that collectively they are plotting the emergence of a new world order.'

'Sorry to interrupt, but how does that involve Alastair?' asked Dougy.

'I'm not altogether sure but what I can say is a new world order will involve religion in some way because over the centuries we have seen the power that religion holds over people. You don't have to believe in any form of god to be affected by it, particularly when it involves indiscriminate wholesale slaughter.'

Ally butted in.

'So this Bilderberg Group is setting out to use my grandson as some sort of talisman, believing that he is sent from God to lead the forces of good against the forces of evil and Jackson is the man they have entrusted with making sure this happens.'

'That seems to be the drift of it, I'm sure, over time, Jackson thinks his new church on Iona will attract a massive following just as the first church built there did,' said Iain Sherrie.

'Well he can think what he likes, Jackson won't get his grubby hands on Alastair again,' said Sara.

Mary moved close to Sara and took her arm.

'Over my dead body,' she said, and Ally knew she meant it.

'Can I say something sir,' asked Sergeant Burns.

'Aye, go ahead,' replied Iain Sherrie.

'Well sir, we're stuck here for a while, provisions are limited and Jackson has the whip hand, it's snowing like the clappers and nothing can get in or out until the weather improves so we can work this to our advantage.'

'How do you mean?' said Iain Sherrie.

'Nobody knows this area better than Ally and me, he's farmed it all his life and it's been my beat for the best part of twenty years, I reckon we can outwit Jackson and be away before he realises it,' said Sergeant Burns.

'Go on,' said Iain Sherrie.

'Well sir, if you can phone your superiors and get them to pin Jackson down at the farm, then an RAF search and rescue helicopter crew will fly us out of here, they're not put off by a bit of bad weather, they rise to a challenge like this, they'll do it for me,' said Sergeant Burns.

'I didn't know you had such influence, Angus,' said Ally.

'Aye my friend, and that's not half of it,' he replied.

'What else had you in mind,' asked Iain Sherrie.

'If a terrorist gang is on its way then we'll need some armed protection, probably more than we've got here, so what better place to hide out than a military establishment.'

He now had the attention of everyone in the room.

'You mean RAF Leuchars,' said Ally.

'Aye Ally, that's exactly what I mean.'

'It could work,' said Iain Sherrie who was already punching numbers into his mobile phone.

He moved to a corner of the room and spoke to his boss. His body language indicated that he was being taken seriously.

'OK, thanks; I'll give them your response,' he said.

'We have a minor difficulty; Gabriel Jackson was right when he said that powerful forces where supporting him. Already the police have been told to back off and the media are again being given restricted access to the story,' said Iain Sherrie.

'So where does that leave us?' asked Dougy.

'We will be air lifted out and taken to Leuchars as Sergeant Burns suggested, but we have to accept that Jackson will meet us there...'

Before he could finish, Dougy was on his feet, his face bright red, his speech almost incoherent.

'Not bloody likely, I'd rather stay here and take my chances,' he yelled.

'Unfortunately, that may not be an option, it's unlikely we'd survive if attacked, let's talk it through,' said Iain Sherrie, his voice calm but tinged with emotion.

'Whose bloody side are you on?' shouted Dougy.

Iain Sherrie ignored him and took charge of the situation.

'Right, let's get things into perspective, we can't stay here, the authorities won't risk Alastair's life. They are under orders from on high to reunite Alastair with Jackson so that plans already under way can be realised,' he said.

'It's this damned Bilderberg Group that you spoke of isn't it,' said Dougy.

'It looks that way, everyone in this room, and that includes young Farai is dispensable, except for Alastair of course,' said Iain Sherrie.

Dougy buried his head in his hands. The phrase 'catch 22' was real, they were in a trap and the only way out was to succumb to the wishes of people with enormous power who meet under the guise of engaging in general discussion concerning the world of politics and enjoying 5 star hotel accommodation. The sinister truth was now apparent to him; this is what it had all been about since the day of Alastair's birth. From the moment that bright celestial body appeared over his birth place enemies of the West had conspired to eliminate him, and without Gabriel Jackson interceding when he did, the forces of evil would have succeeded. The terrorist threat remains high, a gun battle would result in casualties on both sides and he felt sick at the thought of any of his family being killed or injured. Feeling the gentle touch of Sara's hand on his shoulder, he raised his head.

'We have to leave,' she said.

Dougy nodded.

'OK Iain, tell your boss to get things organised, we're leaving, in the meantime let's start clearing some snow.' he said.

Within half an hour of the call being made, a search and rescue helicopter hovered above the cottage and a crew member winched down.

Priorities for evacuation were soon agreed. Wrapped in protective clothing, Dougy and his family were winched through driving snow into the helicopter. Iain Sherrie and his officers would stay in the cottage, acting as a decoy should an attack come. It was a heroic act of selflessness and Dougy prayed that the helicopter would return in time to get them out. The aircraft turned into the murk and at full throttle flew off towards RAF Leuchars where transport was waiting to take its passengers to the warmth and safety of the officers' mess.

The helicopter refueled and took off, heading back to the farm. Dougy felt relief that Iain and the others would soon be rescued and brought to safety. What he didn't know was that the crew had orders to pick up Gabriel Jackson and bring him to Leuchars, and only then would they return to complete their mission at the cottage. Iain Sherrie was ordered to dig in for a while longer.

Chapter 22

It had stopped snowing by the time the helicopter arrived over the farm house. Gabriel Jackson had cleared a space outside from where he stood looking upwards, gesturing to be winched aboard. This was the same ruthless, armed individual who had terrorised a local pub landlord and his customers, so the helicopter commander took no chances, his aircraft would not be compromised. Jackson was hauled in, propped against a bulkhead and held at gunpoint. He raised his hands in mock surrender, giving up his automatic pistol without a whimper, and then settled back to enjoy the flight. He would soon be reunited with his beloved Joshua, that's all he cared about.

As a way of reassurance the Sea King flew low over the cottage, but encroaching darkness ruled out a return flight so Iain Sherry and his men would have to wait until daybreak. There was still no information as to the whereabouts of the terrorist sleeper group; these people are experts at evading detection. Their intelligence is usually accurate but the news blackout would have come in time to stop any details of the evacuation being made public. Despite mugshots and profiles of the group being posted on the police data base three men in their late teens turned up in Inveraray posing as hill walkers without any checks on their identity being made. They were plausible, spoke with distinct Scottish accents and fitted quite easily into the surroundings. They booked into the Crown Hotel, used cash to pay for two nights bed and breakfast and ordered a snack from the bar meal menu, all quite normal. One or two locals in the bar began chatting to them, questioning their sanity for wanting to walk the hills in this weather but the young men were well equipped with trekking gear, maps and the latest satellite navigation device. What they didn't reveal were the semi-automatic pistols, grenades and suicide belts rolled up in waterproof clothing hidden away in three large overfilled rucksacks that they kept close by.

The conversation moved from hill walking to other things. The young men casually asked why there were so many police vehicles in the town. They listened to the story of how a large black man with a gun had threatened the landlord and customers of the Crown Hotel and how the men in the bar had stood up to him. It was a heroic tale, embellished a little over a few beers, but impressive nonetheless. They feigned dismay when told of the landlord being forced, on pain of death, to take the gunman to the McKay farm. The men pretended to be intrigued by the story and asked what was so special about the McKay farm for it to be of interest to such a violent man. The police had said nothing to the townspeople so rumour mongering had taken hold. Why had Dougy and his family returned home from Zimbabwe? Was there a connection between the large black man and Dougy's wife? Why had the search and rescue helicopter been flying around? Before going to their rooms the men had managed to wheedle directions to Ally McKay's farm from a local man who, by then, had had his fair share of McEwan's heavy. Away from prying eyes weapons were checked. Sleepless, they sat waiting for the first rays of dawn hoping the snow would stay away, giving them a chance to begin the trek to where they thought Alastair would be. Similar to those who had gone before, this would be a one way trip, death meant nothing to them. The plan was to get as close as they could to their target then detonate the belts- no one would survive.

A bright winter sun rose over the town, sparkling on the still waters of Loch Fyne, the day looked fair. Eager not to raise suspicion the men ate an early breakfast, chatting amicably to the middle aged waitress who served them. Later, fully equipped for walking, they appeared in the foyer.

'Well bonnie lads, the forecast's good but the snow hasn't shifted much. My advice would be to stay on the road for as long as you can. The ploughs have been out so it shouldn't be too bad. Can you tell me where you're heading just in case,' said the landlord.

'We're just thinking about walking by the loch today, there's no point in taking too many risks, we'll do the hills tomorrow' one of them said.

'Hold on a minute, I've had a thought,' said the landlord.

He disappeared from the bar to return a few minutes later carrying three sets of skis and walking poles.

'I've had these in the back for ages, they only get used now and again, you can borrow them,' he said.

It was only when the police called by an hour later and left some posters on the bar of the Crown Hotel that the landlord recognised who his guests actually were – ruthless killers who had conned him and his customers into divulging information that might result in multiple deaths. Anger nagged at him, first Gabriel Jackson now a bunch of assassins, what the hell was going on in this quiet little Scottish town?

***

Iain Sherrie nodded his thanks to Sergeant Burns as a mug of black sweet coffee appeared at his side. The crumpled, unshaven appearance and bloodshot eyes betrayed a man who'd been propped up in a chair all night. He'd snoozed, even dreamed a little but proper sleep had eluded him. Stretching the kinks out of his arms and shoulders he gulped the scalding liquid, draining the mug at one go. His mobile phone vibrated, the Sea King had developed a fault so their evacuation would be delayed by at least two hours. He was told about the men at the Crown Hotel and that armed police were on their way but the terrorists had a head start so they needed to be at a state of readiness. Adrenalin surged around his body; tiredness was replaced with alertness that comes from a heightened central nervous system. It was fight or flight and as they had nowhere to go, flight was out of the question. The MacKay's were safe so he could focus on defending his position without worrying about them. Two things were in his favour, the first being that the enemy would be in the open and the second was that his officers were crack shots. He still felt deep anger at the gunning down of the two officers at Taynuilt. There was a score to settle, perhaps today was the time to put things right.

The assassins made good progress, reaching the deserted farmhouse in under the hour. Gabriel Jackson had left the front door open, a bedroom window swung on its hinges. The talkative man in the bar had divulged information about the cottage and powerful binoculars trained on the windows soon gave them what they needed.

A plan was agreed, the attack would be mounted from different sides. They couldn't estimate what kind of resistance awaited them but prior knowledge of the slaughter of the group on Iona made them ultra cautious. Gabriel Jackson was a ferocious fighter and for all they knew he was at the cottage.

By mid-morning the air temperature had risen a few degrees above freezing and there was enough heat in the sun to cause the snow on the steep farmhouse roof to thaw. The assassins took heart from this, they finalised their murderous preparations before skiing silently towards the cottage. Their plan was to attack from the front and sides. They would be in the open but the odds were on one of them getting near enough to detonate the belt and complete the mission entrusted to them.

Sergeant Burns shouted a warning only seconds before bullets raked the cottage. He'd sighted one of the men moving at speed, firing indiscriminately, creating a diversion whilst his comrades made their attack from the sides. With the butt of his firearm the sergeant smashed a window, took aim and brought the attacker down with a single shot. Blood pumping from a fatal chest wound stained the snow where the man had fallen.

'Got you,' muttered Sergeant Burns, but his self-congratulation was short lived as bullets hit the cottage from the sides and back. A grenade exploded near the back door, blowing it open. The second killer was upon them, he reached to detonate his belt but the finger on the trigger of a police issue assault rifle was a fraction of a second quicker. The remaining man threw himself over the body of his dead colleague into the cottage where a salvo of bullets cut him down but not before he'd armed his belt. A violent explosion ripped through the building leaving nothing but carnage and burning debris to greet the crew of a Sea King helicopter that hovered overhead twenty minutes later.

Chapter 23

In the privacy of his office, the station commander told Dougy and Ally what had happened at the farm. It was almost too much to take in. Dougy's ashen face was enough to tell his wife and mother that something dreadful had taken place. Ally could not hide his grief; the son of his old school friend had perished defending them. He and those who were with him had paid an awful price, it had happened on Ally's property so any thoughts of returning would have to be shelved until forensics and the Military Intelligence had finished raking through what was left of the cottage and doubtless the farmhouse would be picked over in the search for evidence. His entire property was a crime scene; Ally feared that he and Mary may never be allowed back. The only person who appeared unphased by the outcome was Gabriel Jackson whose temporary billet was in another part of the air base. A cell in the guard room had been modified to offer additional comfort to what was already there, but the freedom of the base was denied him.

Questions flooded into Dougy's mind. Why did rescuing Gabriel Jackson have to take precedence? Who gave the orders? How did the killers avoid detection before it was too late? Someone must carry the can for this but he knew it would be hushed up just like earlier atrocities. The media would be given a watered down version of things, once more the freedom of the press was to be trampled on. The landlord of the Crown Hotel would receive a visit from the police threatening prosecution if he disclosed anything to the press other than what was contained in a carefully worded statement. A grave faced Chief Constable appeared on local and national television to talk about what he described as a 'tragic loss of life in a terrorist incident'. He praised the bravery of those involved and said that through their actions a known terrorist group had been eliminated. He said that investigations would continue into the incident and 'no stone would be left unturned' in his force's commitment to containing terror threats to the region. Seasoned newspaper editors didn't go for this; they demanded their democratic right to the whole truth, arguing their readers deserved nothing less. Banner headlines in the popular press pulled no punches. 'What are they hiding?' asked one. 'What the hell is going on?' asked another. Photographs of Inveraray were used to illustrate articles that probed the reasons why this quiet little town in the Highlands should be at the centre of a major incident. 'Not since the Clearances has there been so much blood in the snow,' wrote one reporter in an article high in conjecture but lacking in substance. Secret orders on MoD headed paper marked 'for your eyes only' were faxed direct to the commanding officer. They contained highly classified coordinates to a place that offered sanctuary and security. A concession was that Alastair's parents and brother could stay with him and have access but Gabriel Jackson was given total control. Once airborne, coordinates would be transmitted to the helicopter's computer. Radio silence was to be maintained throughout the flight and conversation between the pilot and his passengers kept to minimum.

A room adjacent to the Officers' Mess was chosen as the venue for a highly charged briefing during which the conditions were read out. Two armed military police officers stood in the doorway facing the polished oak veneered table around which the briefing took place. Two others guarded the main door. They too had their orders, no one in, no one out until the commanding officer said so. As each condition was put to them Gabriel Jackson nodded in agreement, he had no wish or need to speak as it was all being done for him. A warning hand on Dougy's shoulder prevented him from rising to his feet. Instead he expressed his feelings from his chair.

'People, good people, have died defending our freedom from this tyrant,' he yelled, pointing an accusative finger in Gabriel Jackson's direction, 'Now you are saying that their deaths were pointless, I can't agree to your conditions, God what a nightmare.'
Sara leapt to her feet, glaring at a military police officer who approached her, daring him to touch her. Dougy took her lead; they stood together, joining hands. It was a sign of solidarity; instinctively they knew that despite their anguish and deep resentment at how they and their family were being bulldozed into Gabriel Jackson's grasp,

145

they would stay together as a family, opposing any attempts to split them up.

'Can my parents come with us?' asked Dougy.

The commanding officer turned to Gabriel Jackson.

'Well,' he said.

Gabriel Jackson thought for a moment before replying.

'No, I cannot accept responsibility for their safety.'

'Don't worry, they'll be well looked after here and the authorities will ensure their house is put back to rights,' said the C.O.

Deflated and dispirited, Dougy and Sara sat down. They had to agree or lose Alastair, this time for good. Their silence and Sara's quiet tears told its own story. They acquiesced. An air of finality entered the C.O.'s voice.

'OK, that's settled then, you leave in an hour.'

The MacKays were left alone to say their goodbyes. Dread entered Ally's heart at the realisation that he and Mary would probably never see their grandchildren again. To them, this was a final farewell and the pain was unimaginable.

Once again Dougy and Sara were being forced to flee. RAF transport ferried them across to the far side of the base where a fully fuelled Sea King was warming up ready for its flight to a destination known only to a few. Sabotage, even in military establishments, can happen and the helicopter had been guarded day and night. The flight had been entrusted to the same pilot who had lifted them out of the cottage. This was to be his last job before retirement. He'd enjoyed his time in the RAF, being decorated for bravery along the way; his promotion to Squadron Leader had come later than expected but as his wife pointed out 'better late than never'. The promotion had boosted his service pension. Search and Rescue can be perilous and stressful work but there was no apparent danger in this last mission, straight there and straight back then he could put his feet up and enjoy the fruits of his labour. For two or three days he'd felt a bit out of sorts but put it down to a virus, there was a lot of it going about.

Before belting in he checked his passengers for comfort. Gabriel Jackson took the co-pilot's seat. Much of the rescue equipment had been removed so that Dougy and his family could sit in the main part of the aircraft. Clearance for takeoff was given and for several minutes they hovered, awaiting instructions. Across the other side of the airfield two small figures waved forlornly but it was more of a gesture than anything else. The flight coordinates were transmitted and the helicopter turned south, away from the Highlands, on a course to somewhere in England. Flying in cloud at 2000 feet the aircraft had reached its cruising speed of just under 140 miles per hour. Thickening cloud stopped Dougy from recognising any of the countryside below and Sara busied herself with keeping the children happy. Alastair, who was of an age to take an interest in his surroundings, was inquisitive about the helicopter. His constant pointing and asking 'what's that daddy,' soon had Dougy wishing his son would find something else to occupy his mind. He didn't have to wait long. Gabriel Jackson noticed the pilot was perspiring freely, his face a sickly pallor. The heart attack was massive causing the pilot to slump forward, deeply unconscious. Summoning his considerable strength Gabriel Jackson attempted to pull the unconscious pilot back into his seat. He was an experienced pilot but not on helicopters. Different skills are needed than those for fixed wing flying but he was sure that if he could move the unconscious Squadron Leader far enough away from the controls he could stabilise the helicopter which by now was in real danger of spinning out of control.

'I can't move him,' shouted Gabriel Jackson, his voice betraying more than a hint of panic.

Dougy tried to go forward to help but was thrown off his feet; he stood no chance of reaching the pilot. Sara was desperately trying to hold on to her sons but the violent movement of the helicopter ripped Alastair from her grip. Unrestrained, He rolled to the floor. At that exact moment the nose of the aircraft dipped, propelling Alastair towards the cockpit where he came to rest an arm's length from the stricken man. The boy reached out and touched the unconscious pilot's hand. In an instant, calmness replaced fear; an orange glow shone from the sky, dispersing the clouds, flooding the helicopter with its light, it was as if time had been suspended. For a moment Dougy thought they were dead and had entered a parallel existence. The pilot's body twitched, his eyes opened and he lurched into an upright position.

'What the hell's going on, what happened?' he demanded.

'Just fly the helicopter,' said Gabriel Jackson.

Control was reestablished and the helicopter resumed its planned course. Gabriel Jackson now had the advantage, with just a touch the boy had brought them back from the brink of certain death. Dougy and Sara would have witnessed this and be hard pressed to find any explanation other than a miracle to account for the pilot's recovery. Even they must accept that the boy Gabriel Jackson had re-named Joshua was special.

Two men and a woman, all wearing hooded coats, waited in the shadows of woodland near to where the helicopter put down. No evidence of buildings or other signs of civilisation existed. Two large black cars, their windows darkened and with powerful, silent engines ticking over, waited one behind the other on a narrow track that disappeared behind the trees. Gabriel Jackson led the way from the helicopter towards the welcoming party. The men greeted him with a brief nod of their heads and the woman with a superficial kiss on the cheek. They engaged in brief conversation then moved apart. Despite efforts taken to disguise her appearance, Sara recognised Rachel.

Dusk had fallen and as the helicopter left, a dusting of snow that covered the ground blew in their faces but they were not in the cold for long. Holding Farai close to her and gripping Alastair's hand Sara ensured that they would not be parted, now or at any other time. Addressing Sara, Rachel said,

'Gabriel will travel in the lead car with the bodyguards and I will ride with you. Dougy and the children will travel in the second one.'

Sara and Dougy had no knowledge of what had gone on between Rachel and Gabriel Jackson, his mistreatment of her and the secret vow she made to herself that he would never be allowed to abuse her again. She remained armed at all times, as much for her own protection as that of the people she had once again been reunited with. The cars sped along the track for about a mile then joined a dual carriageway. Dougy remained silent, his experience in dealing with the two people who once again had entered his life was to stay quiet, ask no questions but stay alert for opportunities to regain control of his family. Sara was not so reticent.

'Where are you taking us this time,' she asked in a nonchalant, almost couldn't care less voice.

The response was predictable.

'Sorry, you will have to wait until we get there, but it is not far.'

Sara shrugged her shoulders before re-joining her husband in silence. They slowed; the crunch of gravel replacing the smooth hum of tarmac. A driveway, lit on both sides by old fashioned street lamps and guarded by imposing iron gates, led them towards the end of their journey. Dougy checked his watch. They'd been travelling for about half an hour.

'Well here we are, once inside we will tell you why you have been brought here,' said Rachel.

'Can't wait,' said Dougy, his voice rich in sarcasm, but at the same time remaining troubled by what had happened during the helicopter flight. Did Alastair really bring the pilot back from deep unconsciousness? Where did the bright orange light come from? Has Gabriel Jackson been right all along?

They had been brought to a place that even in the gloom looked imposing; it had that strange feeling of being partially derelict yet cared for. They followed Gabriel Jackson beneath a narrow arch leading to a dimly lit paved courtyard, enclosed on two sides by a high red brick wall and on the other sides by the building itself. The lighting, though poor, was enough for Dougy to see that the building was a ruin. Where glazed windows once looked out across the courtyard there were now openings surrounded by crumbling stonework. Decades or even centuries ago an ornate wooden door, probably crafted from oak, may have formed the main entrance to grand opulence. All that remained was a gaping black hole in the side of the building. It was obvious there were no creature comforts to be had here, yet the night was drawing in, it was cold and snow

149

threatened. Sara drew the children closer to her. Dougy rounded on Gabriel Jackson.

'Is this your idea of a bad joke, the bloody place hasn't even got a roof,' he yelled.

'It has, you're standing on it,' came the reply.

Gabriel Jackson walked towards the hole in the wall.

'Follow me.'

Reaching inside he flicked a switch illuminating a stone staircase leading downwards beneath the courtyard. Sara drew back, this was a descent into the unknown and she had no trust in Gabriel Jackson. Dougy took her arm, she was trembling, almost petrified.

'It's OK, you'll be fine, I'll stay with you,' said Rachel, but her words of comfort were lost on Sara.

'What choice do we have, we can't stay in the open all night,' whispered Dougy to his wife.

The soft light in the stairwell cast its inviting glow around Gabriel Jackson as he stood framed in the doorway. His large impassive face displayed no emotion, Joshua was back with him. Reluctantly, he'd had to compromise by allowing the family to stay together but that was a small price to pay, the future of the foundation church on Iona was secure. The existing Abbey there would become nothing more than a visitor attraction; it was out of its time. The two thousand year old gospels espoused by St Columba and enshrined in the Book of Kells had lost their power to guide lives. Consumerism, greed and debauchery had taken over, so before the world sunk into an abyss from which there would be no escape, a new religion with new gospels and new commandments had to become a reality. A completion date for the church had been agreed with the backers, and on that day Joshua would be presented to the world. More churches were planned in countries across the globe. A massive recruitment drive had been put in place to persuade likeminded people to worship at the feet of the chosen one, who would of course have Gabriel Jackson by his side.

Together, the MacKays entered the stair well. Rough stone steps curved one way and then the other until reaching the bottom. Dougy counted each one. In all there were 33; apart from being a long way down there was nothing significant in that number so he dismissed it from his mind. Reaching the bottom of the steps Gabriel Jackson pushed on a heavy wooden door. It opened silently to expose spacious accommodation that took Dougy and Sara by surprise, and this was just one room. At the far end were two ornate panelled doors, suggesting more rooms beyond. This place belonged to someone with money and exquisite taste. Modern furnishings, expensive wall decorations including original portraits of important looking people and a mock Tudor fireplace within which a real log fire burned gave the room a welcoming feel. Dougy felt some admiration for whoever had built this place but hoped he would not be expected to clean the chimney.

'Follow me and I will show you to your living quarters,' said Gabriel Jackson.
They did as he asked, following him through the door at the far end of the room. A short narrow corridor led to a suite of guest rooms each with en suite facilities and a small kitchen.

'You are the only ones in residence so take your pick, I'll meet you in the main room in an hour,' said Gabriel Jackson.
Sara did the choosing and settled on one which had a double connecting door to an adjacent room. The children would have their own space to play and sleep but she was already feeling claustrophobic. They couldn't live like this for long, as a family they were used to the great outdoors, so no matter how palatial their accommodation, this arrangement would soon become intolerable. At least on Iona they had a window and were able to walk by the sea, enjoying the glorious scenery, breathing fresh unpolluted air. In the cottage they had freedom to come and go, but all that had gone. Here they would be imprisoned, comfortable yes, but Gabriel Jackson had set his mind against them being free. This became evident at their meeting in the main room. He sat near the fire, Rachel at his side. They were talking in low voices but as Dougy and Sara approached they abandoned their discussion. Dougy and Sara were invited to sit with them. A few pleasantries passed between them before Gabriel Jackson laid out his plans and his demands.

151

'By now, I am sure, you will have noticed the absence of any means of remaining in contact with the outside world, no telephone, no radio, no television, but I will bring you a daily newspaper and a few magazines.'

'Condescending bugger,' thought Dougy but then insisted on The Scotsman being his preference.

'All your daily needs will be provided for and Joshua will recommence his preparation for the work that lies ahead of him.'

'Tell us more,' said Dougy.

Because Gabriel Jackson was firmly in charge his reply contained no menace only a steely determination.

'I mean exactly what I say; he will spend each day with me. He will be in contact with the Lord through prayer and meditation and he will continue his studies, growing in perfect faith free from the distractions of the outside world. Only a small number of people know we are here and they are sworn to secrecy. This house has an extensive walled garden where you can walk whenever you wish but please do not attempt to leave or contact anyone.'

'How long are we here for?' asked Sara.

'That I cannot say, but when the new church on Iona is ready I will go there with Joshua. The building will be consecrated in his holy name and then we will return here. All I can say is that Joshua will remain under my instruction until his fifteenth birthday. '

'But that's years away yet, are we to stay here for all that time?' asked Dougy.

'Joshua will, yes, but if you wish to leave then arrangements can be made. However, there will be no way back. Joshua has already shown his powers and these will increase as he grows older. My hope is that you will stay,' said Gabriel Jackson.

The last statement took Dougy by surprise.

'Have you had a change of heart about us then, what are you actually suggesting?' said Dougy.

'I am saying that Joshua will need the normality of family life to support him as he grows. As he will not be mixing with other children the presence of his brother Farai becomes important. Rachel will also

152

be living here with us and she will help you in whatever way she can, so you see everything is being done to ensure your comfort and support.'

'Only for as long as we toe the line,' muttered Dougy.

Gabriel Jackson smiled but did not reply. Instead he placed another log on the fire and settled back into the well-padded leather chair that he'd claimed as his own. Rachel passed round a plate of sandwiches and cakes.

'Is there anything else we can talk about, surely you must be curious about this place and why we brought you here,' said Gabriel Jackson.

'What exactly is it, this building?' asked Dougy.

'In the morning I will take you on a tour, but I can tell you that we are living beneath what was once an abbey,' said Gabriel Jackson.

'I might have guessed,' muttered Dougy.

'Joshua has to be somewhere safe and what better place than here,' interjected Rachel.

Sara was surprised that Dougy didn't correct their son's name; he had always done so before.

'So what's different about this place, it seems we can be found no matter where we are,' said Dougy.

Gabriel Jackson's raised hand prevented Rachel from continuing.

'Enough for now, all will be revealed tomorrow.'

Picking up a poker he prodded the burning logs. Unblinking he stared into the fire. Although appearing to be in a trance he was actually praying, the words were indecipherable, he was praying in a language known only to himself, and presumably God. Dougy and Sara rose to leave but Rachel signalled for them to remain. She placed a forefinger over her lips, requesting silence until Gabriel Jackson had finished. The praying lasted about ten minutes. When he had finished, Gabriel Jackson dropped the poker noisily onto the stone hearth, rose from his chair and left the room. His living area lay beyond the second door, it was here where he could meditate and pray uninterrupted.

Then Rachel spoke.

'Before we part for the evening there is something else that needs to be resolved and that is the naming of Joshua. The boy is not yours to bring up as you wish. Granted, you are his earthly parents but his reason for being here rests outside your understanding. You have to accept this and also accept that his name is Joshua, it is the name ordained by God and he was baptised as such by a representative of God. You must relinquish the name you gave him for his own sake and for the sake of humanity,'

Dougy recalled what his friend Superintendent Iain Sherrie had said about the higher power that was manipulating things to justify its own ends. This was an earthly power not a heavenly one, yet he remained deeply troubled by his son's ability to bring consciousness back to someone who was in a coma. He also knew that if things carried on as before, his son would begin to suffer a crisis of identity. In his heart, Dougy knew that Rachel was right and that he and Sara would have to make a decision or risk losing their son, this time for good.

'We'll talk about it,' he said.

The following morning both he and Sara met with Rachel.

'We will refer to our son as Joshua, but as his given name is that of my father it will not be forgotten,' said Dougy.

Rachel smiled and left to inform Gabriel Jackson of their decision.

Chapter 24

January 1ˢᵗ 2006

A misty, cold morning greeted the New Year but Gabriel Jackson insisted on his promised tour of the grounds. He paraded them around lawns, woodland and gardens. He showed them a picturesque lake, home to many varieties of flora, fauna, water birds, wildlife and shielded on all sides by dense bushes and trees. They noticed things that gave clues to the status of the estate's owners, such as a pets' grave yard where beloved dogs and even a horse were laid to rest beneath a canopy of pine trees. An ice house and various wooden carvings placed alongside the trails raised speculation about who owned the place. But perhaps the most spectacular of all was an enclosed garden in which statues and carvings proliferated. Roses and other flowers grew here, it contained a maze and a children's playground, but why? There were no children here apart from theirs, and it was too well established to have been built specially for them. It was when they discovered what had probably been an area where a cafeteria and shops once thrived, that the ruined abbey and its parkland had at one time been open to the public, perhaps recently. A shallow ford crossed a narrow road, but large concrete blocks on either side curtailed its use, effectively closing the road to through traffic, however, most sinister of all was the contingent of armed police that patrolled a high perimeter fence. It seemed to Dougy that this was to be their life; to decide otherwise would again mean abandoning their elder son. Throughout the tour Gabriel Jackson was friendly enough but when questioned about ownership of the abbey he became distant, diverting the conversation.

'Do not bother yourselves about such matters, let us be thankful that Joshua is safe and that his preparation will be uninterrupted.'

'Well alright, but I'd like to ask one more thing,' said Sara.

'And what is that?' replied Gabriel Jackson.

'A birthday party for Joshua, can we have one please.'

155

'Well of course. We are now one big happy family, Rachel and I will be pleased to attend.'

Sara hadn't expected this, not only had he agreed to the party but he'd invited himself and Rachel. Was nothing private anymore? Sara also pushed her luck by suggesting they might belatedly celebrate Christmas as well but Gabriel Jackson would have none of it.

'Let's celebrate Joshua's birthday and leave it at that shall we.'

As usual Gabriel Jackson dominated things even down to choosing Joshua's presents. He arranged for a wide selection of toys to be brought to the house, each one gift wrapped and heaped in a neat pile close to the fireplace. Enjoying Joshua's obvious glee at opening his presents and Farai rolling about in the discarded wrapping paper restored a semblance of normality to their lives, but Dougy was saddened that his parents could not share in their grandson's birthday. Also in that morning's copy of The Scotsman he'd read of funerals that had taken place during the past two days. The names of the deceased were police officers who it was reported had given their lives in the fight against terror. Among the three names listed was that of Sergeant Angus Burns but what puzzled him was the omission of a fourth name, that of Superintendent Iain Sherrie. Perhaps his funeral had been held previously, but even so it was odd that no mention of his heroism was included in the extensive coverage of the awful events that had led to the carnage at their cottage.

His thoughts were soon put to one side, after all this was his son's birthday and a game of 'pinning the tail on the donkey' had him laughing and joining in the fun, particularly when Gabriel Jackson missed the donkey by a good distance. Rachel moved closer to Sara and whispered in her ear.

'See, he is human after all.'

Sara felt disinclined to respond.

By the end of the evening any frostiness between the two women had thawed, their previous friendship being partially rekindled, which pleased Sara because Rachel's influence with Gabriel Jackson could prove useful. What she didn't know was that Rachel still held a grudge against Gabriel Jackson for the physical abuse she'd received at his hands when Joshua had been rescued that day on Iona. Her resentment of him was buried deep and would stay there unless any violence towards her was repeated, then he'd better watch out.

Later, when the children were in bed, Dougy and Sara relaxed, having enjoyed their son's celebration. Gabriel Jackson was having his own way so he had no reason to make life any more difficult than it already was, for which they were thankful. They talked about their situation and what the future may hold for them and the boys.

'I fear for Alastair, or should I say Joshua. He is only three yet Jackson seems to have planned out his entire life. We have to be sure that he is not taken from us again, even when he goes back to Iona at least one of us must be with him,' said Dougy.

Sara nodded, she was now convinced that her first born son had a special gift, she had seen it on the helicopter but his conception had not been the result of a visitation by a higher power as such a thing had happened only once before in the history of the world. Both her sons were Dougy's and that was a fact.

Dougy changed direction.

'I wonder if Iain is actually dead,' he said.

'Why, what makes you unsure,' asked Sara.

Dougy retrieved The Scotsman from the floor by his chair and passed it to Sara.

'Have a read of page six, there's a report of the funerals of those police officers killed at the cottage and there's no mention of Iain.'

Sara scanned the report then read it carefully. It was meticulously worded, almost as if it had been written by someone other than a newspaper reporter. It spoke of a terrorist atrocity at a location near to Inveraray. It praised the dead officers for their outstanding bravery. There was a short biography of each one but no mention why the farm cottage was targeted or who the terrorists were. Above all, Superintendent Iain Sherrie had been white-washed from the report; it was as if he had never been there.

'It's very strange, particularly as we were told no one had survived the attack,' said Sara.

'Well, perhaps he did and for some reason it's being kept quiet,' replied Dougy.

'Strange, very strange,' repeated Sara.

Chapter 25

The resuscitation team at Edinburgh Royal Hospital had never seen such horrific injuries on someone who was still breathing. Iain Sherrie owed his tenuous hold on life to the skills and dogged determination of a search and rescue paramedic. For half an hour in deep snow he'd worked on the Superintendent's decimated body. Stemming blood flow from ruptured blood vessels and stabilising multiple fractures was a priority before he could be winched into the helicopter. Triage was a formality; he was critically injured and needed immediate lifesaving treatment. Surrounded by armed police the stretcher was hurried from the helipad to a waiting ambulance. In minutes Iain Sherrie was in resus, a consultant barked out orders that were obeyed without question. Blood loss and shock had put the injured officer at the very edge of death but this is the territory where resus teams spend most of their time. To lose a patient is seen as failure but keeping Iain Sherrie alive challenged even their considerable skills. Cross-matched blood flowed into his veins, but much of it was lost internally through splenic haemorrhage. His blood pressure was at a critical level and life seemed to be ebbing away, then he flatlined.

'Shock him,' ordered the consultant.

The resuscitation machine wined and electricity banged into Iain Sherrie's chest. No response.

'Try again.'

No response. Despondency swept through the team, they'd lost and it hurt. The consultant looked up at the clock, ready to call the time of death. Her registrar urged one more try. Another bruising charge of electricity flowed through the paddles, shocking the heart muscle, causing Iain Sherrie's body to arch then drop back onto the trolley. They waited, more in resignation than hope. The monitor flickered but the line stayed flat. Then a bleep and the line spiked, settling into sinus rhythm.

'We have him back, well done everyone,' said the consultant in a voice that barely disguised her emotion.

A surgeon operated there on the resus trolley, removing the damaged spleen, sewing up damaged blood vessels. He peered into the abdominal cavity as a suction machine cleared a reservoir of pooled blood. There was no seepage, the sutures held and Iain Sherrie's blood pressure began to rise. The team worked on him for another hour before he was ready to move to a bed in the ICU. His injuries were consistent with those seen on a battlefield - shattered limbs, deep lacerations and severe facial burns. The prognosis remained critical. Pins and bone grafts to repair shattered legs and a long and painful course of cosmetic surgery to reduce facial damage lay ahead, after which the spectre of increasing immobility and permanent pain held at bay by addictive opiates waited to haunt him.

As far as the media was concerned there were no survivors of the incident at the farm cottage and apart from the Chief Constable, Iain's wife Janet was the only other person allowed near him. A 24/7 armed police guard made sure of that. To avoid breaches of security the authorities insisted on Janet staying at the hospital. A visitors' room was fitted out with the basics and she moved in. Nurses received strict orders not to talk to anyone outside the Unit about their patient. All others involved with his rescue and treatment had been reminded of the penalties of breaking the Official Secrets Act. Iain Sherrie was an official secret and it had to be kept that way.

Early summer 2007

Almost two years had passed without incident yet Dougy remained ever doubtful that they could remain hidden for much longer. Joshua's enemies had no respect for human life and were committed to the boy's destruction. He'd convinced himself that somewhere they were plotting their next assault; their intelligence homing in on Joshua's whereabouts. Yet Gabriel Jackson seemed blissfully unconcerned about any of this. To him the place was impregnable, its perimeter sealed and the air space above the ruined abbey continually monitored against surprise attack. Joshua's preparatory education continued and the access arrangement agreed with Gabriel Jackson was honoured. Rachel and Sara walked in the garden, they fed wild

160

fowl on the lake and Farai laughed at the antics of grey squirrels that populated the woods.

As a family they picnicked during the fine summer weather, and Sara's contentment showed. At the end of each month a black limousine appeared at the main gate. It took Gabriel Jackson to a nearby private airfield where he boarded a small helicopter provided by a local businessman sympathetic to the cause. The flight to Iona was to check on progress with the new church and to reinforce the need to maintain construction targets. Many centuries before, a progress chaser in the shape of St Columba berated the devil for frustrations experienced when constructing his monastery. Slight delays caused Gabriel Jackson to take his anger out on the builders, implying dire consequences should the church not be ready on time. His aim of dedicating the church and presenting Joshua on the boy's 5th birthday must not be thwarted. Once satisfied, and having led his band of monks in a prayer for God's strength to carry on the sacred work, he flew back.

***

For nine months of hell Iain Sherrie had been under medical in-patient care. Physiotherapists had inflicted an exercise regime that reduced him to tears of pain mixed with those of frustration. He would never be the man he once was, which for someone like Iain Sherrie was almost unbearable. It consumed him. Despite psychiatric intervention, dramatic mood swings directed at the nurses and his wife, followed by deep remorse, became a serious problem. Being the only survivor of the suicide bomber he constantly questioned why he was the one to escape death, why did his colleagues have to die and not him? His mind often strayed to the previous killings on the shores of Loch Etive and tears were never far away. The black dog of depression was a constant companion.

Bit by bit, as strength returned to his body, physiotherapists were no longer seen as torturers and psychotherapy was having the desired effect. His mood began to lift and in time he became fit enough to be discharged home from the hospital. A permanent limp and the possibility of further surgery on his damaged body ruled out any hope of him returning to even a desk job, should one be available, and he was invalided out of the police service on full pension. Secrecy still surrounded him and boredom was soon to be a problem, his mind began to dwell on negative things and fearing a return to his depression he set about making contact with his closest friends. Surely he was allowed to do that, living a hermit's life was not for him, so he called the farmhouse.

'Hello,' answered a familiar voice.

'Ally, this is Iain Sherrie, how are you keeping?

For a moment Ally was lost for words but soon regained his power of speech.

'God, I thought you were dead, how are you?'

'Look Ally, I think it best if you and Mary come over for a couple of days, we've a lot to catch up on, can you manage that?'

'Aye, I'm sure we can, where are you staying?'

That evening, when met at the door by a man with such grave disfigurement, Ally and Mary found it impossible not to show their feelings.

'Aye, I'm not a pretty sight but come in, we've a lot to talk about.'

Over tea and homemade scones Iain Sherrie and Janet listened to the entire story of how Dougy and his family were taken to an unknown destination and how Ally and Mary were desperate to see them again. Iain Sherrie suggested they go back to Iona and ask some questions.

'You'll never make it man,' said Ally.

Ally's comment was like waving a red rag at a bull. Iain Sherrie struggled to his feet, for him this was defeatist talk. He faced Ally, his determination obvious.

'We'll go, and that's that,' he said.

Ally saw a mirror image of his own personality in this man, unwilling to admit he was unable to do something even though his body was screaming at him to have more sense.

Janet tried in vain to persuade him to reconsider.

'I know you are worried about me so come with us,' he said.

Reluctantly, Janet gave her blessing to what she saw as a foolhardy venture, but one she could do nothing to prevent. Checking the ferry times they decided to sail the following afternoon. Finding 'off season' accommodation would be easy; they'd pose as visitors looking for a few days of peace and rest. Although Iain Sherrie had been involved in a previous rescue attempt, his altered appearance would only attract glances of pity, not recognition. Even so, to avoid raising any suspicion they agreed to travel under assumed names.

December 2007

A hotel adjacent to the Abbey offered bed and breakfast at an affordable price. Mary had had the foresight to suggest they took sufficient changes of clothing for an extended stay so they booked in for the week, after all why not mix a bit of business with pleasure. Their first evening was spent in and around the locality, looking like another group of pilgrims visiting Iona. The more serious part of their reason for visiting Iona would begin the next day with gentle questioning of local people who they hoped would be forthcoming about the family that once lived at the Abbey, picking up bits of information here and there that may give clues as to the whereabouts of Dougy, Sara and their children. Expectations were not high but they remained hopeful that someone may just be able to help. One thing was certain though; Gabriel Jackson would strike a chord with many people, a man like that could never remain unnoticed for very long. In recent times the island had been raked with gunfire, killing and mayhem which would have left indelible memories in the minds of those affected by it.

They paid the entrance fee and walked along the path to the Abbey. Scaffolding hid some of its qualities, but once inside they felt a sense of the powerful history that is Iona, it was all around them. They'd each visited the Abbey at other times in their lives but there is always something new to see, to wonder at. A smartly dressed man wearing a tour guide's badge who Mary guessed was in his mid-forties had just begun a tour around the Abbey. He was interesting, smiled a lot and responded to questions. About 10 minutes into the tour Ally asked a question, not about the Abbey but about other places they might visit whist on the island. Whether the guide was caught off guard or whether he meant to give out the information, Ally's question prompted a priceless response.

'Well, there's a new church being built on another part of the island that you may consider visiting,' said the guide.

He explained its whereabouts but before he could continue the tour Ally pressed him further.

'Oh aye and what sort of church would that be, is this place being closed then?'

There was deliberate naivety in the question.

'No, the Abbey is not being closed, well not as far as I know. The new church is a private venture being constructed by a group of monks that used to live here. Their boss or at least I think he's their boss, visits on the first day of each month from the mainland. He uses a helicopter so he must be wealthy,' said the tour guide.

Iain Sherrie joined in the conversation.

'What's this man look like,' he asked, trying hard to remain matter of fact.

'Well, I've seen him a couple of times, he's a very big man, black, over six feet, South African I think,' replied the tour guide.

There was muttering from others on the tour that the guide was having his time monopolised and what did all this have to do with the Abbey. One forthright woman insisted that they get on with the tour.

Later, over lunch, they talked about what the guide had said and agreed to pay the new church a visit that afternoon.

'It sounds promising, the boss man could be Gabriel Jackson and if he is, well we could be on to something,' said Iain Sherrie, falling back on his policeman's instinct.

'Look Iain, I don't want to seem overprotective, but you're struggling, I think you should rest this afternoon, we can always go tomorrow,' said Janet.

'Don't fuss so lass, I'm OK, nothing a dram won't put right,' he said.

Arguing with him served no purpose and that afternoon they set off to walk to the new church. Iain Sherrie reluctantly agreed to Janet buying him a stout walking stick from a gift shop. She'd argued that with this to lean on he'd complete the distance there and back. They had to go at his pace and the need to rest every fifteen minutes meant the walk to the new church took far longer than would normally be the case. It was 2pm before they arrived and Iain Sherrie was exhausted, his breathing was laboured and his skin had taken on the fragility of ancient parchment.

'I told you so, you're going to kill yourself,' said Janet, her voice showing concern and anger.

A monk who was working on the roof turned and seeing Iain Sherrie's distress climbed down his ladder and hurried across.

'Can I help,' he asked.

'My husband is weak, is there anywhere he can rest?'

'Wait a moment.'

The monk went into the church and a minute or two later returned carrying a lightweight camp bed.

'He can rest on this, I'm afraid it's all we have.'

Iain Sherrie nodded his gratitude and Ally and the monk lowered him down. A rolled up blanket was placed beneath his head and they carried him into the church where he could rest for a while.

Ally scrutinised the simple yet impressive interior of the building. He'd been in a few churches during his life; they'd all followed the familiar architectural form of a chancel and nave, a crossing and transept, an altar, pews, lectern, pulpit and font, yet apart from an altar constructed of plain oak there was nothing else. The plainness of the building was reflected in a floor tiled with local stone and a roof supported by joists hewn from Scottish pine, nothing fancy but built to last for centuries. A portable heater fed from large propane cylinders kept the church interior warm. Despite its plainness the building exuded calmness and a tranquillity that within minutes had taken Iain Sherrie from pain and discomfort to a restful restorative sleep.

'Please stay for as long as you wish, but forgive me, I must finish my work, Father Gabriel would be most upset if things were not as he would want them,' said the monk.

'Who is Father Gabriel, is he the man in charge?' asked Ally.

'Well, yes but the church is to be dedicated to Joshua,' replied the monk.

'Who is Joshua,' asked Ally.

'He is the chosen one who will lead us to victory,' replied the monk.

'Oh, when does this dedication happen?'

'The day after tomorrow, on the 5th anniversary of Joshua coming into the world, it will be a glorious day, please come, but get here early. Now I must really get on with my work,' said the monk.

They'd be there alright even if Iain Sherrie had to be piggy backed all the way.

Chapter 26

Darkness had fallen, taking the temperature down with it. Had circumstances been different, a brisk walk back would have kept the cold at bay but Iain Sherrie slowed progress to a crawl. Mary, always the pragmatist had a pocket torch tucked away in her anorak and was able to light their way along the rough path. Iain Sherrie insisted on walking unaided but before long he was stopping every few metres, his breathing laboured. Janet moved closer to Mary and whispered.

'There's no way he'll walk all the way back to that church, even after a day's rest.'
Her words carried in the thin night air.

'Have faith woman, I'll not be a burden,' snapped Iain Sherrie, but his pain wracked body told him otherwise. His relief at seeing the distant Abbey lights was palpable.

'Thank God,' he muttered.
Leaning heavily on Ally, Iain Sherrie made it to his hotel room where he slumped into an armchair, utterly spent. After half an hour enough strength returned for him to undress and get into bed. Janet climbed in beside him, prayed for her husband and fell asleep.

A thin beam of bright early morning sunlight found its way through a chink in the heavy velvet curtains, catching Janet's face, wakening her. She reached out to her husband's side of the bed but it was empty. The flickering numbers of a radio alarm clock read ten minutes to eight. She sat up, switching on the bedside lamp; Iain was fully dressed, sitting in a chair. He glanced across at his wife.

'Sorry, did I wake you?'
'No, but you should be in bed, you need to rest.'
On shaky legs, Iain Sherry got up, went to the window and drew the curtains. Sunlight flooded in.

'Only a fool would stay in bed on a morning like this, anyway I need my breakfast.'
Janet smiled; *he must be feeling better.*

A selection of newspapers, delivered to the island by an early morning ferry, was in the hotel reception. Ally, up and dressed since seven o'clock, scanned a couple of tabloids before settling to read a story about the Archbishop of York and a dramatic gesture he'd made in opposition to Robert Mugabe's reign of oppression in Zimbabwe. Under a banner headline about the Archbishop getting hot under the collar there appeared a more considered report that described how he had cut up his clerical collar whilst appearing live on a television show. The churchman had said that he would replace his collar only when the despot Mugabe was out of office.

The report explored the significance of this gesture and suggested that it was a powerful one. The dog collar is not just a badge of office it is a sign of the priest's holy calling and is recognised by people of different faiths across the world. Since the 6th century, clergy have identified themselves in the general community with a form of dress that is specific to their work. The dog collar is thought to have been introduced in the late 18th century. A quote from a Church of England spokesman said that the Archbishop's actions were '*certainly no empty gesture. What he did is a very big deal.*'

Over breakfast, Iain Sherrie borrowed Ally's paper; he studied the report, nodding in agreement with what was printed there. His time with MI5 had been spent in countering the terror threat from Mugabe's corrupt regime. To him this justified all that he'd worked for, at last someone as significant as the Archbishop of the Northern Province of the Church of England had taken a stand. Inwardly he rejoiced at the Archbishop's call for action and for a voice of reason to permeate through to world leaders in the hope that they could convince neighbouring South Africa to move against this despot. Military action wouldn't work, there had to be another way, a powerful voice, a voice of hope giving ordinary people courage to rise up against injustice. Iain Sherrie had lost friends and colleagues to acts of terror. He'd suffered terrible injuries at the hands of brainwashed people who had no other aim but to kill a boy who their master thought would galvanise world opinion against him and the foul regime he represented. A powerful realisation that the fight must go on, ignore

168

the pain and deformity, remain part of it. Breakfast crockery rattled as he brought his fist down on the table, startling other guests.

'We have to be there, tomorrow we have to be there,' he ranted.

'Alright calm down, we will go but the main reason is for Ally and Mary to see their grandson again and to listen for clues as to where the family is being kept,' said Janet.

The day was spent resting and talking. Ally and Mary were excited at the prospect of seeing their eldest grandson again and Ally even entertained the possibility of grabbing him from Gabriel Jackson's clutches. Not a chance, he would be too well guarded, the idea was fanciful. Outside, the mercury inched above zero, and as evening approached it fell back to minus 3; it was sure to go lower. A dusting of snow greeted the morning and as she contemplated the walk ahead of them Janet Sherrie feared for her husband's wellbeing, but he was upbeat and bullish about things. *I'll just have to go with the flow,* she thought. Remembering what the monk had said about getting there early, they arrived at about 10.15am, expecting a large crowd. During the slow walk over, Iain Sherrie reflected on the recklessness of it, he feared that amongst the crowd would be an assassin, mingling, dressed ordinarily, waiting for an opportunity to strike. At least he expected some sort of security check to be carried out. Well he was right about that. Numbers were low, only two dozen or so people but the monks were armed and organised, nothing escaped their scrutiny, bags were searched, people frisked, questions asked. The friendly monk, who had helped Iain, spotted them and allocated a good vantage point directly facing the church door where Gabriel Jackson and Joshua would eventually emerge. A hastily rigged wire fence encircled the church; *'it wouldn't keep my cows out never mind a terrorist,* thought Ally.

'When does it start, this dedication?' asked Mary.

'The moment Father Gabriel arrives.' replied the monk.

'Oh, so where is he coming from?'
The monk wouldn't be drawn.

'I'm afraid that is top secret, even we don't know,' the monk said.

169

He's a lying toad thought Ally, *of course he knows, he must know.*

'Do you hear that,' whispered Janet.

'Hear what,' asked Mary.

Janet pointed to the approaching helicopter as it skimmed low over the sea, heading towards them. It flew straight in, landing on a nearby patch of ground. Two figures emerged, one carrying the other. The rotors continued to turn as if the pilot was to take off immediately but he didn't, which to Iain Sherrie was a sure sign that a quick turnaround was planned.

It seemed strange that for such a supposedly momentous occasion the crowd remained small, consisting mainly of curious islanders, tourists and a rookie journalist who looked bored and fed up; giving the impression that he'd rather be somewhere else. A label pinned on his coat lapel announced him as, 'Jamie McArdle, Junior Reporter, Oban Advertiser'. Noting this, Iain Sherrie thought that with such a powerful organisation bankrolling the operation Iona should be overflowing with national press and politicians, but not so. Their hotel was a third full and as far as Ally could see only a couple of other guests were there. As the doors opened, to suggest there was mounting excitement would have been an exaggeration, a low murmur, yes but that was all. The monks moved to form into two lines between which Gabriel Jackson walked, carrying Joshua. Upon reaching the end of his Guard of Honour, Gabriel Jackson stopped. Instead of a speech he lifted Joshua above his head for all to see, presenting him to the people. Mary wanted to cry out to her grandson but Ally gripped her arm and shook his head. As if drawn, Iain Sherrie moved closer to the fence. His watched as Joshua was lowered to the ground. In an instant there was mutual recognition; Despite Iain's facial disfigurement Joshua knew this was the man who had helped rescue him from Iona. He recognised his grandparents and with a cry of joy tore himself from Gabriel Jackson's grip and ran to where they stood. Stopping in front of Iain Sherrie he reached through the fence and touched the crippled man's hand. Joshua's gentle touch was like something he had never felt before. A bright orange light descended, enveloping him, blinding him. In that instant he felt an overpowering peace. He was healed.

Iain Sherrie dropped to his knees; drained and weeping openly. Janet saw that her husband was whole again and knelt at his side. Ally and Mary stared at their grandson, unable to fully take in what had happened. They too knelt beside their friends. Joshua was scooped up and removed from the scene and the helicopter whisked him away. The dedication would have to wait for another day but the reporter had the story of a lifetime and he wasn't about to keep it to himself.

Within half an hour the story of Iain Sherrie's healing had been emailed to the Oban Advertiser news editor. The reporter waited for the usual accolades that follow a release of such ground breaking news. It was bound to go national; after all he'd witnessed a miracle. His editor dismissed the story as a hoax and emailed back some well-meaning advice about drying behind his ears. The young man would have none of it, he was standing only a few feet away from where it happened, he'd seen it with his own eyes, he'd seen the light surround Iain Sherrie's body and witnessed the scars disappear from his face. He'd watched in disbelieving awe as the crippled man rose to his feet and danced a jig on legs that were strong again. This wasn't a hoax and he would prove it but there was no background to go on. All he had were instructions to cover the opening of a new church on Iona and report it, which should have been a routine, boring assignment. He would get a few names and the odd quote then write his story – job done. What he finished up with was an account no one believed and an editor who had branded him gullible. He had to talk to the man who'd been healed, that would give truth to the story. The problem with this was that the small crowd had dispersed and Iain Sherrie was by now locked in his hotel room, having been smuggled there beneath Ally's overcoat. He remained hidden until the time came to catch the next ferry off the island and away from stories circulating around Iona and an overzealous news reporter whose reputation hinged upon tracking him down.

Gabriel Jackson slammed the car door, his face betraying inner feelings of unbridled anger. His plans for a dramatic unveiling of his prodigy and the launch of the new church had come to nothing. Questions crowded into his mind. *How was it that Joshua's*

171

grandparents had found a way in? Who was the crippled man that Joshua recognised and had healed? It wasn't meant to happen, the man had been standing too close to the fence, what a disaster, but there was nothing on the car radio. He'd expect the press to be buzzing with the story, there were people who had witnessed it, someone must have taken a photograph, yet the airwaves carried no mention of the miraculous events on Iona that morning. He could only surmise that his faithful monks had buried the story. An unbelieving newspaper editor had also put paid to any mention of it in the local press, something he may come to regret. Gabriel Jackson had to regroup and try again; too much had been invested for things to fail. Gradually, his rage calmed and rational thought took over. *Why did the MacKay's kneel with the healed man and the woman, did they know them or was it a spontaneous gesture?* Then it hit him, the crippled man was the one who had shot him in the leg, the one who had taken Joshua from him. Up till then he'd thought Iain Sherrie had perished in the bombing but now he was back on the scene, completely healed and no doubt already plotting with the MacKay's on ways of discovering Joshua's whereabouts. They may have to move again, go on the run and hide out somewhere else. The thought appalled him. Gabriel Jackson wasn't the sort of man who panicked but he would have to be proactive and tell Dougy and Sara what had happened, because Joshua certainly would.

Chapter 27

The story of Iain Sherrie's healing broke in the most unexpected way. Upon returning home he and Janet contacted Father Kilkenny, their local Catholic priest. An urgent appointment was made for them to be at the presbytery first thing in the morning. Janet had maintained her churchgoing but Iain had distanced himself from the faith, blaming the demands of his job but knowing that it was more than that. Once, he'd been a devout Christian but then began to question why there was so much suffering in the world, where was God in the earthquakes and the terrible plight of children in areas where starvation and extreme poverty snuffed out lives before they'd really begun. Why were despots like Mugabe allowed to get away with persecution and such awful cruelty? He hadn't been aware that Father Kilkenny had travelled to the hospital and prayed at his bedside. Horrified at the extent of Iain's injuries the priest had once given him the last rites. Later, he'd called at the house a number of times just to ensure that Janet was coping and to spend some time with Iain in general conversation, usually about football.

Father Kilkenny answered the door. He was a small slim man in his mid-fifties, always serious looking and the epitome of politeness. Facing him, in the half light of a drizzly Scottish morning, stood two figures, one with his coat collar turned up, the top part of his face in the shadow of a peaked cap. The other had no need to conceal her features and they were invited in. Iain kept his face hidden until the presbytery door had been closed behind them.

'Well my friends, what can I do for you?' asked Father Kilkenny in his engaging southern Irish accent.
Beneath the hall light Iain removed his cap and his overcoat.
'Holy Mother of God,' said the priest, crossing himself.
Father Kilkenny reached out to touch the flawless face. There were no bumps or lumps, no scars and no suture marks.
'Watch this father.'

Iain ran up and down the presbytery stairs, repeating the feat two steps at a time before throwing his arms around the astonished priest in a bear hug, laughing hysterically. Two hours later Father Kilkenny had the whole story and confronted with the evidence, he had no alternative but to believe every word. His problem now was what to do with the information. These were truly extraordinary revelations, that should they get out would create enormous anguish for the two people seated on his old leather couch. Not only would their lives change forever, their house constantly under siege, but Iona would be overwhelmed by people seeking out their own miracles. Yet here was an event that, unknown to Father Kilkenny, was not the first act of healing performed by this small boy. He avoided hasty conclusions about a 'second coming' but the bishop had to be told. Not to do so would put Father Kilkenny in an impossible position. Burying knowledge that would transform religious belief wasn't an option. Father Kilkenny asked for permission to disclose what had been said that morning. Reluctantly, Iain and Janet Sherrie agreed, providing no mention was made of Ally and Mary MacKay.

Were it with anyone other than a trusted and respected parish priest, the bishop would have dismissed the telephone conversation as the ravings of a crank, but he listened. When Father Kilkenny had finished, the bishop thanked him and gave instructions to keep Ally and Mary safely inside the presbytery for the time being and he would call back. The tea pot was refilled and they waited for the bishop to make his promised call, which came within the hour.

The impact of what the bishop said left no doubt in Father Kilkenny's mind that what Iain Sherrie had told him, and the evidence before his own eyes was that a great happening had occurred. It was as well that following his return home from hospital, Iain Sherrie had led the life of a recluse, refusing to be seen in public, even his closest neighbours had caught only glimpses of him behind net curtains. His healing had to be kept secret until such times as people much more senior to the bishop declared otherwise. In the short time between the bishop being informed and his return conversation with Father Kilkenny, the whole matter had been relayed on a secure line to the

Prime Minister, who was already in possession of a 'for your eyes only' dossier on Joshua. Gabriel Jackson had sent a constant stream of information to key people; it was part of the agreement he'd negotiated to secure funding for the new church, the twenty-four hour protective cordon and a helicopter whenever he needed one. Yet what had happened during the aborted dedication could not have been predicted, but it had to be dealt with. Under the circumstances it was as well that just a handful of people were there. Already his mind was working on how best he could use Iain Sherrie's healing to his own advantage. What he didn't know was that others would soon be making the decisions; his inability to carry through the dedication as originally planned was, to those at a higher level, a failure of trust. The call to a meeting came swiftly and for once Gabriel Jackson had to be subservient, he had to listen as those around him examined his failings in the most incisive way possible. He was left with little of his personal and spiritual dignity intact and a clear understanding that if he failed again, Joshua would be taken from him and he would be cast into the wilderness.

Upon his return, Rachel could only wonder at Gabriel Jackson's contriteness, but pity for this broken, shrunken man wasn't in her heart. His seniority at the high table had counted for nothing, to them he was a servant and that is how they'd treated him. He confided in Rachel whose initial thoughts were that he'd reaped what he'd sown. Gabriel Jackson had treated her unkindly and she felt a satisfaction that someone had given him a taste of what she had had to contend with. But this lasted only a short while and then her concern for Joshua took precedent. Gabriel Jackson's possible reaction to the thought of losing him horrified her. Whatever freedom the boy had may be lost, isolated forever from his family, force fed religious dogma like some battery chicken. Fear of the wilderness was enough to shape Gabriel Jackson's response to the threat of being sent there. It was the ultimate punishment for disobedience and failure. He'd been responsible for sending a few poor souls to the dark place himself and they'd never been seen again. In the privacy of her room Rachel dialled up a number from the contact list of her mobile phone.

Mary MacKay responded to the phone with an expectation that it was Janet Sherrie calling to give her an update. She settled back onto the couch, preparing for a long conversation.

'Hello Janet, how are things?'

'This is Rachel, you know, Sara and Dougy's friend.'

'Oh, sorry I was expecting someone else, what can I do for you,' replied Mary.

Rachel had no time for formalities.

'Please listen, what you saw at the new church will place Joshua in peril. Gabriel Jackson will imprison him; he will never see his parents or you again. You are his only hope.'

Mary sat bolt upright, she called to Ally who hurried from the kitchen. He was motioned to sit beside her and put his head to the phone.

'Go on,' said Mary.

Rachel spoke in low tones.

'I will meet you at a place not far from where your family is staying, it is imperative that you are there.'

'Quick, get a pen,' said Mary to Ally.

Mary scribbled down directions and a time.

'Can you repeat it,' she asked, but Rachel had rung off. Mary hoped she had recorded things accurately.

'We're going to need some help with this, it's a long way from here,' said Ally.

Mary nodded and made a call of her own.

Iain and Janet Sherrie said they would go but an explanation of how complex things had become meant that a meeting with Rachel could have consequences far beyond yet another rescue attempt. Iain Sherrie's healing had thrown open gates that had previously been firmly locked against outside interference. The new church on Iona was to be symbolic of a staged seismic shift in religious influence across the world with Joshua as a figure head, but now things had changed. This boy was truly remarkable, so remarkable that there was no other being on earth like him, his potential for change and revolution being so great that he must continue to be protected from harm. Joshua's actions at the new church had moved things forward to a point where members of the Bilderberg Group had convened an extraordinary meeting to discuss the situation. The rapidity of this illustrated the urgency and seriousness that disclosure of this boy's powers would have on the world's millions of believers. The effects would be mind-blowing.

The Bishop's Office left no room for any misunderstanding. The instructions given to Father Kilkenny were to ensure that Iain and Janet Sherrie stayed out of the public eye, their freedom curtailed until orders to the contrary were received. Never before had Father Kilkenny disobeyed his bishop, he was under no illusion that to do so would almost certainly put him on a collision course with his earthly boss. But he told himself that life would be boring without the occasional risk, anyway early retirement sounded quite attractive. He wished Iain and Janet Sherrie God speed and prayed for their safe return.

The sun was still to rise when they set off. It was good for Iain Sherrie to drive the Volvo again, so powerful and liberating. Several times Janet reminded him to watch his speed; they must not attract the attention of motorway police, computers being checked and identities revealed was something they could not afford to happen, their mission would be stopped in its tracks. The temperature outside the car registered minus 2 but the main roads had been well salted overnight. Once on the motorway the journey south was quick, by midday the Volvo had crossed into Robin Hood County. An hour, that's all they had to find the meeting place. On the map it was clearly marked as a large area of parkland off the A614.

'There it is,' said Janet, pointing to a road sign indicating a right into Clumber Park.

A stone archway leading down to a long avenue of trees marked out the entrance. Iain Sherrie drove onto the grass, it was where Rachel said she'd be, they were on time but she wasn't.

'We've come a bloody long way to be stood up,' remarked Ally.

Mary shook the thermos flask.

'It's as well I filled it up when we stopped,' she said.

Time passed. The comforting warmth of the tea helped to ease their disappointment of having made the journey for nothing.

'I need to pee,' said Ally, easing himself out of the car.

He stood in the shadow of the arch grunting in relief, when a small grey Datsun turned into the park entrance, moved to within a few feet of where Ally stood, and stopped. The driver got out and walked towards the Volvo. Behind her back she was carrying something in her right hand.

'Christ, it's a gun.'

Hot tea had steamed up the windows; she had the advantage of surprise, this was an ambush.

Ally zipped up and moved to where he could get a better view. He had no way of warning the others, yet he must do something, but what. Frost damaged stonework on the arch had crumbled, leaving a few pieces lying in the grass. Ally picked up the largest of these and hurled it. The stone struck the woman a glancing blow on her left arm. She cried out in pain, the gun fell from her grasp. Wrapping his arms around her in a bear hug, Ally held on with all his strength.

'Let me go you idiot, I'm Rachel.'

Instantly Iain Sherry was out of the car.

'OK Ally, let her go,' he said.

Ally relaxed his grip.

'Why the gun?' asked Iain Sherry.

'I had to be sure it was you, I can't take chances, now let go,' she said, pulling herself away.

Ally picked up the gun and handed it to Iain who removed the clip and put it in his pocket.

'OK, let's talk,' said Iain Sherrie.

'Not here, get back in your car and follow me,' replied Rachel.

It was all about trust, but there were four of them and only one of her so numerically the odds were stacked in their favour. Iain Sherrie kept a safe distance behind Rachel's car; she appeared to know where she was going. Within minutes she indicated for them to pull off the road onto a wide grassy verge that on one side edged up to woodland. On the opposite side was a cricket pitch overlooked by more trees and at the far end an old pavilion with a thatched roof, looking as if it belonged to a time when the sun shone all day and cricket was a game enjoyed by landed gentry. Rachel locked her car and stood as if waiting for the others to join her. Iain Sherrie lowered his window. He had her gun so felt no threat.

'What now?' he asked.

Rachel beckoned.

'Come with me, but hurry.'

She walked at a fast pace around the fenced off perimeter of the cricket pitch towards the old pavilion. Daylight, such as it was, had begun to give way to dusk and the temperature hovered just above freezing, it was going to be a cold night and they still had nowhere to stay. Iain Sherrie removed Rachel's gun from his pocket and replaced the clip; if this was a trap at least he could defend himself and the others, but the last thing he wanted was another fire-fight, he might not be so lucky next time. Rachel had already reached the pavilion. Its windows were boarded up against vandalism and the sturdy wooden door defied anyone to break in. Mary gripped Ally's arm and shuddered as she imagined rats nesting in the thatch, this place may be alright during the cricket season but now it gave off a sense of haunted isolation. Rachel waited for everyone to catch up then took a key from her coat pocket. She flicked a switch and a power saving bulb struggled into life. Its low intensity glow was enough for them to see dusty plastic chairs stacked against a wall in readiness for next season. They each took a chair and sat shivering in the cold dank interior of the pavilion, listening whilst Rachel talked. What she said took their minds off the discomfort of their surroundings; she spoke about Joshua and her fears for his safety. These fears were grounded in the unexpected healing of Iain Sherrie. The anger shown by Gabriel Jackson had plunged new depths; she feared that because of his miserable failure to launch the new church and the effect on him of his meeting with those in authority, he was no longer rational. His plans had been plunged into chaos. In Joshua he had a boy whose healing powers had been seen only once before in the history of humankind and Gabriel Jackson had recalled the cruelty and suffering that this event had provoked. The hunt for Joshua by those who sought to destroy him would intensify. Rachel presumed it was only a matter of time before the whole world knew of this remarkable boy and she had reached a crucial point in her relationship with Gabriel Jackson that saw her loyalty being jettisoned in favour of keeping Joshua alive. The purpose of her meeting with the four of them was to pass on the responsibility. She told them where Joshua was being held, it was only a short distance away and they must waste no time in deciding what to do. She had put her trust in them, particularly Ally and Mary because of their blood relationship to Joshua.

'Has anyone got a mobile phone,' she asked.
Iain Sherrie nodded and Rachel logged his number in her phone.

'Within the next two hours you will get a call from Dougy,' she said.
Then demanding the return of her firearm, she ushered them out of the pavilion, switched of the light, locked the door and hurried away. By the time they had reached their car she had gone, her tail lights receding into the distance.

'Let's get away from here and find somewhere to stay,' said Ally.
In the glow of the car's interior light he studied a road atlas.

'There's a town not too far away, we may be lucky to find a B&B there.'
They agreed to his suggestion and within a quarter of an hour were searching around New Ollerton for accommodation. A small pub on the outskirts of the town gave them what they wanted. The landlord was quite pleased to see them as business was slack; in fact they were the only ones in residence that night. Mary glanced at her wristwatch; over an hour had passed since they had left Clumber Park.

'Is your phone switched on Iain?' Her voice was edgy with anticipation.

'Aye, don't fret lass,' he said, checking the signal strength.

'I hope Rachel wasn't lying,' said Mary.
Ally squeezed his wife's hand.

'Why should she.'

They sat in the deserted bar, a girl brought two cafetieres of coffee and enquired if they would be eating. Ally nodded and asked for a bar meal menu, they'd order later. Hands wrapped around warm mugs of coffee provided a welcome diversion from the tension they each felt. Iain Sherrie placed his phone on the table, Mary stared at it. *Come on, ring, damn you.* Her son was only a phone call away and she was impatient.

The girl came back with a handful of bar menus; she placed them on the table and began chatting. *Please go away; for God's sake clear off.* The girl must have picked something up from Mary's body language and left. Iain Sherrie's phone rang.

'Hello.'

It was only one word but the tremor in his voice was evident. It betrayed the anxiety that he felt, not only for himself but for Ally and Mary also.

'It's Dougy, can I speak to my dad please.'

'Sure Dougy.' Iain passed the phone across the table.

'Dad, I understand from Rachel that you are close by, just where are you?'

Ally had no idea of their exact location, it was a pub in a town called New Ollerton and that was all he knew. Then he spotted the name of the pub, its address and phone number on one of the bar menus. He gave this information to Dougy who seemed pleased at how near they were.

'Listen Dad, this is really important. What happened to Iain Sherrie was a miracle, Sara and I are convinced that Gabriel Jackson was right all along but he is losing control. Alastair, or should I say Joshua, has a rare and precious gift. You should know that Iain wasn't the first to feel the benefit of this.'

Dougy told his father about the helicopter pilot, the bright orange light and the extraordinary calmness they had felt at the time. Ally recognised this as a feeling not dissimilar to the one that had enveloped them on Iona when Iain was healed.

'Dad, things are running out of control here, I think Rachel is on our side but security is very tight. She still has Jackson's trust but I don't know how long it will last.'

181

'It was Rachel who got us to come down here, she told us of her fears for Joshua but I'm at a loss as to what we can do to help,' said Ally.

Mary could no longer contain herself.

'Let me speak to him,' she said, reaching for the phone.

Ally was pleased to give way, he was floundering.

'Dougy, its mum, what do you want us to do?'

'Mum, good to hear you. You are only a couple of miles away so if Rachel can persuade Gabriel Jackson to let you in here perhaps together we can sort something out.'

'Right son, but Iain and his wife will have to be included, and by the way, there are other things you both need to know.'

'OK mum, I'll talk to Rachel and get back to you.'

Their meal was eaten in an atmosphere of excitement mixed with apprehension. Exhilaration at the possibility of seeing their grandchildren again filled Ally and Mary with great expectation, but it may come to nothing. Rachel was the key and Dougy had to convince her to work on Gabriel Jackson whose mind was so twisted that anything could happen.

Chapter 28

Jamie McArdle may be a junior member of staff at the Oban Advertiser but to have had his story buried under a heap of criticism from his boss had belittled him. He'd written a meticulous piece detailing what he'd seen and felt at the time; it was a piece that should be made public, yet without evidence it was just hearsay. He was aware of the newspaper maxim of never letting the truth get in the way of a good story but he didn't hold to that. He was young enough not yet to have been tainted with the same cynical view of life held by his boss. Jamie just wanted the truth of the matter to be out there with his name on the by line. The news editor's attitude gave him a determination to follow through with the story come what may. He had to identify the man who'd been healed but his enquiries came to nothing. He'd asked for information at the few places that took in paying guests on Iona and one hotelier certainly recalled a man resembling Iain Sherrie's description, but fictitious names and addresses in the guest book just confused things. Every lead led to the same dead end; it was as if the man had never existed, yet what had happened was real, very real. After a while Jamie McArdle began to doubt himself. Perhaps his boss had got it right, this was a hoax and the hoaxer had gone to ground. Others in the office had begun to make fun of Jamie; the jokes and snide comments became unbearable so he decided to turn his back on the Oban Advertiser and go freelance, that way he could probably make a living whilst at the same time following the story that was now in danger of becoming an obsession. The day after telling his boss what he could do with his job Jamie was in the Oban public library trawling through old news reports, looking for anything out of the ordinary that may give a clue to the identity of the man he sought. He read accounts of how the press had been kept at bay over a number of incidents in the area that had occurred during the past two years or so. He read stories about heroic police officers who had given their lives defending the public against terrorism. A Chief Constable had been highly vocal in his praise of these officers. He noted reports of things that to him seemed spurious; there was even an overzealous report about aliens from another universe landing in the Highlands. *Never let the truth get in the way of a good story!* In his mind these stories were connected in some way but it wasn't until he came across a piece on the inside pages of the Edinburgh Mail that he realised what the connection may be. A loosed tongued hospital porter had rung the paper saying that a badly injured man had been taken to the emergency room. He'd speculated that because an armed guard had been placed outside the room that the man was probably a dangerous prisoner from Edinburgh jail or some other person whose identity had to be kept secret. The paper had met with a firm 'no comment' from the hospital and although they tried to make something of it the piece was, by and large, without substance. The porter, who was not named, had said something about the man having his face covered with a mask of some sort but couldn't be specific, but it was enough to spark off the synapses in Jamie McArdle's brain. He juggled with a number of 'what ifs'. What if this man had been burned in an accident, what if he was a police officer involved in one of the incidents he'd read about, but they'd all been killed. He went back through the news reports, checking dates, one of which tied in with the hospital porter's story. The link was tenuous but it was all he had, what if this man was a police officer who had survived the killings. Jamie told himself that that idea was almost as preposterous as the alien story, why would anyone keep something like that secret? Next morning he drove across to Edinburgh. His inclination was to look up the journalist who had interviewed the talkative hospital porter, there may be something hidden away in a notebook that at the time was judged insignificant but now could be highly relevant. *'You never know'*, he thought.

The Edinburgh Mail offices were easy enough to find but parking, as always in the Scottish capital, was a nightmare. Driving round he eventually found a spot in a side street a brisk fifteen minute walk from where he wanted to be. From behind a reception desk a youngish woman dressed in jeans and a T shirt peered at him over a cheap pair of spectacles. Jamie explained why he was there.

'Take a seat, someone from the newsroom will be down in a minute.' She dialed up an extension.

Jamie sank into a leather settee that had seen better days. The reception area was in serious need of redecoration. *They're not doing too well.* It was more than a minute before the eponymous 'someone' joined him. In fact it was more like twenty minutes. A strong handshake had Jamie wincing in pain.

'Sorry to keep you waiting, you know how it is, what can I do to help you?' said a bearded, stocky man from the newsroom. He seemed friendly enough.

'Can we go somewhere a bit more private.' asked Jamie.

The newsman nodded and led the way to a small office at the rear of the building. Jamie had never seen an office quite like this one. On a continuum of tidiness to total chaos, this office was well over towards the latter. Any work space that had once existed was buried beneath piles of paper, a dated PC threatened to fall from its precarious perch on the edge of his desk and a collection of dirty coffee cups resided on top of a filing cabinet that was stuffed to a point where the drawers wouldn't shut. Jamie McArdle's interest was briefly taken with Humbert Wolfe's epigram that hung from the wall immediately behind Frank Macleod's desk.

You cannot hope to bribe or twist
Thank God! the British journalist
But when you see what the man will do
Unbribed, there's no occasion to.

Apart from an office chair the only other place to sit was on a low dusty windowsill. Jamie opted to stand. A copy of the article that had led him here was shown to the newsman.

'I'd like to talk to the person who wrote this.'

'Well young man you're talking to him, the name on the article is mine, Frank Macleod, so why the secrecy?'

'The man in your article, the one with the injuries, it's important I establish who he is,' said Jamie.

Frank Macleod may be untidy but he could smell a good story a mile away.

'Why,' he asked.

Jamie edged his bets; if he told this man everything he would probably lose the story.

'It's just something I'm following up,' said Jamie, trying to stay non-committal.

'Look son, I wasn't born yesterday, you didn't come across here for nothing, now stop wasting my time and tell me.'

Jamie propped himself on the windowsill and told Frank Macleod what he'd witnessed on Iona, how no one had believed him and how he'd been ridiculed by others in the office. When he'd finished, Jamie expected a similar response from the older man but what he got surprised him.

'Let's have another look at what that porter said, it's a while back but as you can see I throw nothing away, now what was the date,' he said.

In complete amazement Jamie watched as Frank Macleod went to the bottom drawer of the filing cabinet and retrieved a dog eared notebook. He didn't have to search for it; knowing exactly where it was.

'Don't look so surprised, it might look like a tip but everything in here is in date order, including all of this,' he said, pointing to the mountains of paper.

Flicking through the notebook he found what he was looking for.

'Here it is, now let's see what he said.'

Frank Macleod hummed tunelessly as he read through his notes then looked up.

'Well, there's nothing here that throws any light on who this man was but I'm intrigued, so how do you feel if we pair up and do some digging, two heads are better than one you know.'

Jamie nodded, the older man probably had contacts that could prove useful but he would have to be watched, this was his story and he wasn't about to give it away. Pulling on a long black coat that wouldn't have looked out of place on an undertaker, Frank Macleod headed towards the office door.

'Come on laddie, no time like the present, let's get cracking.'

'Where are we going?'

'The Infirmary, I bet somebody up there could use a few extra quid.'

Paying for information was not Jamie's way of doing things but this was the big city and his story had massive potential. Frank Macleod was a seasoned journalist and his reporter's instinct was in overdrive, he was determined not to let this one get away, even if it meant ditching Jamie McArdle along the way.

Chapter 29

How Rachel did it was a mystery, but she persuaded Gabriel Jackson to let Ally, Mary, Iain and Janet come through the security cordon into the grounds of the ruined abbey, but no further. The concession did not extend to the abbey itself and seeing Joshua was not part of the agreement, but for this difficult, strong minded man to give way so easily carried a message. Could it be that because he was prepared to communicate outside the tightly controlled environment that was built around himself and Joshua, he was admitting to being vulnerable? Iain Sherrie had been dramatically healed in the sight of a number of people and the possibility of this remarkable act remaining a secret was not something he could take for granted. He relied on the monks to concoct a convincing, believable account of what had happened that may satisfy local curiosity, but what of the few others who were there. He'd expected that he and Joshua would fly into a rapturous reception, adoring crowds would lay metaphorical palms at Joshua's feet, but it wasn't to be. Now he found himself isolated and in danger of losing control over the boy. His initial reaction towards Rachel when she told him of her meeting with Ally and the others was one of betrayal and disappointment. He railed at her, accusing her of going behind his back. He abhorred her deception yet even this dark, brooding man could see the sense in what she had done. The bottom line was to keep Joshua out of the clutches of those who would harm or exploit him. Having the boy's entire natural family on the premises presented Gabriel Jackson with several possible roads to go down, yet in his state of mind he was capable of taking the wrong one. Rachel had his ear and put an option to him that she thought would work in Joshua's favour.

'Let these people in, they have seen Joshua's powers and will work with us. Iain Sherrie is already a devotee; Joshua absorbed his pain, in time others will follow.'

At first, Gabriel Jackson rejected her idea, his anger again boiling to the surface. *Hadn't God given him alone the responsibility of*

188

preparing the boy for his ministry in the world? He had to see this through; the consequences of failure had been spelt out to him. Allowing others into this secret garden of sacred knowledge was unthinkable.

Rachel persisted in her argument.

'Joshua cannot go out into the world knowing little or nothing about what to expect. These people will show him the ways of the world, he can leave here under their protection for periods of time. Believe me when I say that Iain Sherrie will guard him with his life, I know he can be trusted.'

'I am being manipulated by this woman; she wants Joshua to herself and will stop at nothing to get him.'

Rachel interrupted his silent paranoia.

'Perhaps you need time to think about it.'

Gabriel Jackson walked away. He went to his private quarters and prayed for a very long time. The coldness and desperation of loneliness was all about him; he asked God what he should do. Gabriel Jackson had lost his way and he was staring into the vast emptiness of despair, only God could help him now. His prayers had become more urgent, more pleading, *'Help me God, please help me now.'* Then with hardly a sound, Joshua appeared at his side. Gabriel Jackson's haunted face turned towards the boy. He felt a deep sense of relief, for without saying a word Joshua had brought the answer to his prayers. Clarity of thought swept away the confusion and despair. Jackson knew what he had to do. He would let Joshua go.

Rising from his knees, he took Joshua by the hand. Together they left the inner sanctum and moved outside to where Rachel was waiting. During the entirety of Gabriel Jackson's prayers she had not moved from the spot where he'd left her. He spoke in a calm, soft voice.

'God has decreed. Take Joshua to his parents and his brother. There you will make preparations for them to leave. Once you have completed this task you must bring his parents to me.'

Rachel sighed with relief. Her actions had been vindicated, perhaps God had spoken to her also, but she hadn't known it, well not until now. She took Joshua to his parents and told them of Gabriel Jackson's decision. They were overjoyed but Dougy still mistrusted the man who had kept them there all that time. He was also deeply concerned about the teaching that Joshua had been subjected to. It wasn't normal for a boy of his age to be force fed like a battery chicken, but then he wasn't a normal boy, his gifts were not of this world. *'One step at a time,'* he thought. Rachel dialled up Iain Sherrie's number and whilst waiting for it to connect she told Dougy that Gabriel Jackson wanted to see them before they left - *'a fond farewell perhaps.'*

'Hello, Iain Sherrie here.'

'It's Rachel, they're coming out, wait exactly where you are and I will join you in a little while.'

Sara packed only the essentials - clothes and favourite toys. Anything else would be replaced once they had reached Scotland, for that is where they'd be going. In the euphoria of leaving, neither Dougy nor Sara had given any thought to how they would be transported away. Surely not by helicopter, that would be far too much to expect. The answer came when they met with Gabriel Jackson. He was precise and directive.

'Joshua will travel with Rachel. Upon arrival, or soon after she will make contact with Brother Anthony at the new church on Iona, he will be expecting her. Together they will pray for guidance and then she will return to you. Rachel will be Joshua's spiritual guide and remain in charge of his safety until you arrive at your destination then the responsibility to keep him safe will pass to you, but remember, his ultimate destiny is out of human hands. He was sent to us with a life's work that must be fulfilled. The Lord is placing His trust in us; do not be seduced by others who will try to take him from you. Now go.'

Listening to these words Dougy surprised himself as he felt a sense of compassion towards Gabriel Jackson.

'What will happen to you when we've gone?'

Gabriel Jackson allowed himself a brief smile.

'That too, is out of my hands, but today may not be the last you will see or hear of me.'

190

The reunion was emotional but brief. Rachel became insistent; they must not linger. Her car was small and the journey was long. Gabriel Jackson had decreed that Joshua must travel with Rachel, so Sara and Farai would travel with Rachel also. Personal belongings were hastily transferred to the Volvo's spacious boot and they set off, heading north. It was only when Joshua asked a question that Sara realised that in the rush to leave she had completely forgotten to explain things to her son.

'Where are we going mummy?'

'To granddad and grandma's house, you know, in Scotland.'

'Why?'

Sara couldn't lie, anyway Joshua would know immediately if she did.

'We are going to stay with them. You remember, we stayed there once before, your daddy built us a cottage.'

'Yes, I remember?'

Sara waited for more questions but they didn't come. Joshua had fallen silent; her answers seemed to have satisfied his curiosity, for the time being at least. It was an hour into the journey when Joshua asked another question, he blurted it out.

'Will Gabriel be there? I hope he is I really like him.'

Sara was caught off guard; she had to think before answering.

'No, I'm afraid he won't but Rachel will be and you like her don't you.'

'Yes, I like Rachel but she's not the same as Gabriel, he teaches me things.'

'Yes I know but Gabriel has said goodbye and now we will have to look for another teacher won't we Rachel.'

Rachel didn't appreciate having the buck passed to her. She glanced through the rearview mirror at Joshua's eager face and smiled but did not respond. Gabriel Jackson had instructed her to talk with Brother Anthony who by now would have been briefed. The onus placed on Rachel to be Joshua's spiritual guide was enormous; she had to ensure that what Gabriel Jackson had started was taken to its conclusion. Brother Anthony had to play a part but his role was not clear, Rachel was unsure about his background or authority to teach Joshua who had clearly formed a strong bond with Gabriel Jackson. It was a deeply rooted relationship that had released the boy's healing potential into reality. Healing the two men was an instinctive act of love that Gabriel Jackson would rather have kept hidden until Joshua was older, but it was in him to reach out, even at his young age. As she drove northwards, Rachel pondered what Gabriel Jackson had done; he'd passed the load from his own tired shoulders onto those of others. He'd off loaded the responsibility of guarding Joshua from danger onto Dougy whose strong mind could easily throw him into conflict with Rachel, but she hoped this would not happen. Joshua's spiritual development had to be maintained and she was the only one of the group surrounding him who could do this.

The Volvo's near side indicators blinked and Iain Sherrie moved onto the slip road leading to a service area. Rachel checked her mirrors and followed, the road behind was empty of traffic, she had to stay close and parked up in the bay behind Iain Sherrie, almost touching the Volvo's rear fender. Sensibly, Iain Sherrie had parked as close to the main entrance as possible, but in a few minutes they would be out in the open for the first time since leaving the ruined abbey. Rachel felt the coat pocket within which her hand gun nestled. It was an act of reassurance; she readied herself to deal with any threat to Joshua, and then left the car. Sara waited for the others to reach them before releasing Joshua from his seat restraint. Dougy lifted him from the car and handed him to Ally which didn't suit Joshua who wriggled violently, trying to free himself from his grandfather's protective hold.

'Put me down, I don't want to be carried.'
Ally was taken by surprise; his grandson's voice carried the authority of someone much older. He felt a compulsion to do as the boy demanded and lowered him to the ground.

'Don't worry granddad, I won't run away,'
Ally could only stand in wonderment at how the boy had controlled him and the maturity in his response. For a few seconds he felt that he had no alternative but to bend to Joshua's will, there was no threat, just a demonstration of the power that comes from being completely in control of a situation. Rachel watched and realised the extent to which

Gabriel Jackson had influenced Joshua's behaviour. In that moment it became clear that his schooling must continue from a spiritual direction, it had to build on the foundations already in place. Any attempt to integrate him into a normal school, no matter how good, would result in debilitating frustration for Joshua and his teachers. *'I just hope Brother Anthony is up to it,'*

Rachel ensured that both cars were locked and alarmed but decided to stay on watch. She would stretch her legs when the others returned. There was a certain satisfaction as she watched the family, again reunited, walk the short distance towards the services; they looked like an average group of people taking a comfort break, but there was a difference. Rachel had insisted that Joshua remain in the centre, shielded from potential harm and that Farai was carried. They were told to walk at a pace that did not vary and once inside to find a table within easy access of a fire escape. Under no circumstances was Joshua to be left unguarded, not even for an instant. Once inside, Iain Sherrie surveyed the faces of those sat in the café area. He did this with the practiced ease that came from having been one of Scotland's top detectives. Now he was protecting a boy who had healed him from horrific injuries, Iain Sherrie owed him a debt he could never repay, except maybe with his life.

Most of the faces belonged to road users who were taking time to relax, preparing themselves for the next stage of their journey. Others belonged to staff members clearing crockery and wiping down tables. The light buzz of conversation gave added normality to the place, nothing appeared out of the ordinary and Iain Sherrie began to relax. They shared a light meal and returned to where Rachel had been left on guard. The cars were still locked; everything seemed secure, but Rachel wasn't there.

'Back inside, quickly,' barked Iain Sherrie.

The response was immediate, the automatic doors of the service area swung open as the group sought cover. They found a sheltered corner deep inside the complex and surrounded Joshua, protecting him from whatever had lured Rachel from her post. Sara held Farai close to her breast, shivering with fear. Already they had begun to attract curious

193

glances, people around them were getting edgy, *what was going on?* Dougy forced a smile, trying to send a message that there was nothing to get alarmed about. Minutes passed and Iain Sherrie decided to make a move.

'We have to find her, it may be nothing, she could be OK. I'll go to the door and look.'

Dougy's strained smile hadn't worked on some onlookers. In fear they watched the glass panelled doors swing open. Iain Sherrie moved to a position where he could see their cars. At first there was no sign of Rachel, he moved closer and then turned abruptly. He was being hailed from a wooded picnic area adjacent to the edge of the car park where, during warmer weather, people would be sat around, watching children playing on the grassy bank. Today it was deserted except for Rachel who had taken up a vantage point behind a clump of bushes. She revealed herself and made her way across to where Iain Sherrie stood. He was furious.

'What the hell are you playing at, you're supposed to be watching the cars not playing hide and seek'.

'That's what I was doing, watching the cars, remaining hidden to give myself an edge should we be attacked'.

Iain Sherrie could see some logic in this but his anger at her actions remained evident. It was clear that Rachel's priority was to ensure that Joshua remained unharmed and scaring the rest of them witless did not appear to worry her.

'Well, you wait here, I'll fetch the others then you can go inside and freshen up,' said Iain Sherrie who glowered at her as if to reinforce his annoyance. Although chastened, Rachel kept her feelings hidden. Gabriel Jackson had put her in charge until Joshua reached the relative safety of his grandparents' farmhouse, and that is how it would stay.

Chapter 30

Frank Macleod had plenty of experience when dragging information from tight-lipped people especially those who didn't want to get involved with stories that might implicate them. He'd also met plenty of others who took great delight in seeing their names in the paper. Secretly he despised those who would exaggerate in the most outlandish way to achieve this spurious objective, but it didn't stop him exploiting them. Hospital staff usually fell into the 'no comment' category. There was just one rule to observe when approached by the press, say nothing and refer them to senior management. Unless a formal press statement had been agreed then there was little chance of getting anything.

He rarely took no for an answer, Frank Macleod could read people like a book, if there's a chink in the armour of confidentiality he will find it. Charm, relentless probing, hinting at extra cash in the pocket for just a few minutes chat, even barefaced lies, was Frank Macleod's Modus Operandi. Workers at the bottom of the pecking order aren't paid much, they often have problems with management, and they see a lot, so a couple of extra twenty pound notes might just loosen the occasional tongue, if only to get back at the boss. It had worked once so it stood a good chance of working again.

A feeling of unease hit Jamie McArdle as he walked through the Infirmary's impressive main entrance. Robust investigative journalism was one thing, bribery was definitely another. He reflected on the framed piece of homespun philosophy hanging from the wall in Frank Macleod's dingy office. Clearly, this particular reporter could not be bribed but had no conscience about the reverse being true. He'd already formed a plan of action.

'The first thing is to find that porter.'

'How do you propose to do that?' said Jamie McArdle.

The older man tapped a forefinger against his nose.

'Just watch.'

Frank Macleod walked to the reception point and joined a small number of people waiting to be attended to. He displayed no impatience or irritability at being kept waiting; this was a professional at work. Finally, it was his turn.

'Yes sir, can I help you.'

Frank Macleod glance at the name badge pinned to the receptionist's smart uniform jacket. He'd learned the value of addressing a person by their name in the politest way possible, none of this first name bonhomie for him.

'Thank you Mrs Johnson, there is something you can do for me. I'm out of work and wondered if there were any porters' jobs going.'

Jamie McArdle raised an eyebrow; he was already in deeper than he wanted to be.

'You will need to speak to one of our Human Resources people; can I make an appointment for you?'

'Yes, OK. While you do that could I have a chat with one of your porters to get some idea what the job's about?'

Frank Macleod winked knowingly at the receptionist who fell for his charm. She directed him to the dining room.

'One or two of them will be having their tea break about now; you should find at least one who'll tell you how hard they work.' Her voice betrayed a certain irony.

Using a fictitious name that Frank Macleod had given to the receptionist she made an appointment with Human Resources, and then wished him well. The dining room was easy to find and he soon spotted a couple of porters on their break.

'I'll go over and talk to them, you bring the tea laddie. I'll tell them you're my son,' he said to Jamie McArdle who by now had resigned himself to Frank Macleod's deception. He'd let him do all the talking and just look on, acting ignorant.

Jamie McArdle stirred his tea and listened as his colleague convinced the two men with him that he wanted to be a porter, and true to what the receptionist had said, one of them couldn't stop talking. It transpired that he was a union steward who was always in conflict with management. He was gullible and believed everything that Frank Macleod told him. Jamie McArdle was sent to replenish the teas and by the time he'd returned Frank Macleod had all the information he wanted. The union steward had said that if he came to work here as a porter it was in his best interests to join the union. When pressed what could happen if he didn't, the union man told him the story of a porter who just over a year ago had been sacked for talking to the papers about a patient, he'd bragged openly about the money he'd been paid for the story. He was in full flow and dropping out the man's name he went on to stress that because the porter wasn't in the union he became easy meat for management. Now, without suitable references he was unemployable and living in a Salvation Army hostel for homeless men somewhere in the city. This story had become one of the union man's best recruiting pitches and using well-rehearsed body language, Frank Macleod let him see that he was impressed. A quick handshake saw them part company.

'C'mon young Jamie, I think I know where to find this man. It's my bet he could use a helping hand.'

Within minutes they were hurrying along the Old Dalkeith Road. It began to rain. Several black taxis sped by, the drivers blissfully ignoring Frank Macleod's outstretched arm.

'Ignorant sods,' he muttered, turning up his coat collar.

Then one stopped.

'It's about bloody time.'

He opened the rear door and roughly manhandled Jamie McArdle into the passenger compartment before getting in himself. Slamming the door shut he leaned over towards the glass partition and gave the driver precise instructions, promising a healthy tip for a fast trip. The cabbie didn't need any further encouragement; he executed a 'U' turn and accelerated, throwing his passengers back into their seats.

'Where are we going?' asked Jamie McArdle, struggling with his seat belt.

'The Salvation Army hostel for homeless men; it's a place I know well.'

The tone of voice with which Frank Macleod answered the question hinted at respect for the place they were visiting.

He continued.

'A close friend once fell on hard times, his business failed and bankruptcy ruined him. The people at the hostel picked up the pieces and he's now back on track. I ran a story about him – it got a good response.'

'We'll have to tread carefully then, we can't afford to upset anyone,' remarked Jamie McArdle.

The swiftest cab journey Jamie McArdle could ever remember came to an end. As promised, the cabbie pocketed an extra ten pounds and sped away, leaving his passengers standing in the rain at the hostel door. A portly man who Jamie McArdle took to be in his early 50's came out to greet them.

'Hello I'm John Wallace, the duty manager, don't stand there getting soaked, come in.'

Any negative images held by Jamie McArdle were immediately dispelled. The hostel was clean and well lit. A strong feeling of acceptance seemed to permeate the place. The manager recognised Frank Macleod whose article had brought in substantial donations from the paper's readership.

'Well Mr Macleod it's good to see you again, what can we do for you this time.'

He explained about the hospital porter.

'I understand this poor fellow may be staying here now.'

The manager refused to confirm whether this was the case, confidentiality was the bedrock of his relationship with anyone who sought refuge there.

Frank Macleod had to come clean; there was no use in being cagey, that would get him nowhere.

'This man may have information about a story my young friend wants to follow up, Jamie laddie you tell him, he can be trusted.'

Jamie McArdle's face betrayed a reluctance to say a word; had he made a mistake taking Frank Macleod into his confidence? He was beginning to wish he'd followed up the story on his own. It may have taken longer but at least it would be exclusively his. *But it was too late for that now.* So in a low deliberate voice the story was retold. John Wallace listened, nodding every so often as the tale unfolded, all the time his attitude hardening.

'So you hope that by questioning a traumatized, homeless fellow you can find the missing bits that will lead you to the man who was healed by the boy.'

'Aye, that's about it, can you help us?' asked Frank Macleod.

'No chance. Now bugger off the pair of you.'

He was no longer the affable friendly man who had met them at the door. John Wallace's duty of care to the driftwood of society that regularly came across his doorstep was deeply rooted. He was angry, very angry. Nothing would persuade him to risk a reputation of trust that had grown over many years, not even the fifty pounds that Frank Macleod waved at him. John Wallace pushed the money away, threatening to call the police. His anger wasn't lost on a large, bearded man sat watching television.

'Having trouble boss?'

'Nay Jackie these gentlemen are just leaving.'

'Well that's OK then, shall I see them out?'

The man rose to his feet. Frank Macleod didn't give the duty manager time to answer. Jackie had fists the size of hams; he was obviously spoiling for a fight.

'That won't be necessary, c'mon Jamie we're not wanted, even when we've got money to give away.'

The deviousness in Frank Macleod's nature was implicit; money is a commodity that homeless men have little of. The hook was baited and all he had to do was wait to land his catch, which didn't take long. Outside the rain had stopped and Frank Macleod took his younger companion by the arm.

'C'mon, let's walk a couple of hundred yards up the road, out of sight of the hostel and then we'll wait.'

'What for, you blew it back there, I wish to God I'd never let you in on it.'

'Oh ye of little faith just watch and learn.'

'I don't think I've much to learn from you.'

Jamie McArdle's caustic response made no impression; the man had a skin like a rhinoceros. He tried again.

'What the hell are we waiting for?'

'Not what, who, and here he comes.'

The big fisted man from the hostel approached them, this time there was no menace in him.

'I heard you've money to give away,' he said.

'I'm paying for information,' replied Frank Macleod, once again baiting the hook.

'What sort of information?'

'Do you know a man living at the hostel who used to be a porter at the Infirmary?'

'Maybe I do and maybe I don't, what's it worth?'

'Twenty quid if you can arrange for me to meet up with him.'

'Aye, I know him but it'll cost you more than a lousy twenty quid. If John finds out he'll kick my arse out of it.'

'OK, forty quid.'

'Fifty.'

Frank Macleod spit on his hand and held it out. The big fisted man shook and the deal was sealed.

Chapter 31

Ally wasn't one for being away from home for long. Hours before, as they'd crossed into Scotland he'd felt the pull of his own bed with its feather pillows and firm mattress. This was home; it was where he felt in control, after all, as head of the family, his was the responsibility for providing a place where his grandsons would be safe. But deep in his heart he knew that another attempt on Joshua's life was possible, his enemies always seemed to find him, there was no secure hiding place from the terror that had invaded their lives, *they would just have to live with it.* Once over the border Iain Sherrie took the lead. He and Rachel had agreed to approach the farmhouse under the cover of darkness, without lights.

They stopped several hundred yards short of the house; Iain Sherrie waited for instructions. *She was still in charge.* Rachel was taking no chances, she sat staring through the windshield, watching and waiting. The house may be deserted but she had to be sure, very sure that instant death wasn't waiting behind the net curtains. Switching off the interior light she left her car, *no chances, take no chances,* and then, moving to the Volvo, Rachel motioning for Iain Sherrie to wind down his window. The electric motor whirred, he looked up.

'I'll check out the house, you watch Joshua,' she whispered.

'Dougy can watch Joshua; I'm coming with you.'

Rachel seemed relieved at this offer. A fit, alert Iain Sherrie was the sort of man she'd want at her side in a crisis but they'd only one gun between them.

'Ally, give him the door keys. Dougy, you sit in my car, if things go wrong get out of here. Never mind the others, just save Joshua.'

The Volvo's interior light dimmed and Iain Sherrie joined Rachel. She pulled the pistol from her pocket. Although the early darkness was enough to hide them, a faint outline of the farmhouse was still visible. Rachel took the lead.

'OK, in we go, stay close behind me.'

Crouching low they approached the house. *'Damn this gravel,' thought Rachel.* Dropping below the level of a window she raised her head to look inside, her senses on full alert. She saw nothing but darkness; she felt nothing except her own steady, controlled heartbeat, she heard nothing except Iain Sherrie's breathing. Her instincts said the house was empty. She unlocked the front door, without a sound it swung open. Ally was always one for keeping the hinges well oiled, squeaky doors were his pet hate. Rachel crouched in the darkness and waited. Then reaching up she found a light switch. *This is it.* A sixty watt bulb cast its light around the hall way, nothing had been disturbed, the place was as Ally and Mary had left it. Together they checked out the house, switching on lights as they went. Rachel's instincts seemed to have served her well, the place was empty, this part of her agreement with Gabriel Jackson had been fulfilled and she could hand over Joshua to the safe keeping of his parents with the confidence that he was in safe hands. If she had a sense of self-satisfaction it was to be short lived, Iain Sherrie made sure of that.

'The barn, we haven't checked the bloody barn.'

They ran from the house but it was too late. The house lights picked out three heavily armed men in full combat gear. Instinct kicked in, Rachel raised her pistol. She'd die right there defending Joshua. Gun fire would alert Dougy, he'd make his escape.

'Wait Rachel, we mean you no harm.'

The gunman's voice was calm. Rachel lowered her weapon, who were these people?

'I am Brother Anthony and these are members of my order. Father Gabriel instructed me to be here when you arrived. He is concerned about Joshua. Let us go into the house.'

'I might have known, he doesn't trust me, despite everything he said, he still doesn't trust me.'

'Joshua is fine, he is with his parents. I'm supposed to meet with you on Iona so why all this?' said Rachel, pointing at the armed men.

'Just precautionary, nothing has changed; you are to come with me as we have to make plans for Joshua's continuing education.'

Brother Anthony turned his attention to Iain Sherrie.

'We know that you have confided in your priest and that details of your healing have reached the highest level of the Catholic Church and the Government. Your actions were unfortunate. Father Kilkenny, in allowing you to accompany Joshua's grandparents, has already been removed from his parish. A new priest will be in place within days. You and your wife are to go to him and do exactly as he says.'

'And what will that be?' responded Iain Sherrie.

Brother Anthony's thin smile contained no humour.

'I would advise against any disobedience.'

Iain Sherry had faced down threats and intimidation before but this was one of those times when opposition would be futile. Already he was a disciple; they were all on the same side. His response was one of penitence, with bowed head he confirmed acceptance of his position,

'I will do as you say, Joshua must be protected.'

'Go now and bring the others here. Before departing we must confirm our devotion to Joshua.'

Iain Sherrie obeyed without question.

Entering the farmhouse Joshua and his mother led the way. Dougy, carrying his youngest son followed and behind him the others. Once inside, Brother Anthony closed the door. Standing before Joshua he fell to his knees. The other monks did likewise. Then, as if it was the most natural thing in the world, all others in the room knelt before the boy. Brother Anthony, in a beautifully modulated voice, sang his devotions using words that had no basis in any earthly language. Joshua had heard this song many times as Gabriel Jackson had sung it each morning before lessons. The words held meaning and it pleased him to hear them again. As if administering a blessing he placed his right hand on Brother Anthony's head. He then moved among the others doing the same to each of them. It was a moment of serenity that can only come from the presence of someone with the power to invoke deep emotions. In turn they rose to their feet, Joshua took his mother's hand and Brother Anthony motioned to his two companions. He was firm in his direction.

'Come brothers, it's time for us to leave. Rachel, please join us tomorrow at the new church,' and then they were gone.
Eager to get life back to normal, Mary hurried to the kitchen and set about making a meal. Filling the house with appetizing smells would normalise things, apart from which, sitting around their kitchen table sharing supper with family and friends was the ideal way of consolidating new beginnings.

Defrosted homemade vegetable soup reheated and served with chunks of stale bread was all she had. No one complained, they were just thankful to be back together again. When supper was finished Sara bathed her sons and put them to bed. It had been a long tiring day and before the bedtime story was even half read they had fallen asleep. However, the luxury of an early night was not for the others, there was much to talk about and Rachel would be the prime mover in plotting the next phase of their lives together. Iain and Janet Sherrie felt a strong attachment to the MacKays and despite the uncertainties and possible dangers, vowed to share whatever lay ahead. There were no blood ties but the powerful bond of a collective love for Joshua drew them together, through his actions he had opened their minds to the enormous capacity for good that had been invested in him by a higher power. It was the realisation of this investment that had been passed to Rachel who led the conversation. She reinforced that Gabriel Jackson had fallen away, completely spent but the journey towards Joshua's spiritual fulfilment must go on. His gift of love, still in its infancy must be fed and nurtured for without it evil men will continue to trample over people too powerless to resist. Through the sheer power of love a message would go out to others that a galvanizing force more powerful and more effective than any number of bombs and bullets was alive in the world. It was what she said next that left little doubt as to Joshua's true purpose on Earth.

'The seeds of this force were sown more than 2000 years ago and the time is approaching for us to reap the harvest. We have felt

Joshua's power, it is hypnotic and persuasive. We will know when the time is upon us so stay close and be ready.'

There was nothing more left to say so Iain and Janet Sherrie made the short drive home and Ally MacKay opened a bottle of his best Scotch whisky.

Chapter 32

There was much speculation within the small parish as to why Father Kilkenny had left so abruptly. Despite attempts by local conspiracy theorists, no one came up with a plausible reason except that this decent, honest and respected priest had been retired by the bishop. Three days later his replacement was in post, there had been no interregnum, Father Seamus Moloney was parachuted in without consultation or an interview. No one in the parish had any idea about his background, he'd simply arrived. The first and only appointment in his diary was a meeting with Iain and Janet Sherrie scheduled for the following morning at 10 am sharp. Father Moloney's phone call to arrange the meeting was not so much an invitation but an order. So not wishing to get off on the wrong foot with the new priest they dutifully attended as required. Any expectation of a warm priestly welcome was quickly shattered when Father Moloney answered the door. He was a much taller, younger and fitter looking man than Father Kilkenny. The brusqueness of his manner suggested someone who did not subscribe to 'touchy feely' theology, rudeness lurked just below the surface. In his former life ex detective superintendent Iain Sherrie could have dealt with this man, but not now. Recent experiences had softened him, he was vulnerable and it showed. Standing back from the doorway, Father Moloney gestured for them to enter.

'Come in, you must stay, we've a lot to talk about.'

Negotiating an obstacle course of unopened packing cases they followed the father into what was now his study. Iain Sherrie looked around.

'Father Kilkenny must have left in a hurry; his belongings are still here.'

'Please sit.'

They sank into the same well-worn leather couch that once belonged to the previous incumbent. Father Moloney remained standing, looming over them. Running a finger around the inside of his broad, pristine dog collar he began speaking; curt, to the point.

'Father Kilkenny disobeyed his bishop, I will not. You both have knowledge known only to a few others. Father Kilkenny was wrong in allowing you to leave the parish, never mind permitting you to accompany others on their travels. However, Gabriel Jackson was ordered to limit the damage and that is why he passed responsibility for Joshua's wellbeing to Rachel and from her to his parents and grandparents. They fully understand why Joshua has to be guarded. You too must recognise the dire consequences of Joshua's location being leaked, even by accident.'

Iain Sherry nodded; there was no one apart from a retired helicopter pilot who could have better reasons for keeping Joshua safe, and he'd been unconscious throughout his ordeal. The priest continued.

'Those in authority are not pleased with what has happened, your healing was witnessed by others including a local reporter, but as yet nothing has come out. We know that he tried to write a story but failed to convince his editor of its truth. This reporter has left his employment so he may or may not be trying to find another outlet for his story, only time will tell, but we believe he will attempt to track you down.'

'I've plenty of experience in dealing with the press so there are no worries there,' replied Iain Sherrie.

'That's as may be but Gabriel Jackson's aborted launching of the new church taught us lessons that must be heeded. If you are approached by this man or any other reporter say nothing, come straight here, I will deal with it.'

'Suits me, is that all, can we go?'

'No, there is still much more for us to talk about.'

'That means he'll do the talking and we'll do the listening,' mused Iain Sherrie.

The priest leaned back and positioned his hands as if in prayer. He remained silent for a few moments, collecting his thoughts. Then, what he said confirmed Iain Sherrie's suspicions. It became clear that Father Moloney was no ordinary priest; he spoke of the coming together of global temporal and spiritual power sources in the fight against all things that threatened the Christian way of life. At the heart of this conflict lay the massively influential Bilderberg Group with its membership spanning elected governments from all countries where the Christian faith was predominant or under attack. This group means business and when the news of Joshua's birth and the circumstances under which it occurred became known, the symbolism was too much to ignore. Pledging unlimited resources, the group became involved.

'We believe that somehow, heaven and earth became connected, a conduit you might say, and Gabriel Jackson and Rachel came to us from on high. It is now our understanding that Gabriel Jackson has returned to his origins. We will regain the high ground but it will be at a cost. Brother Anthony and Rachel will continue with Joshua's preparation,' said Father Moloney.

The priest paused, waiting for a response, but none came. He carried on.

'It is remarkable how quickly Joshua is maturing. From your own experience you can see this. Mistakenly, Gabriel Jackson in his impatience assumed that Joshua was ready to be presented to his people now, but he was many years too early, we must be patient and await his fifteenth year, for then he will be truly ready.'

'So we have to wait until 2017,' said Janet Sherrie.

'December 31st 2017, to be precise,' replied Father Moloney, whose tone had softened to the point of allowing a smile to flicker around his lips.

'So, what do we do in the meantime?' asked Iain Sherry.

'More to the point, it's what you don't do. You don't say anything to anyone about your healing, especially the media who will sooner or later be knocking on your door. Remember that you carry the mark of Joshua and as such you will support him in doing whatever is asked of you by Brother Anthony and Rachel. You cannot refuse. This, I assure you, will at times be arduous. Now go to your home, pray for strength and make yourself ready,' replied the priest.

'And what of me, where do I fit in?' asked Janet.

The reply was terse.

'You must stay by your husband,' was all Father Moloney would say.

In silence the Sherries walked home, but once behind the closed door of their modest detached house they talked about what the priest had said, to analyse his words. What did he mean by Iain making himself ready, ready for what? He'd told Janet to stay by her husband, but she'd always done that, so did he mean something different? He'd told them to pray for strength, strength to do what? The whole thing was a mystery. They had been given a date confirming Joshua's readiness, but ready to do what exactly? *Questions, questions.*

'I'm going to call Ally,' said Iain.

'Be careful what you say, you know, the phone might be bugged,' remarked Janet.

Iain gave her a quizzical look; their right to privacy may well have been compromised. He'd listened in to a few conversations himself; tapping into a phone was easy for people who had the skills, for him it had become commonplace. Usually there is a tell-tale click or some other sign that the phone had been compromised and Iain listened for any such noise as he dialled his friend's number. There was nothing to raise his suspicions but when Ally answered the call he was guarded just the same.

'Are you and Mary free to come round for a meal this evening?' asked Iain.

'Aye, I expect so but let me check.'

In the background Iain heard Mary say it was OK and they agreed sevenish. It was when Iain switched off the phone that he detected an unusual noise, faint but definitely different, just as Janet had feared, it was bugged. It's a strange thought knowing that someone is listening in to every conversation, recording every word. His mobile may be tapped as well; in fact it was a certainty. Security forces are meticulous in such matters. His paranoia took over, he scoured the house checking for hidden microphones, but his search drew a blank. At least they could engage in small talk over a meal without some nosy eavesdropper listening in, but even so there remained the possibility that he had missed a bugging device. Modern ones are tiny, powerful things that can be hidden in the most unlikely places. He shuddered at the thought of his home being violated in this way and felt a certain level of remorse at having directed similar violations towards others during his time as a police officer. But that was different, those people were known criminals and it was an effective means of collecting evidence. He and Janet were not in that category, they had always been on the side of law and order, tapping their phone was a diabolical act of privacy invasion and Iain felt sick.

Later in the evening, when the four of them sat round the dinner table, Iain threw caution to the wind. He was not going to be a prisoner in his own home, what had happened to the old adage about a man's home being his castle? If anyone was going to decide on whether the drawbridge was up or down it would either be him or Janet, not some faceless goon wearing headphones. Their talking focused on Joshua, his parents and his brother. Normally, a dram or two of whiskey would fuel such an evening but not tonight. Sobriety bordering on reverence guided the conversation, Joshua had laid his hands upon them and their lives were now dedicated to him. Father Moloney need not concern himself about indiscretions, a fact that was made clear by Iain, in a loud voice, assuring anyone listening that he and all those in his house that night had sworn allegiance to the boy. Almost on cue, his telephone rang.

'Hello, Iain Sherrie here.'

'Mr Sherrie, my name is Frank Macleod; I'm a reporter with the Edinburgh Mail, can me and a colleague come round and talk to you? We're staying in Inveraray so we can be with you in a short while.'

'No you bloody well can't, now get off my phone.'
He hurled the disconnected phone into an easy chair, it bounced onto the floor. His face was ashen and his hands shaking.

'The vultures from the papers have caught up with us, they want to talk to me, shit, shit, shit.'
He stormed around the room.

'It's alright love, we won't let them in. Call Father Moloney, he'll know what to do,' said Janet.
Iain Sherry made the call.

'This is Father Moloney, I'm sorry I can't take your call at the present but leave a message and I'll get back to you. In emergencies please call my mobile.'

The priest, in a slow deliberate voice, repeated his mobile number twice giving callers the chance to write it down without the aggravation of listening to the whole message again. Iain's hand was still shaking as he punched in the numbers.

'Hello Iain its Father Moloney, I'll be with you in 5 minutes.'

Iain Sherry sat down, his shoulders hunched as he leant forward.

'They were listening in all the time, Father Moloney's already on his way.'

The Westminster chime of the doorbell had never sounded so threatening.

'Is that you Father?' asked Janet.

Scuffling and cries of pain from the other side of the door startled her. She jumped back, expecting the door to burst open.

'It's alright, you can open the door now; everything is under control.'

Janet recognised the priest's voice and opened the door.

'Your uninvited guests I believe,' said Father Moloney.

He held the two reporters firmly by the scruff of the neck, Jamie McArdle was trying to stem copious bleeding from his nose, and puffiness beneath Frank Macleod's right eye would later become a well-defined black eye.

'Now gentlemen, how did you find us?' asked the priest.

Frank Macleod attempted some bravado, threatening to call the police and report Father Moloney for assault, but it made no impression.

'One more time, how did you find us?'

In between dabbing at his sore nose, Jamie McArdle told Father Moloney what he wanted to know. He even volunteered the errant porter's name, an action that immediately sealed the poor man's fate – the listening device was still active.

Despite having crossed a priest who was a match for the pair of them, Jamie McArdle found himself in awe of Iain Sherry. He'd seen the man's dreadful injuries and how, with a single touch, a young child had healed him. He recalled the bright light and the feeling of total peace. The realisation of being in the presence of a miracle now meant more than just getting his name in print; he wanted to experience that same feeling again. From that moment, Joshua had another convert; Father Moloney sensed this and released him. Not so with Frank Macleod who was unceremoniously dumped in a chair and told to stay silent. Father Moloney had already decided how this belligerent reporter and his youthful colleague could help the cause. He'd inflicted damage so letting them go without anything at all carried a risk that a pack of highly damaging speculative lies may appear in Macleod's seamy rag. So a story about Iain Sherrie's healing could be permissible without lurid headlines or stupid catchphrases. Father Moloney decided to turn the situation to his own advantage, which is why he chose to write the story himself. There would be just enough to stimulate interest without making any dramatic claims. There was always the risk of stirring up further terrorist activity but he reckoned that to be a chance worth taking. He judged that whetting the media appetite at this stage to be beneficial. He would do this without any mention of Joshua or his powers, suggesting other, more ancient powers, may have been responsible. Father Moloney called for a sheet of writing paper, sat at the kitchen table and wrote: -

'A former police officer grievously injured whilst on duty, has experienced what he believes to be a miracle. A recent pilgrimage to the Island of Iona resulted in his injuries being completely healed. He and some friends were standing outside a new church building, which on that day was to be formally opened. He states that during the proceedings a bright light descended upon him and his injuries just seemed to disappear. His parish priest, Father Moloney, believes that something remarkable did happen but is reluctant to say outright that it was a miracle. Whatever occurred on Iona has resulted in a servant of the community recovering his health, something we can all be thankful for. "Perhaps the spirit of St Columba is still at work there, who knows," remarked Father Moloney.

Permission to go ahead with the piece was needed otherwise he'd finish up in the same boat as his predecessor and his political instincts were far too sharply honed to let that happen. Out of earshot he dialled up a secure number on his mobile phone. The bishop's view was to stay ahead of the game. *A lie can be around the world before the truth has laced up its boots.*

The neatly written press statement was handed to Frank Macleod whose response came as no surprise.

'My bosses will never go for that, it's not my style, all that stuff about St Columba, its bloody stupid,'

The paper was snatched from him.

'You've had your chance, the young man shall have it for himself; he'll find a place for it.'

Jamie McArdle nodded; the story was his anyway and he was sure, even in its watered down form and with a photograph of the new church, there was enough to interest a responsible news editor somewhere. And so it turned out. His piece appeared in the supplement of the Scottish edition of a national Sunday paper. Frank Macleod returned to his mundane existence, grubbing around for sensational stories. The warning he'd received from Father Moloney was enough to keep him away from anything to do with healing, miraculous or otherwise.

Chapter 33

As expected, the article attracted some comment as well as featuring in a BBC Scotland Today news report. Critics said it was a cynical confidence trick by a discredited church whilst others used the story to reinforce religious beliefs or to justify the presence of aliens from another world. Seasoned television producers latched on to the 'blood in the snow' story when the Chief Constable had sworn that 'no stone would be left unturned' in the investigation into the killing of his officers by terrorist activity in an earlier incident. Old footage was shown and questions asked. Was this grievously injured police officer who had been healed a survivor from the incident, if so why had his survival not been disclosed at the time? Surely, public interest demanded a complete account of who had died and who had survived. Father Moloney declined to make any further comment on the grounds that he had nothing more to add. However, the bishop held a press conference during which he confirmed that an unknown man had apparently been healed of severe injuries during a stay on Iona. Whilst he had no means of confirming this he said that if it be the will of God for such a wonderful thing to happen then we must give thanks and he urged people to attend their local churches to pray. It was a masterful performance of putting up a smoke screen whilst at the same time urging people back into a diminishing flock. Neither had it escaped him that extra revenue gleaned from the faithful visiting Iona to see where this miraculous healing was supposed to have happened could find its way into church coffers. As before, there were more questions than answers and the bishop felt inner satisfaction that the story would soon be relegated to a dormant existence in the news archives where it would lay undisturbed until the time was right for its resurrection. He'd done a good job, ensuring that Joshua had not been directly linked through the media to Iain Sherrie's healing. Apart from those who knew the truth it remained an enigma for the chattering classes to speculate upon and conspiracy nuts to flood the internet with even more rubbish than usual. However, it had not eluded the bishop and his advisers that those whose mission it was to kill Joshua would have followed this story and making a link between the events on Iona and the flurry of media activity was not beyond them. It was the ultimate imperative for Brother Anthony and Rachel to remain vigilant, day and night if Joshua was to stay within the bosom of his family. Apart from a journey involving lengthy road travel and two ferry crossings, the risks involved in transporting him to and from Iona on a daily basis were too great, so Joshua would be home schooled by Rachel and Brother Anthony. The plan was for them to live at the farm on a monthly rotation and then, when not teaching Joshua, would go to Iona and spend time in contemplation and prayer. The MacKays were pleased with this compromise as it allowed them to be a family and even more important, Joshua's safety had gained an extra layer of security. Also the Sherries were immediately available should they be needed.

This arrangement worked well, Joshua flourished and any anxiety about further attempts on his life subsided to a point where Rachel worried that complacency may erode the security mind-set so carefully nurtured over the past months. Regular drills were carried out to ensure that such a thing did not happen and that readiness remained at peak efficiency. It was irksome to be dragged out of bed during the early hours to defend against a virtual attack but the reasoning was sound and the MacKays accepted it as a small price to pay for keeping their son close. The drills were not always confined to the MacKay's but from time to time involved the Sherries. Iain found it a stimulating experience to be on the front line again; especially when the all clear was given and a full Scottish breakfast was his reward.

December 2009

The rate at which Joshua had grown physically and intellectually was astounding. His seventh birthday was a week away yet the range of knowledge already within his grasp would, if he were older, gain him admission to any of the world's top universities. However, he was still a boy with a sense of impish fun and despite the intensity of his education Joshua played happily with his younger brother who was not showing any of his brother's talents. Then why should he? But age makes a difference and home schooling carries the downside of potential isolation. For a short time on Iona Joshua had interacted with other children but now it was becoming obvious there was a need for him to mix more frequently with children of his own age. Playing with Farai was well and good but Joshua had never experienced peer group pressure, competing against others at sport or just chilling out with other kids. Perhaps the time had come when some of his education ought to be in the local school. *'Gabriel will oppose it?'* thought Rachel. But the decision was hers to make so she talked it over with Brother Anthony, Dougy and Sara before approaching the head teacher of Inveraray Primary School. There was a general consensus that it would be a good thing for Joshua to mix with his own age group but on the basis that it was more of a placement than a permanent arrangement, but the head teacher didn't see it that way. Dougy thought she was a bit on the young side to be a head teacher, *'what would she be, about 27, no more than that,'* he *mused.* But this minor prejudice disappeared when he realised that a wise head rested on those slim young shoulders. It had taken Patricia Nolan two years of hard work to convince the governors that changes were necessary and now in her third year at the school she had instituted a challenging educational experience for her small pupils.

At first the MacKays accepted that Joshua's special gifts and the reasons for him being home schooled must not be disclosed, yet they felt that Patricia Nolan could be trusted with their son's secret, she gave off positive vibes. Joshua seemed to take to her and she to him but as always any decisions concerning disclosure must come from Rachel and that wasn't about to happen. She would argue that the more people who had knowledge of Joshua's gifts the more likely it would be that his security would be compromised. *'Security, security, that's all she thinks about, Gabriel Jackson has brainwashed her,'* thought Dougy, yet he admired her tenacity.

'As one of Joshua's tutors you should meet this head mistress and then make a decision,' said Dougy.

'No, no, no,' said Rachel, thumping her fist down hard on the kitchen table.

'Why not, we both think she can be trusted,' replied Sara.

'That is not the point, this head teacher is one of the new breed who expects children to talk about themselves, and then the others will tell their parents. No, sorry, the risk is too great.'

'Well, how do we prevent the wee boy growing up with little knowledge or understanding of others then?' questioned Dougy.

For once Rachel was stuck for an answer. She'd talked Gabriel Jackson into releasing Joshua from the restrictions of life at the ruined abbey arguing that growing up in a normal family home had many advantages. Yet she was now just as controlling. Her understanding of where the future would take Joshua had never been clear, only Gabriel Jackson and his handlers seemed to hold that vital information, so how important was it for him to develop his own humanity through doing what everyone else does throughout life. If they carried on in the same way Joshua may grow into manhood without the experience of physical love and attachment to someone other than his parents and grandparents. True, on the occasions when he had healed the two men, Joshua showed enormous empathy. Those inside the light felt a powerful love that as he grew would become stronger. Then, almost as if God himself had spoken, the reason for Joshua being on the earth was revealed to her. The simplicity of the revelation and its meaning had been within the grasp of humankind since the dawn of time. Iconic religious figures had spoken and written about it, many had tried to practise it but none had entirely succeeded in making it work on a global scale. Here was a boy sent from who knows where with a gift so powerful, so destructive to evil that from the euphoric moment of his birth he was earmarked for assassination by a superstitious Zimbabwean President who interpreted the heavenly changes as a sign that something so immensely powerful, capable of unifying the people against him had been unleashed. It was almost a replay of events enacted over two millennia ago, the difference being that an angel was not sent just to relay the good news but was one armed with an array of deadly weaponry, his mission being to save the fragile child from an early death and to nourish a gift that in itself carried the potential for personal destruction.

So this is Joshua's great gift. It is a gift that if enabled to spread undiluted, will completely and irrevocably eradicate the evils of the world. It will heal the nations, destroy all that sets its face against peace and reconciliation and like any virus, if the conditions are right, will spread like wildfire. It was as if those in close proximity to Joshua when he unleashed his healing powers had undergone a restructuring of their DNA. Could it be that within the complexities of the human genome there is a coding for love that once activated will destroy the malignancy of hate. Such an organism requires a carrier and in that one brief flash of insight Rachel recognised that beyond any doubt, Joshua was it, yet to release him now was not the right time. Gabriel Jackson had insisted that he must stay within hers and Brother Anthony's influence until he decreed otherwise. Rachel changed her mind and met with Patricia Nolan.

The young head teacher listened as Rachel explained more about her role and how she emphasised that Joshua was a highly gifted child requiring an intensity of education not suitable for other children of his age. She remained unsure that a local primary school, no matter how good, was the place for him. Yet she was sure that for Joshua's gift to be fully realised he must become an integrated part of the human race and not set aside from it. Patricia Nolan was keen to take Joshua into her school as she too had been a gifted child and understood that an intellect such as Joshua's had to be challenged and stimulated. Half an hour into the conversation Rachel began to relate the story of just how special Joshua was. A look of amazement appeared on Patricia Nolan's face as the attempts on Joshua's life were unfolded, it was an almost unbelievable story but to discover that part of it had happened within a few miles of the school was even more shocking. In the same way as others in the close knit community of Inveraray Patricia Nolan remembered the intense police activity of a year or more ago. To discover that Joshua was at the centre of it filled her with horror.

'Poor wee child,' she repeated over and over again.

Rachel sensed that the head teacher's mind was in turmoil. Patricia Nolan rose from her chair; she walked to a window and stared out towards the hills. Then several minutes later and with her back towards Rachel she said,

'I cannot risk the other children's safety by taking him into the school; anyway the governors and the parents association will have to be consulted before any decision is made.'

'That cannot happen, the decision must be yours and yours alone,' said Rachel who had already sensed that the whole idea was a non-starter. No head teacher in her right mind would take such a risk.

'I'm sorry Rachel, the answer has to be no but if I can help in any other way please tell me. Oh, and nothing of what you have said will be repeated.'

Rachel nodded her thanks and left. Patricia Nolan sat down, for the first time in her teaching life she felt a sense of failure, unable to give a place to a boy with such a gift gnawed at her conscience, but she simply could not place the other children in harm's way. She had a duty of care to them, but the dilemma grew in her mind and somehow had to be resolved. She was of a personality type that made it impossible to let something like this rest and two days later she contacted Rachel with a request to meet Joshua in the relaxed surroundings of the farm.

Chapter 34

Still in some doubt as to whether it was a wise thing to do, Patricia Nolan arrived at the farmhouse. Having given up her Saturday to meet Joshua she rationalised that the visit was social, that's all it was. She wanted to see more of Joshua and meeting him here, in familiar surroundings, seemed more sensible than in the sterile, formality of her office. There'd be no commitment, no promises; just a relaxed time with Joshua and his family to get a broader feel for things, then perhaps the dilemma may go away. Mary met her at the door, immediately inviting her in. Traditional Scottish hospitality in the form of drop scones and tea removed any remnants of formality and soon everyone, including Brother Anthony who had been invited, was chatting as if they had known each other for years. Farai seemed bemused and clung to Sara but not so Joshua, he'd met the head teacher before and liked her. Patricia Nolan made a suggestion.

'It's a nice day so how do you feel if Joshua and I had a stroll around the farm, he can show me things and I can get to know him better.'
Glances were exchanged between Rachel and Brother Anthony betraying their opposition to this suggestion.
'Why not, it seems like a good idea to me,' said Dougy.
Sara agreed, on the understanding that they went no further than the barn. Earlier feelings of bonhomie were in danger of evaporating, until Patricia Nolan said,
'Well perhaps grandma might like to join us.'
Rachel smiled and the tension eased.
'All settled then,' said Mary, swapping her apron for a cardigan.
An enthusiastic Joshua showed off his granddad's tractor and other bits of machinery to an attentive Patricia Nolan who in return asked questions about the farm. Joshua surprised her with his understanding of how things worked.

'Och, he's a quick learner, he'd make a good farmer,' said Mary with obvious pride in her voice.

They walked for a few minutes before resting on a coarse wooden bench purposely placed to capture scenic views across the fields to the hills beyond.

'This is where granddad sits sometimes, he likes it here,' said Joshua.

'I'm sure he does, do you like it here as well,' asked Patricia Nolan.

'Yes, I like it better than the other place I go to.'

'Oh, where is this other place?'

Joshua looked up at Patricia Nolan but did not answer.

'He means Iona,' said Mary.

Gentle probing yielded nothing except the sort of responses expected from a boy of his age. There was nothing in his behaviour to suggest anything other than normality. A bemused Patricia Nolan took him by the hand. Here was a small boy who she had been told was amazingly gifted, yet on this showing he was quite ordinary, much the same as any of the others in her school, so why all the fuss? She judged that if the circumstances surrounding him had been different she'd take him; there'd be few problems. Her initial reluctance to give him a place was based solely on the need to maintain a safe environment within the school and this had to remain a top priority, she could not allow her natural teacher's instinct to overrule common sense but it was becoming difficult to resist Joshua's appeal. He hung on to her hand as they walked slowly back to the farmhouse. Mary stayed a few steps behind, watching as her grandson's amazing capacity for love moved through those lightly held hands. All he needed was to touch another human being and the transfer was complete, Patricia Nolan felt utterly amazing, she had experienced love before, towards her partner, her own child but never anything like this. Joshua was sharing his gift in a way that forked lightning finds its most direct route to earth. Patricia Nolan was a person who had an affinity for caring; she was susceptible to Joshua's influence and so his gift of love found an easy route and buried itself into her heart. She had to find a way around her

221

reservations; Joshua could not be left in isolation, being in the company of other children had to be the right thing for him. She would talk again with Rachel, Brother Anthony and Joshua's parents.

If Rachel needed Gabriel Jackson's counsel it was now. She tried his mobile in the forlorn hope that he may still be connected. It was a number that only she had and to her surprise a voice mail message in his unmistakable deep resonant voice invited her to call him at any time on another number that Rachel memorised and stored. Her strong instinct for security told her this may be a trap, impersonating Gabriel Jackson's voice could easily be achieved by someone skilled enough, yet there was something in the tone that was uniquely him, so she took a chance and dialled up the number. He responded immediately.

'Hello Rachel, I've been expecting a call.'

'You just knew I couldn't manage without you didn't you.'

Knowing that Gabriel Jackson held firm views on Joshua's education, Rachel described her dilemma. He listened without interruption. When she had finished he stayed silent, considering his reply. Rachel expected him to rebuff the idea of Joshua entering a normal school so she was more than mildly surprised when he agreed to it.

'I have no objections providing Joshua's spiritual programme continues undiluted and that he is protected from harm.'

'That's the problem. The head teacher knows about Joshua and previous attempts on his life and whilst she is very keen to have him in her school there remains the real possibility of another attack. She has a duty to ensure the safety of others. Anyway where are you, can we meet to talk about this face to face?'

'No, those who control me will not allow it. This conversation will have to be the last time we communicate through direct means but please reassure Patricia Nolan that Joshua and the others will be safe, you have my word.'

'How do you know her name? How can you say such a thing? Please Gabriel, tell me where you are.'

'Trust me; no harm will come to any of you. Brother Anthony and his monks will see to that.'

'How can you be sure? The school authorities won't allow armed guards on the premises and that is the only way Joshua will be protected.'

'You are wrong. I must go now. Just trust me and trust Brother Anthony, but above all, trust God.'

Gabriel Jackson terminated the call. Rachel felt like screaming. It was typical of the man, he'd left her with unresolved questions, demanding that she trust him but why should she? He'd never been able to prevent previous attacks. Granted, he was good at fighting them off but he had to be on the premises to do that. Also how did he know Patricia Nolan's name, she hadn't told him so who had? Was it Brother Anthony going behind her back? Gabriel Jackson had said that no further direct contact was possible, with her at least. Brother Anthony may well be Gabriel Jackson's mouth piece but direct confrontation would achieve nothing as he'd probably deny everything. It seemed to Rachel that the matter of Joshua spending some of his time in a normal school had already been discussed and agreed beforehand. Letting slip the head teacher's name was confirmation of this. She felt hurt and isolated. Once again Gabriel Jackson had used her, knowing all the time that Joshua's future was not in her hands but in his and those of Brother Anthony and Patricia Nolan. Rachel didn't blame the head teacher, to some extent she felt for her because Joshua was already so far ahead of the other children and almost certainly was on a different intellectual level to his teachers.

Patricia Nolan showed genuine delight when told of Gabriel Jackson's agreement to Joshua joining her school. With reservations, Rachel passed on what had been promised about the boy's personal protection and how this will extend to the other children. There was zealousness in Patricia Nolan's eyes, Joshua had really got to her, she was now his and Rachel had no doubt that when the school authorities met him they too would fall under his spell. She felt a shudder extend the length of her spine. The seeming impossibility of Brother Anthony and his band of monks being able to guarantee the sort of protection that Gabriel Jackson had promised struck her with enormous force. They could not be in two or even three places at once and the thought of what could result from a concerted terrorist attack filled her with horror.

'Just trust me and trust Brother Anthony, but above all, trust God.'

What did Gabriel Jackson mean by this? Trust him to do what; she had no idea where he was or the company he was keeping. Invoking God's trust was all well and good, she felt some comfort from this but how could such trust deflect a bullet from a high powered assault rifle or disarm a suicide bomber? So there had to be something else, something that would be powerful enough to throw an impregnable, invisible cordon around the area. Sleep evaded her as she pondered the dilemma that Gabriel Jackson had given her.

'...but above all trust God.'

At 4 am Rachel closed her eyes, not to sleep but to pray. She asked God for a sign, anything that signified his presence in all this. Rachel had enough experience of God to know that His ways are full of mystery but she needed more than a promise, she wanted a revelation, nothing less would satisfy her.

The weak sun of a winter's dawn struggled over the horizon, casting early morning rays across the fields. Sitting up, Rachel rested her tired body against the headboard of the single bed that Mary had made up for her in the spare room. Her mind was still full of the previous day's happenings but in a strange way she felt less anxious and more relaxed about the whole scenario of Joshua going to a small town school. After all, the arrangement was only for a couple of days each week during which time he'd do things that interest children of his age. She told herself there may be some regression but this should easily be countered by the intensity of the instruction he received from Brother Anthony. Throwing off the bed clothes Rachel felt the cold of the morning. Mary had loaned her a dressing gown, not the most stylish garment she'd ever worn but warm and cosy just the same. Noise from downstairs told her that others were already up and about, and the strong aroma of coffee drifting up from the kitchen overcame any reticence Rachel may have had about being seen in public wearing an old fashioned dressing gown.

Brother Anthony had stayed the night also but in his case the bed had been one made of straw in the barn. It was his own choice to sleep in such a primitive way; he'd never experienced the luxury of a modern well sprung bed and doubted that he could sleep on one anyway. Rachel was envious of his rested appearance. He'd obviously slept well and none of the doubts that had haunted Rachel had disturbed his slumber. Rachel found a chair next to Brother Anthony who was sitting in contemplation near the Aga. The perceptive monk turned and noticing the heavy bags under Rachel's eyes, declined to ask how she had slept. Instead he greeted her in a gentle, kindly way then returned to his semi trance like state. Rachel had often marvelled at the way monks can do this. At any time they will disappear into a world of their own, only to return when it suits them. It could be down to the nature of their calling or some special relationship with God, but it was a common characteristic that Rachel had become used to. She blew the steam from her drink, sipped it and waited until Brother Anthony raised his head. Staring straight ahead he spoke in a whisper.

'Father Gabriel is concerned that you do not trust him with Joshua's safety. Believe me when I say that you must restore your trust for he is in a place where all things are possible. No harm will come to the boy or those around him.'

'Please do not speak in riddles, tell me where Gabriel is and why you are so sure that he can protect Joshua,' replied Rachel.
A deep sigh came from beneath Brother Anthony's cowl.

'Above all things Father Gabriel told you to trust in God for it is from Him that protection will ultimately come. Believe me when we say that is all you need to know. Tomorrow, Joshua and his parents will meet the school authorities, but I am sure it will go to plan.'

'And what plan is that?' asked a bemused Rachel.
Brother Anthony realised he had spoken out of turn. Now he had to say more or forever lose Rachel's already fragile trust.

'Once Joshua's place at the school has been agreed we will meet at the new church and there I will confide everything I know. I am sure Father Gabriel will understand.'

Rachel felt a sense of smug satisfaction for she had broken through the wall of secrecy so jealously guarded by the two men. It was clear that Brother Anthony did not know the true personality of Gabriel Jackson whose ability to understand another's point of view did not exist, especially when it involved him changing direction. She thought he'd done it earlier when agreeing to Joshua entering a normal school but had now discovered it was all part of an agreed plan, how could she have been so naïve?

Chapter 35

Monks were still working on the new church when Brother Anthony and Rachel arrived, having sailed across on the mid-morning ferry. Throughout their journey from the farm hardly a word had passed between them. A few passengers shot quizzical glances in their direction as it was not usual to see a robed monk on the ferry, but nothing was said and Brother Anthony didn't seem to notice anyway. The Spartan interior of the church had been kept at a comfortable temperature to allow its use as a living and worshipping space. A wooden table and chairs dominated one side of the church and an assortment of sleeping equipment was scattered around the place. A large propane gas cylinder that fed the heater also provided fuel for a two ringed cooking stove supported on a wooden cupboard containing essential culinary utensils and crockery. A monk was busy stirring a large tureen of soup that would serve as the midday meal. A wooden cutting board, upon which a pile of roughly broken chunks of warm home baked bread rested, sat on the table. Brother Anthony invited Rachel to join him and the monks for the meal.

'We will eat first and talk later,' he said.

The keen sea air had stimulated Rachel's appetite and she felt more able to engage in what might be a difficult conversation on a full stomach, so she willingly agreed to this suggestion. They stood round the table as Brother Anthony said a prayer. When all were seated the thick vegetable soup was ladled out, each one receiving a full bowl and a wedge of bread. Rachel had never before tasted soup such as this, it was sublime and the bread added to her enjoyment. They ate in silence and at the end of the meal another prayer was said. The monks rose from their places and went about their work. They would not eat again until 8 o'clock that evening. She showed her appreciation by offering to clear up after the meal but Brother Anthony refused to allow it. He wanted to spend the next hour at least in conversation and reflection. He beckoned Rachel across to where a small desk and two chairs nestled beneath the main window.

'This is where I do my work, the light is better here.'

He folded a set of drawings that lay across his desk, placing them alongside other documents in a large wicker basket. They sat opposite each other and Brother Anthony began the conversation. His manner was formal and abrupt.

'It is my wish that you know what has been agreed between Father Gabriel and me. It was never our intention to deceive you but he believes that if the plans for Joshua's safety are known only to us then they will not be divulged. He is not aware we are having this conversation but I am sure that by the time we are finished he will know.'

'How, he is not here is he,' queried Rachel.

'No. He is in a place where all things are known and all things are possible.'

'More riddles, why do these people always speak in riddles?'

'And where is that?'

'He is with the master.'

'In Heaven you mean? If that's the case how was I able to speak with him on my mobile phone?'

'Like I said, he is in a place where all things are possible.'

Rachel decided not to pursue this line of discussion. Non-verbal annoyance was aimed at Brother Anthony who moved the conversation onwards.

'Father Gabriel's influence straddles this world and the next. Since passing Joshua's care over to us he has been invested with the power to keep him safe. It is power given to him by God. Father Gabriel has always been Joshua's guardian angel and will forever protect him and those near to him from all harm.'

More questions flooded into Rachel's mind. If someone with a gun or a bomb wanted to attack Joshua how could Gabriel Jackson prevent it from happening? This was a question she asked of Brother Anthony, whose reply was less than convincing.

'I can't say how Father Gabriel will achieve this; I just know that he will. Look at it this way. It is as if he has woven an invisible impenetrable barrier around Joshua. He will know when someone is plotting to harm him and action will be taken to prevent it happening. Two or more of us will go to the source and it will be neutralised.'

'You mean the monks,' asked Rachel.

'Yes.'

Rachel recalled how they had been waiting at the farm and how in previous battles with the forces of evil they had butchered the enemy without a second thought. These are soldiers of God; beneath the anonymity of their robes they represent a terrifying force, an army where each one is prepared to give his life to protect Joshua. Rachel began to see the reason for building the new church. It was a focal point from which Joshua's influence would spread like ripples on a pond across the world.

'In time, when he is sure that Joshua is ready, Father Gabriel will install him in this church as its head,' said Brother Anthony.

'Well, he tried that once before but things went wrong and he paid the price didn't he.' Rachel's sarcasm fell on deaf ears.

'Yes, that was unfortunate for him at the time. For a brief moment he failed to do what he is now imploring you to do.'

'And what is that?'

'Trust in God.'

'Are you saying that what happened on that day was preordained?'

'Not exactly, but think about what has transpired since the policeman was healed. A group of people, including his family, have dedicated their lives to Joshua. They are his first disciples on earth and when the time comes there will be many more dedicated to his new church and to spreading his gospel that love is all powerful. It is a new version of an old gospel that will transform nations across the globe. My sadness is that you of all people seem to be having doubts. From the start you have been at Father Gabriel's right hand, you are just as much an agent of God as he is, yet you seem to be losing some of your faith.'

Rachel pondered these words. Perhaps this was the real reason why Brother Anthony was speaking to her. Did he consider that she was no longer suitable to be involved in Joshua's preparation? Was she to be replaced by Patricia Nolan? The truth was that she had been touched by Joshua's power, she was close to him and he liked her but had the time come for a change in his life? Against her wishes he was to attend an ordinary school, mixing with ordinary children. Was this God's doing or was it just another way of airbrushing her out of the picture. She asked Brother Anthony that very question.

'No, that is not the case; you remain an important part of God's plan for Joshua. You will work with me at the church, for it is here that the child will spend the greater part of his time. Patricia Nolan is God's chosen person to guide Joshua in secular ways. It is all a matter of balancing out his life to include those things that are non-spiritual. His mission is to be in the world, not immune from it.'
It was then that Brother Anthony made the most startling revelation of all.

'When God's only begotten son Jesus Christ was here on earth he preached a message based on love. It is the opinion of a group of powerful leaders throughout the world that this message failed and when the news spread of Joshua's birth they saw it as a sign of hope that a new dawn may be approaching. It was not a coincidence that Father Gabriel appeared seemingly out of nowhere as Joshua's protector and through certain channels he latched on to the group. It had money, resources and the political will to ensure that he could do the work entrusted to him by God. Rachel, you were also sent by God but in a different way. From the moment of your conception it was preordained that you were to become an instrument in guarding, protecting and nurturing a boy whose mission was to rekindle the message of love first preached by Jesus Christ more than two centuries ago.'
Rachel had always felt a deep connection to Gabriel Jackson but could not fully say why, but now she was beginning to understand, and the implications were potentially awesome.

'Are you saying that Joshua is Christ reborn?' questioned Rachel.

'No, Joshua is himself. The success of his mission will depend on those who surround him. He will be borne on the wings of angels to where his presence is most needed.'

'And where would that be?'

'Wherever innocent, defenceless people are ruled by fear and despotism. Through this church he will give power to the destitute, to the poor and in so doing will strike fear into the hearts of those who mercilessly trample them into the dust. Even when a despot falls, another will spring up in his wake so the mission will not be without bloodshed. The head of the monster must be severed and its roots destroyed before the seeds of love can take root. Joshua already has the power to heal individuals and as he matures that power will be extended to the healing of entire continents.'

Rachel recalled the parable of the sower which now made more sense to her. Joshua was the sower who had been sent out to sow the seeds of love. Some will fall on stony ground and the yield will have no roots and be withered by the heat of the sun, some will be sown amongst thorns and will be choked before they have time to grow strong. Yet some will fall on fertile ground and the yield will be abundant, perhaps up to sixty times. She was immediately struck by the metaphorical meanings within this parable and why Joshua himself had to be placed in the fertile ground of a school where he would grow in his understanding of others. It all made sense to Rachel, she no longer saw Patricia Nolan as a threat but as an ally in whatever battles lay ahead.

Chapter 36

Sara and Dougy were no different from other parents taking their child to school for the first time. True, they had been parted from Joshua before but feelings of anxiety associated with this stage of their child's life were natural. The risks had been explored and accepted, so after a hug and kisses Joshua seemed content to be led into school holding Patricia Nolan's hand. The arrangement for Joshua to spend two days a week at the school had been put aside for the first week to give him chance to settle in. The head teacher had sorted out a table for him. He'd join three others, Bethany, Kate and George. It was Bethany who didn't think much to having a stranger dropped into their cosy little circle. She showed her annoyance by deliberately ignoring him, whereas the other two, captivated by Joshua's charm, took to him straight away.

Joshua was introduced to the class and the day's activities began. It soon transpired that Gabriel Jackson had taught him well for he was able to read faster and with much greater accuracy than his classmates and his ability with numbers was amazing. By the middle of the week questions were already being asked by the staff about Joshua's suitability for this type of education. Was this really the place for him? These serious doubts came to a head during Friday morning's reading practice when each child was asked to bring a book from home to read out. Joshua's choice was a children's story written in Modern Hebrew that he read faultlessly and then for the benefit of his classmates, translated it into English. There was no pretension about this; Gabriel Jackson had come to expect it. Yet during the free time when others played together Joshua stood alone in a corner. At home he'd play happily with Farai yet at school he was initially awkward and unable to join in with the others. Surprisingly it was Bethany who went to him and held out a hand. Joshua took it and from that moment any ill feeling Bethany may have had towards him evaporated. Even for someone so young she felt the power within him and from that moment they became firm friends yearning for each other's company during the times when Joshua was not there.

Over the weeks it became a problem, during his study time at the abbey his concentration often wandered, his mind was elsewhere. This pattern of behaviour was unexpected so Rachel and Brother Anthony had to find a compromise or Joshua's spiritual development would suffer. Similarly, neither Patricia Nolan nor any of her teaching colleagues had experienced this kind of thing before. The relationship between the two was in itself spiritual, Bethany's education went into decline, Kate and George took the brunt of her moodiness, parents became involved, including Dougy and Sara, so a solution needed to be found, fast.

The solution came not from a meeting of adult minds but from Bethany and Joshua. Joshua's strength of character and extraordinary charisma had rubbed off on Bethany. Together they were a formidable pair, some would even say scary, and the control they exercised over the situation left no option but to keep them together throughout the school week otherwise the potential for disruption would be immense. Brother Anthony, Rachel and Patricia Nolan agreed that Joshua's entire education would be carried out within the school so at least when he wasn't with his spiritual teachers, free time could be spent with Bethany and the others. Brother Anthony spent that evening in prayer. He asked for a sign that the decision to teach Joshua in this way had the blessing of a higher power. It was in the dead of night that a deep, subconscious voice woke him. Startled, he sat up, staring into the darkness, expecting to feel the presence of another being. For a while he stayed quite still, listening, there was no one there. He whispered into the night, no response. Eventually he lay back and sleep overtook him. It was then that the message came through and in the morning Brother Anthony had no doubt that the decision was the correct one.

The new arrangement for Joshua's schooling bore fruit of such magnitude that Brother Anthony had long since dismissed the idea that it was anything other than the actions of a divine being that had caused this to happen. Bethany settled and things returned to normal, well, as normal as possible with Joshua as a pupil. During the days when he was in class he continued to study the books that Brother Anthony had given him. His capacity for concentration never wavered and he became a role model for others who followed his example. All round test results improved, much to the delight of the school authorities. Farai had started at the same school. Although just a normal boy he did have an outgoing and engaging personality which was quite remarkable considering he had constantly been in the shadow of his brother.

December 2011 brought with it the usual cold snowy winter. At this time of the year Ally and Mary were well accustomed to being cut off from the town, but this time it wasn't so bad. The tractor fitted with its ancient snow plough ensured that Dougy was able to keep the surrounding tracks clear enough for access to out-buildings where their small herd of cows would spend the winter. The barn was well stocked with feed so there were no worries on that score. The snow came in flurries rather than in huge amounts and council grit spreaders made a good job of keeping main roads clear so local traffic could get around unhampered, which was as well because a party had been planned and all the children from Joshua's class were invited to his ninth birthday celebrations on New Year's Eve. Dougy spent most of the morning clearing what snow there was from the farm track. Last year the snow was so bad that any celebration had to be limited to the family. Not so this year, the party would be fantastic. There'd be plenty to eat, snowball fights and lots of presents. What more could a 9 year old boy want? Above all, Bethany would be there, so making his day complete.

The farm house looked resplendent. Christmas decorations had been replaced by birthday bunting. Outside a big 'Happy 9th Birthday Joshua' sign, tied to the fence, flapped in the cool wind. Mary had made enough sandwiches, jellies and the like to feed an army. She had an old fashioned view about birthday parties. Children came to them to do three things, eat, play games and make as much noise as possible. This one was to be no different. Mary said they owed it to Joshua who had missed out having his friends round last year so this had to be a double celebration. Dougy made a wry comment that one lot of food would have been plenty which his mother ignored.

'Just wait and see, those bairns will go through this lot like a plague of locusts,' said Mary. She made room for yet another plate of homemade strawberry jam sandwiches, placing it at the edge of the table where it balanced precariously.

Even for a boy of his age Joshua was tall, he seemed to grow more each day without the addition of much weight. Although Sara fretted over her son's slight build, Mary said Dougy had been just the same as a boy and that he'd fill out. The first of the guests had arrived. Joshua met them at the door, his eyes lighting up at the size of the wrapped presents they each carried. One by one the others arrived except Bethany who probably had the furthest to travel. As time went by Joshua's joy turned to melancholy, she was now half an hour late and the food was disappearing. *'Where was she, what had happened to her? Surely she hadn't forgotten his birthday.* The telephone rang, it was Bethany's father saying they were on their way but an incident had closed the road. The police couldn't say for how long. He said to tell Joshua that Bethany will be there as soon as possible. Before Bethany's father rang off he remarked on something that set Dougy's pulse racing. Alongside the police cars were two hooded monks who appeared to be carrying firearms. Immediately he knew this was no ordinary incident, danger threatened and Dougy could take no chances. He told Sara and his parents about the conversation. Without alerting the children Ally went round the doors and windows, locking and bolting them against what may be out there. Stout wooden doors and heavy duty double glazing fitted since the time when Iain Sherry was so grievously wounded gave Ally some reassurance that his house was better protected than it was then. He went to where his shotgun was locked in a cupboard, took it out, pushed two cartridges into the breach and then put it out of sight but within easy reach. *'Better than nothing but no answer to high velocity rifles or a suicide bomb.'*

'Can we go outside and make a snowman,' asked one of the boys.

'Why don't we stay in the warm and play some of the games I used to enjoy when I was a child,' said Mary.

Dougy nodded his appreciation at her quick thinking and soon the house echoed to the sound of children playing postman's knock, blind man's bluff and other games that none of them had played before. For a while the games took Joshua's mind off Bethany, he'd convinced himself that she would soon be there but after an hour when there was still no sign his edginess increased.

'Where is she daddy, you said she would be here.'

'She will be son, just be patient a little longer.'

The house phone rang, Ally picked it up, he expected the worse but it was Bethany's father.

'The road has been closed indefinitely so we turned round and are now at home, can you get Joshua to the phone, Bethany wants to wish him a happy birthday.'

Joshua displayed a mixture of relief and disappointment. At least his friend was alright and he listened with some amusement as she sang Happy Birthday to him but it was not the same as her being at his party. He described the games they were playing and that a slice of birthday cake had been saved for her. As their conversation went on Joshua's interest in his party waned, a chat between two friends became increasingly intense to a point where Bethany's father suggested that she should meet with Joshua later, joking that his phone bill was going up by the minute. But it was no joke to Bethany who became tearful. Throwing the phone to the floor she ran upstairs to her bedroom, slamming the door with such a resounding bang that a picture hanging on the landing wall slipped sideways. Bethany's phone was still switched on and Joshua heard the background commotion. His friend's distress was too much for him, he ran to the door, trying to get out. He had to be with her, it was his nature to bring comfort, to reach out. Bethany was in need and not to be with her was unbearable but it was the noise of wheels crunching over impacted snow that caused Dougy to pull his son away from the door. Outwardly he was calm; inwardly he felt a sense of panic that he must not show.

'Get the children to hide under the table; it's a party game I used to play.'

Ally unlocked his gun cabinet but did not immediately remove the weapon; he had to be sure that no other option remained before taking a step that was irretrievable. The vehicle stopped, blue flashing lights reflecting off the snow. Ally's hand closed around the gun, it was their only means of defence. His eyes turned to the children as they hid expectantly under the table. The thought of any harm coming to them filled him with horror, he would do his best but the chances of repelling a well-planned assault were zero. A request that was probably more of a command was shouted from outside.

'Hello in there, it's the police, open the door please.'

Dougy didn't believe a word of it. The dialect may have been Scottish and the voice that of a female but it didn't mean anything, Mimicry was well within the capabilities of terrorists.

'We're armed and ready to shoot anyone who tries to break in,' shouted Ally.

Then there came a more familiar voice

'Dougy, this is Iain, things are OK, you can open the door, there's no danger.'

'Come to a window and show yourself,' said Dougy.

Iain Sherry's familiar face appeared at one of the downstairs windows.

'OK, but stand back, there's a shotgun pointing straight at you.'

Ally took the key from his pocket and tossed it to his son. Taking a deep breath Dougy opened the door to face Iain Sherry, Brother Anthony and two armed police officers.

'Come in and join the party, then you can tell us what all this is about,' said Dougy.

Iain Sherry bowed his head in Joshua's direction.

'As it happened it was a false alarm but Brother Anthony was concerned enough to alert the police that an attempt on Joshua's life was about to happen.'

'It's always good to see you Iain but where do you fit in to all this,' asked Dougy.

'I carry a lot of intelligence about the area so when Brother Anthony received news of a possible attack he thought I could be useful, apart from which I would gladly sacrifice my own life to shield Joshua from any form of harm, just as you all would.'

'Yes we would, but who tipped you off, where did the information come from,' asked Sara.

'It came from a source that is above all of us. Messages reach me in a certain way. Remember, Father Gabriel implored us to trust God, he will not fail us,' said Brother Anthony, looking heavenwards.

'Well that's as maybe, but thankfully his warning this time was a long way out', interjected Mary from her position under the table where she'd turned the whole thing into a game. 'Can these bairns come out now, we need to get them home.' she asked.

'Aye Mary, the road's open so we can expect a few anxious parents to arrive any time now,' said Iain Sherry.
He'd hardly finished the sentence before the first of several vehicles pulled up to take the children home. It was a party they wouldn't forget in a hurry. When the last of the party guests had departed Brother Anthony convinced the MacKay's to let him stay the night just in case Father Gabriel's warning had been misinterpreted and danger still lurked in the vicinity.

'I'll stay as well, if that's OK,' said Iain Sherry.
The police officers agreed to patrol the area until dawn.

'Just in case, you never know,' said one of them.
Apart from Joshua and Farai no one at the farm slept that night and Mary assumed the position of tea maker, something she had become well accustomed to.

Chapter 37

There were no more scares, so later the following day Brother Anthony was given a ride back to Oban by Iain Sherry. He'd left Rachel in charge at the new church until his return. The two monks who had been seen at the road block had already made their way back. Brother Anthony remained puzzled. Gabriel Jackson does not raise false alarms so all he could think of was that the fault was his and he had somehow misinterpreted an ordinary dream. But it was no ordinary dream, it had been so powerful and compelling; something had gone wrong which meant the threat remained. He reassured himself that Father Gabriel would contact him again if he needed to, nothing was more certain than that.

On arriving at the church, extreme tiredness overtook him. He told Rachel what had happened at the farm and shared his concerns about Joshua. She urged her companion to sleep, if only for a few hours. In his gentle way Brother Anthony thanked her and lay down. Sleep came in an instant. Rachel placed a blanket over him; she sat beside his bed, watching and waiting as he slept, for if a prophetic dream did manifest itself she must be ready. The extent of Brother Anthony's physical exhaustion was such that only a slim chance of him summoning an effective response to any form of evil remained. Rachel had to take over; after all they were in it together. Reflecting on his handsome features she watched him sleep. It was a troubled sleep; he tossed and turned, several times throwing the blanket to the ground. Patiently, Rachel replaced it and continued to sit by him, waiting and listening. Then, two hours into his sleep, Brother Anthony began to mutter, incoherently at first, but then with increasing clarity. Only the voice was his; the words were those of Gabriel Jackson. He addressed her direct.

'Rachel, Brother Anthony woke too soon. He heard me correctly but only part of my message reached him. Those who plot to kill Joshua remain active and must be eradicated. Take the monks to a

239

place high in the Glen Coe mountain range for there you will find these men. You cannot afford to wait, go now.'

Bathed in sweat, Brother Anthony awoke. His face was drawn and pale, his hands shaking uncontrollably.

'I dreamt but can remember nothing,' he whispered.

Rachel chose not to tell him what Gabriel Jackson had said. Preventing him from leading the monks on a mission that had been set for them would be impossible. Once again, Gabriel Jackson had given the responsibility to her. Brother Anthony had to rest, allowing his body time to recover. Glen Coe in winter is formidable and no place for a weakened man, or indeed for anyone who is not physically fit and well prepared for survival in one of the most dangerous highland regions of Scotland. Glen Coe has an infamous reputation borne out by the massacre of 78 members of Clan MacDonald by an army made up from Clan Campbell and lowland Scots in 1692. It is a place scarred by treachery and Rachel shuddered as she recalled the helicopter shot down there by terrorists as a result of Gabriel Jackson's duplicity. Was this a baited trap waiting for her and the monks to walk into? Jackson was very good at sacrificing others to serve his own interests and even though he was now in a place outside of the earthly domain he remained under the control of powerful influences and Rachel felt as if she and the others were nothing more than cannon fodder. It wouldn't surprise her if Gabriel Jackson had become jealous of Joshua's relationship with Bethany; after all it was something over which he had no control. Rachel put that thought to the back of her mind, she must do everything in her limited power to save Joshua for the great things that he would do in the world.

The monks were assembled, briefed and set to work readying themselves for the battle that lay ahead. As a body, these ferocious fighters were prepared to make the ultimate sacrifice. Specialist combat equipment including body armour, all weather fatigues and tents, up to date high velocity weaponry, and satellite navigation devices had been stashed away as if in readiness for this type of situation. Each monk had a survival pack containing food supplements and liquid. Transport came in the form of two rugged Land Rovers that, up until now, had been kept under cover in the garage of a local man; Brother Anthony certainly had an eye for detail. Having double checked that everything had been loaded Rachel climbed behind the wheel of the lead vehicle and drove to where the ferry had docked. There were no other vehicles waiting to go on board, so apart from several foot passengers they had the boat to themselves. The ferry pitched and yawned as it made the rough crossing which gave fellow passengers something else to think about other than a dozen men and a woman in combat gear. The road journey to Craignure took more time than usual, a large amount of snow had been heaped on either side of the narrow road but even with four wheel drive engaged, care had to be taken, they had another ferry to catch and Rachel didn't want to spend valuable time rescuing a stranded Land Rover. Passing places had been dug out so hold ups were kept to a minimum and they left Mull with enough daylight still remaining to reach the village of Glencoe. Villages were used to all kinds of visitors so a couple of Land Rovers carrying soldiers on routine military exercises were likely to attract no more than a cursory glance and probably a wave.

Pine trees bordering a small lochan provided enough shelter for them to spend the night and Rachel had no scruples about bedding down in a tent with a couple of monks. Insulated from the cold in a sleeping bag designed for mountainous environments she settled for the night. Three monks volunteered to take turns at keeping guard and together cleared a patch of ground for a fire, which was risky, but they were well hidden amongst the pines. Every scrap of wood was wet with snow but these men were survivors, they piled up dead bark from beneath fallen trees that was dry enough to burn. Reluctantly the fire took hold; it spluttered a few times threatening to die but with coaxing the flames became stronger, casting flickering shadows across the ground. The monks sat cross-legged on a spare ground sheet, trance-like they stared at the flames, before two fell to sleep in the sitting position. The other remained awake for the first watch, his highly tuned senses combined in readiness to filter the natural sounds of the night from those of an alien presence.

As he kept watch the temperature plummeted to well below zero; it was the sort of paralyzing cold that ate into the bones bringing a rapid onset of hypothermia. He glanced at his sleeping companions, their breathing was regular and even, the cold had not penetrated their high quality mountaineering gear but he kept the fire going just the same. As well as providing warmth it was a living entity giving its own brand of company, he derived a strange pleasure from poking it with a stick and seeing sparks fly from the angry flames. The first watch dragged its way through the night and then, as if an alarm clock had gone off in his head one of the sleeping monks awoke to take his turn on guard. This became the pattern and when dawn came in a flurry of snow a stout wooden tripod made from green branches cut from a spruce held a bubbling pot of coffee above the flames. As if drawn by the magnetic odour Rachel and the others crawled from their tents. No conversation passed between them as they squatted at the edge of the fire, chewing on breakfast bars, gulping down the scalding liquid. Ten minutes was all Rachel allowed for the meal, then she stood up, coffee dregs creating a brown stain in the snow where she'd thrown them.

'Let's clear up, check our equipment and plan a strategy for the hunt.'

Terrorists were just quarry to be hunted down and shot on sight, no quarter given. Rachel spread a map of the region on the ground, there were many square kilometres to cover and the enemy would be well dug in to escape the cold. Sweeping a hand across the map, Rachel gave her thoughts on the situation.

'If Father Gabriel is to be believed the enemy is somewhere in the mountains so to survive they will be well equipped. They will be camouflaged and almost impossible to detect. So where do we begin to search, has anyone any ideas?'

There was no verbal response to Rachel's question but together as one body, the monks moved to the Land Rovers. Rachel had not experienced this sort of robotic behaviour before, she realised they did not need a map; they were being guided by something or someone else.

'Gabriel Jackson, he's in their heads,' she thought.

Rachel relinquished command, her driving seat being taken by a monk. She was relegated to sitting in the back. The Land Rovers moved off, heading towards the mountains taking their occupants to an inevitable battle with the forces of evil. The Three Sisters of Glencoe came into view but it wasn't these that interested the monks, for it was the highest peak in the Glen, Bidean nam Bian, they were being guided to. They came to a halt at the foothills, from here it was a hard slog on foot, but first the monks had to decide on the direction to take. Ignoring Rachel they collected in a huddle. She heard low murmuring but nothing more from the group before they moved off towards the steep slopes. One of the monks had taken the lead and the others, all heavily armed, fell in behind him, their backpacks holding essential survival equipment including lightweight tents, food and water. Rachel had to decide whether to go with them or remain with the vehicles. She chose to stay behind and moved into the driver's seat of the first vehicle, watching as the monks disappeared round a snow covered outcrop. These wild, desolate mountains generate their own unpredictable weather systems that have caught out even the most experienced of climbers. It began to snow again, and as the weather closed in Rachel doubted the wisdom of what they were doing, but they had come too far, a deadly threat had to be neutralized. Briefly, she closed her eyes and prayed for the success of the mission and for the safe return of the brave monks.

Once again darkness brought extreme cold. Rachel wrapped a thick blanket over her battle dress. She had resisted turning on the engine to heat the cab but uncontrollable shivering changed her mind. Within ten minutes the heater was pushing out warm air, gradually dispelling Rachel's discomfort. She felt sleepy but resisted closing her eyes, staying alert could mean the difference between life and death. Habitually, Rachel touched the holster carrying her side arm, its fully loaded presence reassured her and she settled back into the seat to wait. The sharp crack of gunfire startled her. Sound carries for long distances in the mountains so there was no way of calculating how far away it was. The dashboard clock told her the monks had been gone for eight hours but the weather would have slowed their progress. Then it came, a distant rumble gradually swelling to a roar. Tons of snow disturbed by shock waves from high velocity gunfire was on the move down the mountainside creating an irresistible force, burying everything in its path. Fear struck deep into Rachel's heart. Had the monks been buried along with the enemy? Rational thought was abandoned, should she go and search for them? Then common sense kicked in. She must stay with the vehicles, the monks were highly trained and resourceful, if any group of people could survive in these conditions it was them. Rachel waited.

No more sounds of gunfire reached her. A clear night lit by a bright moon gave a reasonable field of vision partially hampered by flurries of snow swirling in a moderately strong wind. Every now and again she activated the windscreen wipers, pushing the soft snow to one side. Running the engine had kept the cab at an optimum temperature, but for how much longer. The fuel gauge registered half full, perhaps enough to get off the mountain and reach a filling station. Taking no chances, Rachel decided to wait in the other vehicle, that way diesel usage was evened out, but whatever she did only a finite amount of time remained before her own survival took precedence. She snacked on breakfast bars and bottled water. Just once she relieved herself in the snow, an activity she had no wish to repeat, although it did give her a chance to stretch tired and aching limbs. The warmth of the Land Rover's cab welcomed her back from a brief excursion, it seemed to wrap its arms around her and at first Rachel dozed then she fell deeply asleep. The sharp pain of leg cramp woke her, she had been asleep for only half an hour or so but felt that she had betrayed the monks. She cleared the windscreen of snow, and rubbing a hole in the condensation, Rachel looked out. The moon seemed even brighter, lighting up the mountain landscape in sharp relief. Then movement caught her eye. Furiously she rubbed at the accumulating condensation that came with every breath; she picked out a figure stumbling in the snow towards her, then several others. Rachel drew her sidearm, if they were not the returning monks she was in deep trouble. She switched off the engine, but then its noise may have been what led

244

them in. Removing her blanket Rachel slipped the door lever. Once outside she slid to the rear of the Land Rover, guessing she'd be better protected there. Her firearm ready, she stood with her back to the tailgate. The leading figure was now a few metres away, Rachel heard his feet crunching down on the freezing snow. She calculated he was in range, and taking a deep breath to steady her hands she spun round the side of the Land Rover to face him. Standing, feet apart, her gun held in both hands at arm's length she was ready to fire but the man had fallen to his knees. A gaunt face looked up at her; it was one of the monks. She reached out, helping him to his feet. By now the others were back, some half carrying, half dragging their comrades. They had survived, but at a cost. They'd come equipped with battlefield first aid supplies but for two of them this was not enough. So severe were their wounds that Rachel only partially stemmed the blood loss. The men were dying and there was little she could do to prevent it.

'Let's get out of here while we can,' shouted Rachel.
She climbed into the driving seat of one vehicle; an uninjured monk took the wheel of the other.

'Damn it.'
Rachel cursed and thumped the steering wheel. She should have turned the Land Rovers to face the way out of the foothills; a major error by her standards. Now the snowbound track was fraught with danger. They couldn't reverse; going forward was hazardous enough with hidden rocks lying in wait beneath the snow, so there was nothing for it but to turn the vehicles. Standard turning manoeuvres were out of the question; they had to be shunted round bit by bit. It took an age but eventually they succeeded. Rachel was in the lead and with headlamps on full she crawled her way along where she thought the track was until the main road appeared. Tall posts along each side of the road guide drivers away from snowdrifts that can swallow a car and its occupants. Rachel led the way into Glencoe Village where she would try and get help for the injured monks. There had to be a doctor here at least. A local priest found it hard to believe Rachel when he answered the door to her frantic knocking, pleading for help. Thankfully, he took her at face value and a phone call soon had a doctor at the house but

the injured men had died en route. Rachel blamed herself but in reality these men had no chance, their injuries were too severe and their blood loss too great. They had led the assault, taken the brunt of enemy fire, making it possible for the others to overcome a small but determined group of terrorists, leaving their bodies to be buried beneath the snow. In contrast to their fatally injured comrades the remaining monks had suffered only minor wounds and frostbite. As they were all in battle dress, giving the appearance of soldiers, Rachel kept quiet about the true reason for being there; as it was she'd have enough difficulty getting the bodies of two men back to Iona for burial without adding to her problems. Instead she thanked the priest and the doctor for their help before reminding them of the Official Secrets Act. Her warning had no basis in law but they didn't know that.

The Land Rovers were refuelled before reaching Oban and the bodies of the dead men concealed beneath equipment, one in each vehicle. Habits were pulled over battle dress and the monks travelled together in silence as the ferry made its choppy way to Mull, from where the journey to Iona was straightforward. Brother Anthony insisted on digging the graves and performing the committals himself. Two simple pieces of the same stone used to build the church marked both burial places. Rachel was the last to leave, having remained at the gravesides to pray and reflect on the bravery of two fallen monks who had taken the highroad back to where they belonged. It was then that Brother Anthony decreed that wherever in the world a monk falls in defence of Joshua his remains will be returned to the new church for burial in ground consecrated for martyrs.

A debrief of the surviving monks revealed that as well as killing a band of terrorists, a large arms cache had been destroyed. The terror group had built this up in the belief that no one would think of looking halfway up a mountain for it. It was also revealed that the avalanche heard by Rachel was deliberately triggered by the monks to bury any trace of their deadly work. That night Brother Anthony enjoyed a dreamless sleep. Gabriel Jackson was well pleased.

Chapter 38

The first six months of 2012 passed without incident other than Joshua maintaining his astonishing rate of learning. He and Bethany drew closer as friends, and largely due to Joshua's influence she too had moved ahead of the class. Jokingly, Dougy had remarked to Sara that they should begin planning for the wedding whilst knowing that such an event was unlikely to happen. It was difficult to accept that whatever lay in store for their eldest son could not be determined by them. Theirs was a bit part in the wider scheme of things and the inevitability of losing him to the powerful forces that controlled his life was never far from their thoughts. They had knelt before him, dedicating their lives to him. Next year would be Joshua's final year at the local school and as far as Dougy and Sara were aware, no plans had been made for him to move to a higher school in the area. No one seemed to have much of an idea what was happening, or at least no one was letting on. They had become well accustomed to Brother Anthony's ability to avoid answering questions whilst remaining convincing that there was nothing to get concerned about. *'If it's God's will then it will happen,'* was his stock response to whatever was asked of him. Then with praying hands and a slight bow of the head he'd walk away. Dougy had to admit that everything that had been promised about keeping Joshua safe had been fulfilled, perhaps God was working away somewhere in the background, anyway it would be good to know what the future held for Joshua's schooling.

Rachel welcomed the start of the long summer break. Events had tired her and in passing she remarked to Dougy that a period of time away from it all would not go amiss. The first week in July brought a hot spell of weather and the forecast was good for the next few days. The winter battle in the Glen Coe Mountains had been kept secret, so as far as Dougy was concerned there had been a settled period of calm and everything was under control. He recalled what Rachel had said about needing a holiday, not too far away but far enough to make a change from the farm.

'That sounds good, I've forgotten when we last had a holiday,' replied Sara.

'Well I think the bairns would like a proper seaside holiday, you know, buckets and spades,' said Dougy.

Sara smiled, having spent her childhood in Zimbabwe the idea of a bucket and spade holiday didn't have the same appeal as it did for Dougy who was clearly recalling his childhood days.

'We used to stay in a caravan at a wee place up from Oban, it was quiet and plenty of sand to dig, the bairns would love it, a few days there would do us no harm.'

'Alright, but we must tell Brother Anthony what we are doing, he might not like the idea of Joshua being anywhere but here,' said Sara.

His face the picture of solemnity Brother Anthony listened as Dougy outlined their holiday plans. A few days at the seaside, that's all it was, surely there could be no objections, but Dougy should have known better than to expect a straight yes or no from this infuriating monk. As usual he prevaricated, questioning the wisdom of such an idea; even so, Dougy detected a softening of Brother Anthony's resistance. For a moment it felt as though he was half expecting this request and his initial reluctance but a smoke screen. Dougy shrugged off this feeling and waited for Brother Anthony to respond.

'You may go on your holiday providing Rachel accompanies you.'

But he omitted to add that he'd be hovering in the background, unseen but missing nothing. Sara warmed to the suggestion, it was a reasonable compromise. Dougy wasn't so happy, couldn't they just once have some time together without someone looking over their shoulder, but then he grudgingly agreed.

'Right, now we have to tell the boys and it's my bet we'll be taking Bethany along with us,' said Dougy.

His assumption was accurate, Bethany's parents took the view that if they stopped her going their lives would be hell for weeks to come so there was no argument, she could go.

Dougy had some local knowledge so he checked on the internet then rang around guest houses and cheaper hotels in the area. Being the height of the season there were no vacancies in any of them. By the time Dougy had exhausted all the possibilities, a cloud of despondency had settled over them. Sara put a brave face on the situation.

'Well Dougy you tried, perhaps we'll have better luck later in the year.'

Dougy put an arm around her.

'Yes, but the weather is so good and the bairns are really geared up for it, what a shame to disappoint them.'

Brother Anthony had been listening and for him to make a helpful suggestion took everyone by surprise.

'Maybe I can be of assistance, have you thought about camping, the children will find it most agreeable, I'm sure you'll find a campsite with space, they can't all be full.'

'What a great idea but what about Rachel, she'll have to have her own tent, but I don't suppose she'd mind that too much,' remarked Sara.

Dougy's excitement at spending a few days under canvas was almost childlike.

'That's settled then, there's a camping shop in Inveraray. I'll get a couple of tents and other bits and pieces there then we'll be on our way soon enough.'

Sara was a bit more pragmatic.

'It will take a bit more planning than that but I'll get things organised so we can start out first thing in the morning, Bethany will have to stay the night and Brother Anthony can arrange for Rachel to meet up with us at the campsite once we know where it is.'

Brother Anthony nodded in agreement and made a call to Rachel on his mobile. He moved out of earshot and spoke at the level of a whisper.

'It will happen just as we planned. You will join them and then carry out Father Gabriel's instructions to the letter. He was specific in my dream, you must not fail him, is that understood?'

'Yes, fully understood.'

Brother Anthony finished the call and rejoined Dougy and Sara as they made plans for their holiday.

'Any idea where you're going yet?' he asked in matter of fact way.

'Not yet, but now we're camping, all we have to do is find a place with a vacant pitch, just as long as it's near a beach,' replied Dougy.

He Googled campsites around Oban and came up with a holiday village that had a few pitches left. He rang the number listed on the web page and within a short while had booked them in. Again Brother Anthony gave himself some privacy and informed Rachel, telling her to leave right away and check out the place.

'Be sure to check the distance from the camp site to the sea, be very accurate about it, we can't afford any more mishaps.'

Rachel understood, they had managed to retrieve the situation in Glen Coe but any more failures… well it wasn't worth thinking about.

Brother Anthony continued,

'Tomorrow I will return to the church. Once the instructions have been carried out you must call me as I have things to do.'

'I understand,' said Rachel.

The call ended there and Brother Anthony made himself useful helping with the holiday preparations. Sara couldn't believe how laid back he was about it. Now the narrow minded Brother Anthony who previously had put Joshua's safety before everything was helping them prepare for a holiday that potentially could put Joshua at risk. Tents are not the most secure places and whilst Rachel was going to be there and doubtless armed, the risks were still greater than if they were staying in a guest house.

Her thoughts were soon diverted as Dougy called her to come and see the equipment he'd purchased, or to be more accurate what Ally and Mary had bought for them. A family tent to sleep six and a small pup tent for Rachel were stacked neatly in the back of the 4X4. He'd taken advice from the store owner and bought good quality sleeping bags, a portable gas stove and anything else that would add to their comfort.

'Do you think that tent is big enough for Rachel, from the picture on the box it looks really tiny,' asked Sara.

'We're only away for a few days, I wasn't going to spend a lot of money on a tent just for one person, anyway she'll manage OK,' replied Dougy with more than a hint of mischievousness in his voice.

Bethany's arrival increased the air of excitement. She had had a seaside holiday before and amongst other bits and pieces to play with, she'd brought a well-used bucket and spade and lots of little paper flags on sticks to adorn the many sand-castles she planned on making. Sara noticed Joshua's puzzled look, he was being prepared for many things in life but making sand castles was not one of them.

'It's alright sweetheart, I'll buy you and Farai a bucket and spade each when we arrive. I'm sure Bethany will show you how to make sand castles,'

Bethany nodded gleefully; it made a change for her to know something that Joshua didn't. An early start was planned, so that evening the children went to bed earlier than usual. Brother Anthony retired to a corner of the barn that served as shelter where he said his customary evening prayer, but this time he added something extra. He prayed for success as he and Rachel prepared to carry through the mission entrusted to them upon which the future of the new church and Joshua's part in it depended. Not without compassion he prayed for Dougy and Sara for he knew that the joy of their holiday would be short lasting, but then it was the will of God that had spoken to him through Gabriel Jackson and therein was the mystery.

Chapter 39

The holiday park was everything they expected it to be. Rachel had arrived and met them at reception. Taking it upon herself she'd negotiated a pitch close to the edge of the camp-site from where the gentle whoosh of surf breaking over a sandy beach could be heard. A cloudless sky and warm sunshine added to the carefree atmosphere of their surroundings. Rachel watched with some amusement at the head scratching and constant reading of instructions that accompanied putting up the family tent. Initially Dougy's pride wouldn't let him accept help from other campers but in the end he had to capitulate, otherwise Sara concluded they'd be sleeping in the open air. Much to Dougy's annoyance, Rachel's smaller tent had virtually erected itself and she'd obviously enjoyed watching his own feeble efforts. She had to admit the family tent was an impressive structure with its spacious living accommodation and separate bedrooms. To Joshua this was a novelty, something to be explored and wonder at. Of course, Bethany's parents had a similar tent and she took pride in sharing her expertise in the art of camping with her friend. She took Joshua on a grand tour whilst at the same time claiming one of the two smaller bedrooms for her own use.

'This one is mine,' she said, unzipping the flap far enough to crawl inside.

'Why,' asked Joshua.

'Because…'

'Because what.'

'Just because…'

Dougy listened to the conversation with some amusement; he took Joshua to one side.

'Don't argue Joshua, you can't win boy, you'll understand one day.'

The benefits of Joshua's time at Inveraray School soon became apparent. His initial extroversion had long since been replaced with an outward looking approach to life and he and Bethany quickly made friends with other children on the site. For a while Farai clung to his mother but then he too ventured out to splash about contentedly in a nearby paddling pool. Keeping her distance, Rachel kept a sharp watch on them, her loose top masking the bulge of a holster within which the loaded 19mm Glock 17 nestled. The last thing she needed was another attempt on Joshua's life, especially in a crowded holiday park. Rachel looked on as Joshua attracted others to him; she likened him to a candle, pulling moths towards the flame. He was hypnotic and where he led, others followed; even older children didn't question him, for he was that kind of boy. Like the Pied Piper of Hamelin, he played an irresistible tune to which, one day, the world would march. They enjoyed their games until the appetizing smell of a barbecue brought them back to the tent. During his hunting trips in Zimbabwe Dougy had survived on meat cooked outdoors and his skills transferred quite easily from a crude wood fire to the sophistication of a portable gas barbecue. Rachel joined them in their supper. Outwardly she projected peace and contentment, yet inwardly her mind had already moved ahead to the following day and what she was to do in the name of Gabriel Jackson. Whilst the family chatted and relaxed in each other's company, Rachel remained on the edge of things, she wasn't one of them so why get too involved. Before he went to bed Joshua kissed her lightly on the cheek, it was a kiss that spoke volumes. '*He knows, I'm sure he knows,*' thought Rachel.

The pup tent offered more comfort than its exterior suggested. Rachel slept partially dressed, keeping her firearm within easy reach. Rising before the others to take advantage of the public showers she wrapped her gun inside a towel, which she placed in a small dressing case holding clean clothes for the day. She slipped her mobile phone down the side of the towel. Rachel padded in flip flops across the grass, there was no one else around so for the time being she had the building to herself. The shower was amazing, it wasn't the kind of lukewarm shower usually associated with campsites. This one shot jets of hot water, stinging her skin, revitalizing her, removing any remaining traces of sleepiness. Her expensive shower cream did what it said on the bottle and she waited for the last trace of foam to disappear down the plug hole before leaving the cubicle. Rachel pulled on a white T shirt and a pair of baggy red shorts; she had to stay in the background. A vital task had been given by Brother Anthony and today was the day that she would be called upon to do what was expected of her. Her entire being must remain focused, ready to respond. Brother Anthony communicated in riddles so she had no understanding of what form the happening would take or from what direction it would come. Because she had been instructed to find a pitch close to the beach, Rachel assumed that the sea had some part to play in the mysterious event, but that was all. Joshua's cheery voice startled her,

'Hello Rachel, how was the shower?'

'Lovely and hot, mind you don't get scalded,' she replied as Dougy and Sara shepherded the children past her, but Bethany had to have the last word.

'I don't know why we have to have a shower; we're going in the sea later.'

Sara smiled and took no notice.

Stowing her flip flops, Rachel walked barefoot to her tent. Although it was still early the grass felt warm and comfortable between her toes. She kept the shower block within her field of vision, staying alert. Everyone going in was scrutinised, the way they walked, their body language, what they were carrying, anything out of the ordinary that marked a person out from the crowd. After fifteen minutes and no sight of the MacKays she began to feel agitated, surely it doesn't take that long to shower, even with three children. She moved towards the entrance, not exactly expecting trouble but prepared for it just the same. Usually, children are naturally noisy when they are together but the brick built shower block absorbed any sound. She ran the last few steps before colliding with Dougy. Relief replaced anxiety but Dougy was not amused. He placed both hands on her shoulders, gently moving her away from him.

'Rachel, what are you doing? We're OK. I can look after them you know.' Dougy's clipped Scottish accent gave an edge to his feelings.

Rachel did not reply, Dougy's understandable annoyance soon turned into an apology, he'd agreed to Rachel being there so he must expect her to breathe down his neck from time to time. He invited her to have breakfast with them.

'Let's eat then go to the beach, after all that's what we're here for.'

Joshua moved to Rachel's side, taking her hand, gripping it tightly.

'Are you coming to the beach?' he asked.

'Yes; I'll help you make sand castles if you like.'

His grip loosened.

'Good, that will be nice.'

By mid-morning the beach was busy, colourful wind breaks marking off territorial claims to patches of sand that soon turned into construction sites by children eager to build the best sand castle on the beach. As expected, Bethany took charge and before long her past experience at castle building began to show. With some amusement Dougy watched from the comfort of his deck chair as the resourceful girl divided the labour between Joshua, Sara and Rachel without doing much digging herself. *'This lassie has a future,'* he thought. Farai, on the other hand, showed little interest in the grand sand castle project and busied himself making simple sand pies and then knocking them down. Dougy could not remember when he last felt so relaxed.

The warmth of the noonday sun added weight to his eyelids and awareness of what was going on around him waxed and waned as he entered the limbo of semi consciousness. The gentle sound of waves caressing the beach relaxed him further, his head dropped forward and he fell asleep. Sara did not awaken him; Rachel was more than capable of watching over Joshua. It was good to see Dougy so relaxed, something that had become a rarity. He worried a lot about his sons and deserved to be left in peace for a while, she felt sure nothing was going to happen, even when the sky appeared to darken across the horizon. Initially, he hadn't noticed the abruptness with which Rachel stopped playing with the children, it was when she ran to the water's edge and stood with arms outstretched facing the growing darkness that Sara fiercely shook Dougy awake.

'What the hell…'

'It's Rachel, look at her.'

The sky was darkening in a way that accompanies a total eclipse of the sun. People all along the beach turned to watch, more in awe than fear. Rachel walked through the waves to meet the darkness. Farai and Bethany took Sara's hand but not Joshua. He too had gone to the water's edge where he stood like a rock, facing out to sea.

'Go to him Dougy,' urged Sara.

Dougy moved to be with his son.

'It's alright daddy, it's alright.'

Dougy felt transfixed as the sea washed over his feet. The darkness was now almost upon them, the temperature had fallen several degrees. In the instant before it completely enveloped the beach a bright orange light appeared at its centre. Growing in intensity it caused Dougy to look away, yet Joshua was able to maintain his gaze without discomfort.

'I am going to be with Rachel,' he said.

Dougy offered no objection as his son moved to where Rachel stood. Her arms remaining outstretched, she looked down and smiled, it was a radiant smile, the sort of smile depicted in images of angels painted by artists of the old school that hang in major art galleries of the world. Joshua moved nearer to Rachel, they appeared almost as one. The light had waited for this moment, it enclosed them and in an instant they were gone. The darkness retreated, allowing the sun to return its warmth to the beach. Dougy moved from the water, turning he made his way to where Sara stood. Like him, she was calm and accepting of what had happened. She motioned Dougy to look around. Doing so he witnessed people on their knees in the sand, some were praying, others just silent. Then Bethany began to cry.

'Where is Joshua, I want Joshua.'

Sara had no answer; she just held the young girl's hand, until her weeping subsided.

Collecting their things they began making their way to the camp site. The holiday was over so the sooner they returned to the farm the better, anyhow, Sara was keen to hand Bethany back to her parents. Approaching their pitch Dougy was taken aback to see the figure of Brother Anthony busy dismantling the tents. He'd already packed away Rachel's tent and had made a start on the larger one. Dougy felt angry and betrayed.

'He knew all along, that's why he was so eager for us to come here, I'll bet Gabriel Jackson is behind this; it's got his stamp all over it.'

Brother Anthony looked up as they approached. He held out his arms in greeting but they were ignored. Instead Dougy faced him down, demanding an explanation of why his son and Rachel had been taken and when they were coming back. Brother Anthony did not answer directly.

'Please, let us return to the farm and I will tell you then where Joshua is. All I can say now is that he will come to no harm and is perfectly happy.'

Arguing with Brother Anthony was a pointless exercise; the tents and equipment were loaded into the 4x4 for the journey home. Bethany began to cry again.

'Where is he, tell me where he is,' she sobbed.

Sara cuddled her until they reached the farm, by which time she had cried herself to sleep. *'It's funny how children do that,'* mused Sara.

Brother Anthony had gone on before and was waiting at the farm. He stood silently in the doorway, head covered, arms encased in the sleeves of his robe. He'd said nothing to Ally and Mary but by his demeanour it was clear that something had happened.

'Where is Joshua, what in God's name has happened,' said Ally, his voice fraught with concern.

'Ask him,' replied Dougy, shaking an accusative finger at Brother Anthony.

'Well, where is he, where is my grandson?'

Brother Anthony said nothing; he moved inside the house and sat at the kitchen table. Dougy and Sara followed him. Mary took the still sleeping Bethany from Sara and gently placed her on the couch. Farai sat on his mother's knee. Brother Anthony raised his head and began to speak.

'I am sure you feel antagonistic towards me for what has occurred but...'

Dougy did not allow him to finish, his anger at boiling point.

'You duped us into going to that place, you and Rachel plotted to get us there, was it Gabriel Jackson's doing?'

Sara touched Dougy lightly on the arm.

'Let him go on,' she whispered.

'Father Gabriel has been visiting me in my dreams. He is in another place not of this earth. The bright light that took Joshua up was indeed Father Gabriel. In his present form he was only able to materialise over the sea and that is why Joshua had to be near or in the sea when the time came for him to be taken up.'

This time it was Mary who interjected.

'Taken up to where, will we get him back?'

'He has been taken to the Place of Angels where he will stay until he is of the age when it is foretold he will return to fulfil his mission. His earthly education has been completed. You may see him again but I cannot say for sure as I have no knowledge of the place where he will again be returned to earth; as with many things that Brother Gabriel does, it is a great mystery.'

'Where is the Place of Angels? Is it in heaven?' asked Mary.

Brother Anthony waited a few moments before answering.

'I cannot tell you, my only contact with Father Gabriel has been through my dreams. I and my fellow brothers will continue with the work ordained to us at the new church. This work will also go on through those who Joshua touched. Even that sleeping child over there will dedicate her life to him. When he returns his mission will have begun, his church will have grown. So my friends, there is much work to do, let us go forward together.'

Without another word he rose from his chair and left. From the moment that Gabriel Jackson had entered their lives Dougy and Sara had lived with the inevitability of this day. To them it was not an ending but a beginning to the next phase of Joshua's mission. They vowed not to fail him for he was their son and despite Brother Anthony's misgivings they would see him again.

Chapter 40

December 2017

Largely due to the efforts of Brother Anthony and his faithful monks the message of the new church had begun to find its way into countries where people needed to hear it most. In these countries despots who ruled through fear, intimidation and torture still held sway and paid little heed to the threat of a global resistance movement whose weaponry came in the form of love and peace. The new church on Iona was a focus for pilgrims, but these were different pilgrims from those usually associated with this holy isle. The New Church website encouraged cyber pilgrims. It was named 'The Community of Love' and provided constant encouragement to converts who logged on through underground information technology centres manned by brave souls, some who gave their lives upon being discovered. But as quickly as the mailed hand of despotism smashed one centre, another sprung up in its place. Social networking sites were full of chatter and stories from people who had experienced conversion. Prominent amongst these were consistent, believable accounts of Joshua being taken from the beach by people who had witnessed it, but it was through financial backing of the Bilderberg Group and deliberate non-interference from the established church that the website and all that it meant to suppressed millions was able to continue. Iain and Janet Sherry broadcast their story of how Joshua had restored the injured police officer to a fully functioning life and Jamie McArdle had a full time job as website news editor. His biggest story by far was to report that the Zimbabwean despot had finally succumbed to old age and the Archbishop of York had restored his clerical collar to its rightful place.

Each December since Joshua was taken from the beach his family had celebrated the anniversary of his birth. It was a time to restore hope that he would return and today, the 31st December 2017 was the predicted date when this would happen. Mary and Sara had prepared the birthday tea. As in previous years Bethany was there, as was Iain and Janet Sherry. As usual an empty chair had been placed at the table. Iain Sherry recalled having been told by Father Moloney that on this date Joshua would be installed as the leader of the new church but first he must return.

'The boy will come back here,' said a hopeful Dougy, 'this is his home.'

Bethany's eyes filled with tears.

'Happy birthday Joshua, come back to me, I miss you.'

Her sentiments prompted the others to raise their glasses and drink to the absent boy, just as they had done each December since Joshua was taken.

There were numerous reports of sightings from around the world but none had been confirmed. Converts were eager to see him, to see what he looked like and digital images began to appear on the website from people who genuinely thought that Joshua had reappeared in their locality. The images were often of poor quality, making positive identification impossible. As the appointed day moved into evening Brother Anthony locked himself in the church and began to pray. He prayed for a sign, anything to say that Joshua had returned just as Gabriel Jackson had promised he would. Two hours passed and still he prayed. Where was the boy? Brother Anthony had to have something to tell the Community of Love otherwise he feared its members may become disorganised and disenchanted. This day had been set aside, to members of the community it was a holy day, the day when the leader of their church had been promised to them. Brother Anthony felt a heavy weight descend upon him; he cursed Gabriel Jackson for his trickery, for leaving him to carry the burden of a leaderless church. His prayers became frantic as deep inside he felt the intense pain of rejection fuelled by rage and disbelief. Another hour passed and Brother Anthony became exhausted. Completely spent he crumpled to the floor where he lay motionless, he'd done all he could, for him this was the end when it should have been a glorious triumphant beginning. He stared at an impenetrable wall of despair; there was no way through and his pitiful wailing caused the monks, who had gathered outside to plead with Brother Anthony to let them in but to no avail, even if he were able to hear them he was not listening;

Brother Anthony was a broken man, he felt, as Jesus felt on the day of his crucifixion, that God had deserted him.

After a few minutes Brother Anthony ceased his wailing. In one last desperate attempt to communicate with God he prostrated himself before the altar and again he prayed. At first he did not notice the shimmering orange light that appeared above him. Then he felt the despair leave him, his depression lifted and in that moment his prayers were answered. The light moved to floor level and Brother Anthony rose to his feet. He turned to face the light and this time his cry was one of joy, for there within its soft glow stood Gabriel Jackson and Rachel with Joshua at their side. Joshua reached out and touched Brother Anthony on the shoulder. This simple act carried the message that Brother Anthony had been waiting for, it was a message of reassurance that Joshua had returned as promised. Gabriel Jackson smiled, bent forward to kiss Brother Anthony gently on the forehead and retreated into the light which then disappeared, taking him and Rachel with it. Joshua had changed, no longer a boy, he was tall and strong, ready for what lay ahead, but first the news of his return must be broadcast to the Community, then afterwards the difficult and emotional task of reuniting him with his family.

Outside, the monks heard Brother Anthony unlock the door of the church; huddled together they feared the worse. Brother Anthony's wailing had affected them and when Joshua appeared in the half light of a winter's moon they stood transfixed, hardly daring to believe what they were seeing. Joshua extended his arms in a collective embrace, these were his disciples, the men ordained to do his work, and they knelt before him. Joshua blessed each one before sending them out to continue the task already begun. Then he spoke directly to Brother Anthony. His voice was one of authority; it projected power and a single- minded purpose, not unlike Gabriel Jackson.

'Brother Anthony, my faithful friend, please take me to my parents, I wish to speak with them and with Bethany.'

'It is late Joshua; there are no ferries, so it will have to wait until the morning?'

'Very well but we must go at first light.'

Brother Anthony agreed and asked Joshua if he should contact his parents first.

'Yes, do it immediately and please ask for Bethany to be there when we arrive in the morning.'

Brother Anthony wondered at why Joshua insisted on Bethany's presence but stayed silent.

***

Since the day that Joshua was taken, his grandfather had kept the kitchen light burning. He said it was there to guide Joshua home, a safe harbour should he need it. That night, as usual, the family sat around the table and prayed for Joshua, it helped them to stay in touch and gave them hope. Iain and Janet Sherry joined in; they were staying over that night. Bethany had been picked up by her father an hour before. Just as Dougy muttered 'Amen' the phone rang.

'Who can that be at this hour?' said Mary.

Ally picked up the phone and before he could say anything Brother Anthony's unmistakable voice announce the good news.

'Are you sure?' questioned Ally. There had been many false reports, was this just another one.

'What is it dad?' asked Dougy.

Ally handed the phone to his son.

'It's Brother Anthony, you speak to him, he says Joshua has returned and he's there on Iona.'

It took just a few moments for Dougy to realise that Brother Anthony was indeed speaking the truth.

'Can you put him on please,' asked Dougy.

'No, he is not the same person that you remember; we will be with you mid-morning tomorrow. He asks for Bethany to be there, can that be arranged?' then abruptly he rang off.

No one in the McKay household slept that night.

'What did he mean when he said that Joshua was not the person we remembered? Obviously he was now older but surely he was recognisable, people don't change that much, there will be something wrong if I don't recognise my own son,' said a bemused Sara.

'Well, we'll know in a few hours,' said Mary.

Sara didn't let it rest there.

'Why did he ask for Bethany, what does she have to do with anything?'

Dougy hugged his wife who was clearly distressed.

'Call it a mother's intuition but I don't think Joshua will be here for long. Brother Anthony will see to that,' said Sara.

Mary felt much the same.

'We don't know where Joshua has been and we don't know where he is going. What we do know is that when he was taken it was not to an earthly place. His gifts are not of this earth. We must accept what he has become. Obviously Bethany is part of the grand plan, it's a shame she'd gone home before Brother Anthony rang.'

'I expect Bethany's parents will have a lot to say about it, it's long past midnight but we ought to ring them with the news and Joshua's request,' interjected Ally.

'Aye, I'll do it,' said Dougy.

Surprisingly Bethany's father answered the phone almost immediately, as if he was expecting a call.

'Och, is that you Dougy, I thought you might ring. You have some news I expect.'

Dougy was taken by surprise.

'So you know - how did you find out?'

'No one told me, but Bethany has been like a cat on hot bricks, she has so much faith in Joshua, it's as if they are telepathically linked.'

'He's coming home in the morning and wants Bethany to be here when he arrives, said Dougy.' Almost as an afterthought he asked if that could be arranged.

'Aye, I don't see that we have any alternative, we'll be there, sometime mid-morning.'

Dougy thanked him and put down the phone. If either he or Bethany's parents had an inkling of what Joshua's intentions were they might not have been so amenable.

The night dragged. Once more Mary found herself making tea and cooking an early breakfast. The morning, when it arrived, was grey and snow clouds threatened a cold miserable day, but the weather was the last thing on their minds as they prepared for Joshua's homecoming. Bethany arrived earlier than expected.

'Sorry to be here so soon but, well you know, Bethany couldn't wait,' said her father.

Bethany's eyes seemed to shine with expectation but apart from that she was surprisingly calm, almost too calm considering she was soon to be reunited with her closest friend. The morning wore on with no sign of Brother Anthony or Joshua.

'Perhaps the ferry was late getting away from Mull.' said Mary.

'The ferry's never late,' retorted Ally.

Tension began to build; the kitchen clock was showing quarter past eleven when a car drew up at the front gate. Mary looked through the window.

'It's them,' she said.

Dougy opened the door, Joshua had come home and emotion overcame them both. His son had grown; he was as tall as his father. Dougy went to Joshua, throwing his arms around him, holding him, trying to speak but words would not come. Joshua embraced his father in return; they hugged each other for what seemed an eternity. Then Joshua looked for his mother, his brother and his grandparents. He went to each in turn, embracing them with the same depth of feeling shown to his father. Farai seemed bemused by it all, he was small when Joshua was taken and had virtually forgotten what his brother looked like. Now, everyone was making a fuss over someone who to him was a stranger.

'It's Joshua, you remember your brother don't you Farai?'

Farai nodded but not in a convincing way and took a step back when Joshua bent to kiss him.

'Don't worry, give him a couple of days, he'll soon come round,' said Mary.

In the background Brother Anthony shook his head, he hadn't got two days. The others stood back, watching, except for Bethany who could not contain herself. The earlier calmness disappeared; she ran to be with her friend. Taking Joshua's hand she led him into the house. Brother Anthony followed at a discreet distance whilst never taking his eyes off Joshua. It was Iain Sherry who first noticed Rachel's absence and asked where she was. Brother Anthony's reply was typical of him.

'She is here with us. You can't see her but she can see us. Please understand I can say no more.'
Iain Sherry realised the futility of a response so did not pursue the matter.

Brother Anthony waited a while longer then asked everyone to listen as he had something to say. Sara held Dougy's arm, she feared that what the monk had to say would not be to their liking, but Dougy jumped in first, speaking directly to his son.

'Joshua, where have you been, what have you been doing all this time. Not a day has passed that we haven't thought about you and prayed for your safe return.'
Joshua remained silent; instead he turned to Brother Anthony who spoke for him.

'Joshua was taken to a place of final preparation. You will see that in the time away he has grown from a boy into a fine young man. He is now ready to go out into the world.'
Dougy shook his head.

'Not good enough, he is still my son and I want to know where he has been for the last five years.'

'Very well, he was taken by Father Gabriel to a place known as the Place of Angels where he lived and continued his studies. It is a secret, holy place set aside from the confines of physical existence yet it provides sustenance for physical and spiritual growth. It is a place where the quest for a new spirituality goes on. That is as much as I can say.'

'Let Joshua talk to us, can he tell us what he did in this Place of Angels,' asked Dougy.

'No, but let me continue with my message to you. Joshua can stay here for just one more hour. He has told me there is something he has to do before going about his work.'

Joshua motioned for Bethany to stand close to him. She smiled and did as he requested. Joshua then spoke.

'During my time away I stayed in touch with Bethany and we became one in a spiritual sense, which means we are bound in such a way that separation is no longer possible. We must travel the road together.'

Bethany's parents did not seem at all surprised; somehow they had suspected as much. It was clear to them that Bethany could never be truly happy until she was with Joshua but the impact of her leaving so suddenly hit them hard. Brother Anthony had words of consolation but the die was cast, preparations were already in place for Bethany to join Joshua in his life's work, Gabriel Jackson had decreed it. Joshua looked for Iain Sherrie, who through being healed had become a devoted disciple. Iain Sherrie carried the mark of Joshua and years before had been told by his parish priest Father Moloney to "Pray for strength and make yourself ready." Now the time had arrived. Joshua took Iain Sherrie's hands in his and once again the retired police officer felt the power of compassion surge through his body.

'My purpose for being in this world is clear; you carry my mark and have proved your faithfulness. You have prayed and waited for this day. Others will listen to you and follow you in my name. Your task is to carry my message to all parts of world, there is no greater work.'

Joshua rested his hands on the top of Iain Sherrie's head, closed his eyes and prayed silently for a few moments. Then he removed his hands.

'I understand now,' said Iain Sherrie, 'I am ready to do as you ask.'

An hour later Joshua and Bethany said their goodbyes, Brother Anthony gave his now familiar little bow, and they were gone.

Epilogue

On Iona, Joshua and Bethany walked hand in hand into the quietness and solitude of the new church. The quest for a new spirituality on earth had already begun and now its promised leader had materialised. During the years of Joshua's preparation everything had been foreseen, the script had been written in another place and from that first astral event in the heavens above Messina to the emergence of Joshua from the Place of Angels there have been no coincidences. Gabriel Jackson, the Bilderberg Group and even the established Roman church, despite the powerful influence they'd exerted, were part of the script. Granted, Gabriel Jackson occupied a leading role but he was a member of the cast just the same. *All the World's a Stage* wrote William Shakespeare, but this is no theatrical play, it is for real. Although still in his teens, Joshua has inherited wisdom and maturity from a source not of this earth. Justice tempered by love formed his being. In his childhood he'd reached deep into the lives of others. His parents, grandparents, Iain Sherry, a stricken helicopter pilot, Patricia Nolan and Bethany understood his influence. Those who felt Joshua's power were immediately won over; the seeds of love already planted have produced a return of one hundred fold. Since the first appearance of the Messiah a time such as this has been awaited by millions of people, ordinary people in lands entombed beneath a dark hatred fuelled by genocide and wanton killing. Yet Joshua does not profess to be anyone other than himself, born of human parents he knows pain and fear, his feelings for Bethany reflect human characteristics. A deep knowledge of prophetic scripture is his guide post, he follows where it leads. For him and Bethany the ancient, dusty Emmaus road has become a modern global highway along which they will travel together, never staying long in one place, moving on, preparing the ground and sowing the seeds of perfect love, recruiting more disciples until time itself determines when Joshua's mission is accomplished. It is then and only then, that the world will be ready for its second cataclysmic event.

Acknowledgements and reference

With thanks to Chris Bulmer, Margaret Wyche, Gwen Grant and members of the Bassetlaw Writers Group for their friendship and support.

Special thanks to the staff and guides of Iona Abbey. Their help and knowledge so freely given during my visits to Iona was greatly appreciated.

Additional factual knowledge gleaned from: -

Holder, Geoff *The Guide to Mysterious Iona and Staffa*, Tempus Publishing Ltd, Stroud Gloucestershire 2007

The book is dedicated to Mary, my wife.

Lightning Source UK Ltd.
Milton Keynes UK
UKOW04f1214230913

217736UK00002B/444/P